# QUEEN of MIAMI

## Books by Méta Smith

*The Rolexxx Club*
*Queen of Miami*

# QUEEN of MIAMI

A NOVEL BY

## MÉTA SMITH

**WARNER BOOKS**

NEW YORK   BOSTON

Copyright © 2007 by Méta Smith

Warner Books
Hachette Book Group USA
237 Park Avenue
New York, NY 10169

Visit our Web site at www.HachetteBookGroupUSA.com.

Printed in the United States of America

First Edition: March 2007

10  9  8  7  6  5  4  3  2  1

Warner Books and the "W" logo are trademarks of Time Warner Inc. or an affiliated company. Used under license by Hachette Book Group USA, which is not affiliated with Time Warner Inc.

Library of Congress Cataloging-in-Publication Data

Smith, Méta.
     Queen of Miami / Méta Smith. — 1st ed.
          p.  cm.
     Summary: "A novel about a famous DJ who, after escaping her affluent upbringing, begins an affair with a man whose violent profession puts her life in jeopardy"—Provided by the publisher.
     ISBN-13: 978-0-446-69853-5
     ISBN-10: 0-446-69853-9
     1. African American disc jockeys—Fiction.  2. African American women—Fiction.  3. Miami (Fla.)—Fiction.  4. Psychological fiction.  I. Title.
     PS3619.M5922Q44   2007
     813'.6—dc22

                                        2006021377

Book design and text composition by Ellen Rosenblatt/SD Designs, Inc.
Cover design by Franco Accornero

*Dedicated with love to the memory of my godfather,*
*Emerick Matthews*

*Also dedicated to all the female DJs*
*and to "Big" (T.D.)*
*because the music sounds better with you*

# ACKNOWLEDGMENTS

I'm gonna keep it short so that I don't get in trouble this time for forgetting people! Thanks to God the Father for allowing his child to have a voice once again. Eternal love to my son, Jordan, for constantly inspiring me and forcing me to take breaks! Special thanks to my family and friends for all of the support and encouragement and acting as managers, publicists, and cheerleaders. Nothing feels better than to hear you say that you're proud of me.

To my godmother, Pauline Springfield: I feel like an idiot for not giving you a big shout out in the first book. I am so sorry. It's my head, not my heart.

Derrick, Dwight, James: y'all can call your cousin every now and then!

Thanks to the writers who have offered me invaluable advice and support (in no order, of course): Karen Quinones Miller, Lyah LeFlore, Steve Perry, James Guitard, Thomas Brooks Joy (that is your name, right?) King, Danielle Santiago, T. N. Baker, Tracey Taylor, Jason Miccolo Johnson, Omar Tyree, J. L. Woodson, Tillis Vaughn, Elaine Meryl Brown, Nikki Turner, T. J. Williams, Terrie Williams, Pearl Cleage, Curtis Bunn, and especially Walter Mosley and J. California

Cooper for saying things that changed my life without even knowing it.

Myra Panache of the Panache Report, sorry I couldn't squeeze you in this one, but you know I *love* talking to you! Call me (Ginger)!

Devi Pillai, thanks a million for being a "sweet" editor. Big up Crown Point! (ha ha) Congrats on the new gig! All the best!

To Linda Duggins, thanks for being a publicist/sister/friend/ confidante/chaperone! You really are a blessing.

Marc Gerald, thanks for looking out and being such a great agent!

Adam Batson, you deserved a mention in the last book. Here it is. Sorry for being mad for so long. You've been a very supportive friend and I love you. Thank you for the past twenty years.

Antonio "Spock" Daniels, thanks for being there when I needed another artistic nerd to understand me. Thanks for quantum entanglement and platonic bubble baths. And of course, thanks most of all (I think) for being the Big to my Carrie. You haven't always been there when I called but you're always on time. Now be there when I call, dammit! And if you think I'm gonna let you play me for six years while I wait, you got me f*&^ed up! Do I *really* have to go all the way to Paris? Seriously though, it's been an amazing journey. No matter what, I . . . more than like you (wink), Tweet.

And a million thanks from the bottom of my heart to all the book clubs, librarians, reviewers, media, booksellers, and especially the readers for your support, which has made this undoubtedly one of the best rides of my life!

Peace & Positive Vibes,
Méta Smith
"The Queen of Bling Fiction"

# QUEEN of
# MIAMI

# INTRO

**M**IAMI IS A CITY OF HUSTLERS. EVERYONE HAS AN ANGLE that they're working. There's so much excess, so much luxury in Miami, that people can't help but want a little bit for themselves. There's only so long that even the most pious and reserved person can sit around in a town like Miami and watch everyone else have all the fun. But fun costs a pretty penny in Miami.

Bottles of liquor that cost twenty bucks in the store are jacked up ten times at a nightclub. The admission to South Beach's clubs is usually $20 or $30, often more. And drinks are going to run around ten bucks a pop. There's also the money that's spent on the gym memberships to stay in perfect South Beach shape, the latest designer fashions because you've got to look good, the perfect haircut, skin care, and cosmetics because you've got to look great to gain entry into this world. Clubbing is an expensive addiction. But just like any other addiction, nightlife junkies find a way to feed their habits.

People find ways to make money, whether they have to rob, steal, or kill for it, and they'll go to great lengths just to have money to blow on superficial shit. And regardless of the state of the economy, the season, what war is going on, or any other variable, on South Beach, the hustlers are the kings of cash. In the words of KRS-One, illegal business controls America, and it damn sure controls South Beach.

The hustlers in Miami add a unique dynamic to the whole nightclub scene. They pump a steady flow of disposable income into the clubs every night of the week. They take flossing to a higher level. They kick it like every day is their last, because it just might be. Hustlers come in every color—from alabaster to indigo—from every social caste, from every corner of the earth, united by the quest for the almighty dollar.

In a city like Miami, the president, members of the media, and the so-called political experts would have you believe that hustlers only come in two shades—brown and black—and from three places—the ghetto, the barrio, or Latin America. But people who know the streets know that the arms of illegal business stretch far and wide, encircling everything we think we know about the world until the lines between right and wrong become so fuzzy that we just don't see them anymore. Anyone, but anyone, can get caught up.

# CHAPTER ONE

*March 2006*

I DRAG MY HUNGOVER BODY OUT OF THE BED, WALK OVER TO my window, and throw back the curtains. There had been a light misting of rain earlier but now the Florida sun is peeking through the clouds, and I'm lucky enough to see a rainbow shooting across the sky. *My pot of gold is on the other side of that rainbow, and today I'm going to get it*, I muse.

It's been a while since I've been up so early, 9:00 AM, but I have a big day ahead of me. To my surprise I don't melt, catch on fire, or explode when I'm exposed to daylight, quite a feat for a vampire like me. I go into the bedroom and nudge the snoring body that's asleep in my bed.

"Time to go, buddy," I say, like a cop moving a derelict sleeping in a doorway. "Get up."

My guest mumbles something incoherent and rolls over.

"Yo!" I shout. "I've got things to do today. You have to leave!"

The man who spent the night with me sits up and rubs his eyes. He shakes out his wild mane of dreadlocks like he's Bob Marley or someone, and grins. I suppose that he finds this sexy, but I just find it irritating. I had my fun and now I want him gone. I have no room in my life for clingy-ass men who don't get the fact that as far as I'm concerned men are only good for one thing, and it ain't living happily ever after. They're about satisfying my sexual needs and then making themselves invisible as quickly as possible.

"Come back to bed," he says, his voice tinged with a Caribbean accent.

"Player, get out of my bed," I say, and I say it real gully because I'm losing patience with this man. How is he going to tell me to come back to bed like he's at home or something?

"I told you, I've got work to do. You don't have to go home, but you've got to get the hell outta here." He frowns but doesn't move, like he's hoping I'll change my mind. I fold my arms across my chest, and give him a look that says I mean business. I call it my subway face, because if you're ever on public transportation you can't sit around looking like a vic ripe for the picking, you've got to look like you'll cut any motherfucker that looks at you funny. That's how I'm looking at him. He reluctantly gets out of bed, puts the wrinkled clothes that lay in a heap on the floor back on his body, and winks. I don't know what the hell he's winking for, because his performance was average if anything and he didn't do anything spectacular enough for me to want to give him another shot.

"Got any coffee?" he asks.

"Nope," I lie. "And I've got a meeting in a half hour, so it's been nice, but I really need you to leave so I can get myself together." I do have things to do, but not for more than three hours. Still he doesn't need to know all that, so I usher him to the door and open it wide.

"It's been real," I tell him. *Real ordinary*, I think in a postscript to myself. I don't know why I have it in my mind that every guy with dreadlocks must be a beast in bed, because that shit isn't true, but still I'm a sucker for a man with a head full of nappy hair and an accent, and the blacker the better.

"Think we can get together again sometime?" he asks.

"I'll call you," I say, gently pushing him across the threshold.

"But I didn't give you my number," he says. It doesn't matter, though, because I've already closed the door and locked it.

I go into the kitchen, turn on my espresso maker, and toast a bagel. I smile to myself as I smear cream cheese on the bagel and take a bite. The Winter Music Conference is finally here, more specifically, the DJ Spin-Off. This is my first year in the contest, but I'm confident that I'll be a front-runner. It's my time to shine. People from all over will finally get a chance to hear what I can do on the turntables. I've been working toward this moment for a few years, and I know I'm ready.

In the music business, everyone has to pay their dues, and I paid mine no matter what anyone has to say. I didn't become one of the hottest DJs in Miami because of my looks, though I've got to admit that being fine doesn't hurt. And I didn't fuck my way into this spot either, although I've done my fair share of fucking. But in this game, it doesn't matter how you look or who you fuck, if you are a garbage DJ, you won't have a career. You might score a gig here or there, but if the crowd isn't feeling you, you won't be back. Hell, you might not even survive the night.

But I don't have to worry about not making it through a gig. I learned my craft from a great teacher, I practice my ass off, and I'm not afraid to be creative and think outside the box. I refuse to play something just because it's popular.

Nowadays, half the popular music is hot garbage; I don't care how much it sells. Don't get me started on how wack rap is today: a bunch of former and current hustlers, writing their own indictments as they tell the feds all the dirt they've done and in some cases are still doing, everything the po-pos could need to build a case and lock their stupid asses away for a long time. I miss real hip-hop, music with a message, music that brings attention to the plight and struggles of unrepresented and underrepresented populations. But there's a big difference between telling people what's going on in the hood because you want things to change for the better, and glorifying everything that's fucked up about the hood and keeps normal, hardworking folks from ever getting ahead.

I guess you could say that I'm a DJ with a conscience. I give the people what they want, yes. But I also give them what they *need*, and I even give them what they never knew they wanted. I'm not dumbing down my sets for anyone. Fuck that. My goal once I step up to the deck is to enlighten minds through music. I can't do that if all I play is the same boring drivel over and over again. Sure I'll play hits and shit, but you better believe that I'm going to throw in classics and sleeper cuts that should have gotten way more pub than they did. I play obscure music, stuff you can't help but dance to, and stuff that you're not going to hear in heavy rotation on the radio. Because in my eyes, even though video may have killed the radio star, the radio star murdered good music.

I grew up listening to all kinds of music. Sure, lots of people *say* that they listen to all kinds of music, but what they really mean is that they turn the dial every now and then rather than keep it parked on one station. But shit, all the stations are owned by Clear Channel anyway, so it's not like the programming is going to be any different. I bet if you look through the record collection of a so-called music lover—

if they're even true enough to music to actually own any vinyl—you'll see a definite pattern of the same old shit repeating itself.

Now I *really* listen to *all* kinds of music. I own everything from Armenian folk music to zouk and zydeco. My music collection includes over 300,000 songs and counting on about 22,000 or so albums and CDs. I've even got some 78 rpm records, cassettes, and eight-tracks in my collection. I've worked everything from bar mitzvahs and Hindu weddings to quinceañeras and sweet sixteen parties in the past, and it wasn't just because I needed the money, but because I wanted to see firsthand what makes people of all races, from all walks of life, leave their cares behind and lose their minds on the dance floor. And *that's* why I can rock any crowd.

But even with my skills, I've had to work twice as hard to get where I am. I could say that sexism is rampant and that people give me shit just because I'm a woman, and I wouldn't be lying or exaggerating, but my possession of a pussy hasn't been my biggest roadblock. I mean, men in this business can be sexist, but men in any business are always thinking with their dicks and fucking it up for the women who are using their brains. That said, life as a DJ isn't as challenging as say, corporate America. Besides there's always a new club, another city, or a new promoter, so there's always a new chance at scoring a gig if you know how to hustle. And for every chauvinist jerk, there seems to be someone waiting to hire me just because I'm a woman, so it all kind of balances out.

What has made me have to work so hard hasn't been resistance from other people because of my gender. Nope, it hits a little closer to home for me. My struggles have come from trying to break free from a prominent, overbearing, and wealthy family. I grew up in the spotlight, with every creature comfort available; money was never an issue. I know it may sound like I have had every advantage in life; hell, a prominent, overbearing, wealthy family got a coked out C student with the vocabulary and enunciation of a third-grader into the Oval Office, so why should it be a hindrance to little old me, right? Wrong! Baby boy Bush has the support of his family, and I definitely don't. When you've got wealth and power on your side, oh, it's a beautiful thing. But when you've got wealth and power fighting against you, it's quite a battle indeed. My relationship with my family has been just like a regular Joe going up against a multimillion-dollar corporation. Winning isn't impossible, but it damn sure is hard.

For as long as I can remember it's been my ultimate dream to work in the music business. I've always envisioned myself as a pop star, but I can't sing, I can't rap, and although I can play the piano and the guitar, I didn't want to be a classical musician, which was the only acceptable music choice my peeps were going to support. I once ran the idea of becoming a recording engineer by them, or working in audio for TV or film, but it was a no go. The Hayes clan wasn't going to have it. So even though it's been long and many a winding road, at least I had the balls to say the hell with my family and follow my heart. Most adults who clash with their families over their choice of career end up giving in to the pressure. And they end up miserable and trapped in a dead-end job until they're too old to work anymore. What a waste! I may not be exactly where I want to be career-wise, but I'm proud that I haven't buckled, that I've held my ground, especially because of who my family is. Standing up to them is hard, and going against them is even harder.

See, my grandfather and father are the Reverend Robert J. Hayes Sr. and Robert J. Hayes Jr., respectively. My grandfather is a civil rights and religious icon, like a living Dr. Martin Luther King Jr., who just happened to be a friend of my family when he was alive. My grandfather's congregation, Sweet Name of Jesus African Methodist Episcopal Church, is on Chicago's South Side and has been renowned for over fifty years for its civil and human rights work both in America and abroad. Rumor has it that Grandfather is being considered to receive the Nobel Peace Prize for his work with AIDS orphans in Haiti and sub-Saharan Africa, as well as his AIDS activism in America. He's respected, admired, and revered. But he also hates most music that isn't gospel. He believes rock and roll kills the soul and rap is the minion of the devil. So he's none too pleased that his only grandchild is so caught up in the secular world of Beelzebub's hypnotic beats, as he refers to today's music.

My grandfather and I get along really well but we'd get along a lot better if he just eased up and accepted the fact that I'm not going to carry on the family legacy of fighting injustice and inequality. Not the way he wants me to. But hell, music has always been a huge part of any struggle, from slavery to civil rights, and I think I contribute to the "revolution" that way. Grandfather keeps telling me he wishes I would *do* something with my life and then whips out his Bible and starts preaching every time I see him. I could try to tell him that I am doing something with my life, but then I'd really get an earful. I love the Lord just as much as anyone else, but he gave us free will, and I just can't will myself to listen to all the sermons.

My daddy is a powerhouse attorney that has been toying with the idea of running for office when his buddy Barack Obama steps down from the Senate and hopefully steps up to paint the White House black. If he wants it, he's got an excellent shot at winning too, because that's precisely what my dad is known for: winning at every single thing he puts his heart and effort into. My dad's the guy that you call when your civil liberties have been violated, if you're a celebrity charged with the murder of your ex-wife and her new lover, or if you're fighting a big business that is responsible for the wrongful death of a loved one. He makes the late great Johnny Cochran look like a loser. My dad's win-lose ratio is phenomenal; he has one of the best track records around. And he has qualities that are scarce in lawyers: honesty and integrity. He's not the lawyer that will use your case to try to shift the attention to his own agenda or use your problems as a photo op; and he won't take on a case if he feels you're full of shit and you're out just to make a buck. Yet he isn't some idealistic dreamer who can't pay the rent because he's out defending the rights of all the downtrodden of society; he definitely makes a pretty penny and his net worth is well into the millions.

I know my dad loves me. But I also know he always dreamed of a son to follow in his footsteps. Although he didn't get a son and I'm an only child, I know he hoped that Daddy's little girl would become a lawyer or a doctor or something professional and I definitely didn't live up to his expectations. He always seems so sad and let down when I'm around him, so I try to stay away because the guilt is a motherfucker, and my dad is a pro at the art of negotiation. If I'm around him too long there's no telling what he'd talk me into! He's tried everything under the sun to sway me, but it's futile because music is my passion. Living without it would be like living without oxygen. I just can't do it.

My father once offered me a Ferrari if I'd just go to law school, but as tempting as the offer was, I stood fast and in the process broke his heart (or so he says when he really wants to lay the guilt on extra thick). I wish I could have been Daddy's little girl, his angel, his princess; I wish I could just be accepted and loved unconditionally and that my family would support my dreams but that's just not the way it is, so I've had to sacrifice all that to be true to myself, to do what I want. My father now refers to me as the most important case he ever lost. Nice, huh? Still, I don't think my choice of vocation would be such a big deal to my father and grandfather if it weren't for my mother's constant meddling and negative vibes.

My mother is a real piece of work. Monique Toussaint LeBlanc Hayes is from an impressive and rich family from New Orleans. Her father was one of the first "colored" cardiologists to practice in New Orleans and was on the parish council. Her mother was a well-known socialite in "proper black society," herself the daughter of a New Orleans doctor. My mother is third-generation money, and her relatives are so sedity that they thought that my father wasn't good enough! They didn't approve of my grandfather's "rabble-rousing" during the civil rights movement, nor were they too keen on my father's "Negroid" features. They're a bunch of Uncle Toms and sellouts, I'll admit, but I'll cut anyone who talks shit about them. They're *my* Uncle Toms and sellouts so even though their way of thinking digusts me, what am I gonna do? You can't pick your family.

Mother's family is *really* into being Creole. They don't really even consider themselves black. Being called African American or African anything is considered fighting words. My mother almost has a coronary whenever I tell her that there's no such thing as Creole and that Black is Black, but it falls on deaf ears. It doesn't sicken me to think that mother's clan is actually proud of the history of rape and forced miscegenation that made them as fair as any white man, with so-called good hair. I think that everyone should be proud of whom, where, and what they come from regardless of the circumstances, and hold their heads up high. What pisses me off is the fact that they think that their "French" blood makes them *better* than other black folks.

My mother is a large part of the reason why I am admittedly somewhat fucked up. When she wasn't trying to brainwash me with her colorist and elitist ideology, she was filling my head with materialistic bullshit. My mother has never heard the saying "make money, don't let money make you." Money is her identity, her security. In her eyes it's just one more thing that makes us superior.

When I was growing up, I couldn't wear anything that wasn't name brand, and when I say name brand I don't mean urban fashion, which was a big no-no in my household. I mean haute couture from the best fashion houses in France, and at the very least the high-ticket items available from Saks, Neiman's, and Marshall Field's. The only exception was the clothing that was custom-made for me at my mother's insistence because so many girls emulated my style, a fact that she was fiercely proud of. I was given my first charge card at the age of seven, and by the time I was sixteen, I had store charges for every major department store, with the exception of Sears and Penney's and the like.

I was never allowed on public transportation, not even cabs, because we had a driver who could take me where I wanted to go, though that fact never stopped me from riding the CTA just to be spiteful. I got a BMW for my sweet sixteen and a Range Rover when I finished undergrad. I got my hair done by a professional stylist every week without fail, but I never had to go and sit and—heaven forbid—wait in a beauty salon. Some of the nation's finest stylists came to my house to do my hair.

So how did a man from a family so proud to be black, a champion of the underprivileged underdog, end up with a woman whose family was ashamed of the melanin in their skin and wouldn't dream of commingling with someone who made less than six figures a year? Aside from the fact that Mother is really beautiful and smart (despite her antiquated, brainwashed way of thinking), it was simple: she got knocked up. My parents were college sweethearts who met and fell in love while attending Howard University. They had a whirl-wind courtship and were married after less than a year of dating, but the real truth is that my father was quite the playboy and was not ready to settle down, so my mom got pregnant on purpose to trap him. Mother smelled the poten-tial money my father was going to make, and she loved how much people practically worshipped my grandfather. Being associated with them made her feel important. She wasn't going to let my father get away, because although he was darker than a paper bag, he was almost like royalty. Their wedding was featured in *Ebony*, *Jet*, and even white main-stream publications. By marrying my father, her place in black society was solidified. I can't say that I'm pissed, though, otherwise I wouldn't be here. And life hasn't exactly been tough financially.

But growing up, I was confused as hell. I was expected to be just as civic-minded and socially conscious as my father's side of the family and there was mad pressure to be this picture-perfect, prissy Black American Princess like my mother and her people, and the two just don't mesh well in my eyes. In Jack and Jill, the elite social club for African American families I belonged to, all of the other kids and the parents were super nice to me, but it was so fake. The fact of the matter was that no one wanted to run the risk of getting on my father's bad side, and my mother was the Queen Bee of Chicago's black upper- and upper-middle classes. One bad word from her and you were a social pariah. One good word and you were in like Flynn. People were always appeasing me to get in my family's good graces.

But what people didn't know, and what a lot of people still don't realize, is that I carried absolutely no clout or influence with my folks. I was the bad seed, always in trouble and wild as hell. I ditched classes, cussed my teachers out, and was what people considered "fast." I lost my virginity at fourteen, and by the time I graduated from high school, I'd had sex with eight different guys. But the crazy thing was I did what I did, not just because it was fun, but because I *wanted* to get caught. I *wanted* to get in trouble. I wanted something in my life to be ordinary and normal. I wanted to be like other kids. But my life was anything but normal, and there were very few things under my control. Everything the public could see was controlled by something much bigger than me. There were advisors and press secretaries all putting their two cents in on how the Hayes should appear to the masses. This wasn't your case of average American parents nagging their kid to make straight A's and wear the right clothes. This was life by tribunal, and although a democracy might be a great way to run the government with everyone having a fair say in what happens, it is no way to live your own life. Everyone, whether they're rich or poor, wants to be able to make their own choices in life.

I have made the choice to be who I am, and not put up any fronts. I'm a Jack Daniels–drinking, hell-raising, take-no-shit kind of woman and, not only that, I'll confess that I'm a bit of a slut, and I don't even care what anyone thinks about it because it isn't going to change. I am the antithesis of everything my parents stand for; in their worlds I just don't fit. I've tried, but I just don't.

Moving to Miami when I finished college was just what the doctor ordered. I was free, at least for the time being, to be whoever I wanted to be. But I had no idea what that was or exactly what I was going to do with my life. My parents cut me off; they changed the terms of my $4 million trust fund so that I couldn't touch my money until they saw fit, which was when I graduated from law or grad school, when I got married, or when they died. None of that shit is gonna happen any time soon, so even though I had it made as a shorty, I had to make a living for myself just like everyone else. My parents thought cutting me off was punishment, but it wasn't. For once, I could be normal. I could make my own choices without their interference and it was worth it.

When I first got to Miami, I tried waiting tables, but I wasn't really good at it. I guess growing up with housekeepers and cooks and nannies put a monkey wrench in any future I may have had in the hospitality industry. So I ended up selling real estate, because I wouldn't have to be cooped up in an office all day. I was pretty good at it too because, if I say so myself, I can show the hell out of a house. I know just what to highlight to satisfy rich folks and make the sale. But even though I made good money, it bored the shit out of me, so I quit. Still, I was able to buy a nice condo on South Beach and upgrade the Range Rover my parents gave me to a newer model, which I promptly had painted candy pink. I even had a nice little stash to live off while I figured out what I was going to do next.

Then I met Kaos. He was one of the best DJs I'd ever heard, and he was as fine as he was talented. We fell in love at first sight, and were together for two years. He had acquired quite a following, and was blowing up as a DJ, but although I loved the music, I got tired of him always ignoring me, choosing to fool around on his turntables instead of fooling around with me. Then it dawned on me. I would become a DJ too. Since I couldn't beat the game, I could join it, and

I'd have a great career in music as a bonus. Kaos was more than happy to become my mentor, and I was a quick study. Once I got a taste of spinning, I was hooked. Kaos used to tell me that part of the reason that he loved me so much was because I loved to spin just as much as he did, and DJing became as much a part of our relationship as making love.

Kaos wasn't just my man and my mentor, but my best friend. We could talk about any- and everything, and he never judged me because of my background. Even though he was from the hood and grew up poor, he was the only person who seemed to "get" my angst about my bougie background. He accepted me at face value and never tried to make me be something that I wasn't. We worked together, we played together, and we lived together and things couldn't have been more perfect. I was the happiest I'd been in my whole life, and we were planning to get married. But one morning I woke up and he wasn't there. Overnight my world changed. Kaos was killed in a motorcycle accident. I was the one who received the phone call from the coroner's office, and I had to identify his body at the morgue. One simply can't go through something like that and then be okay afterward. It's just not possible.

Kaos's death sent me reeling, and it was almost impossible to piece my life back together afterward. There were days when suicide wasn't far from my mind and I wondered how or if I could go on. But I could and I did go on. In the months that followed, I practiced day and night in the walk-in closet we converted into a "studio." There was so much of Kaos still alive in that tiny little room. It was my way of connecting with him. Sometimes I could still smell his cologne, or I'd run across a piece of paper with his handwriting on it, and that and the music kept me going when the going got tough. I eventually started to score sporadic gigs on my own at some of Miami's hottest clubs; I had never worked without Kaos before. I know that some of those first jobs were landed heavily on the merit of my affiliation with Kaos, because I was constantly being labeled as Kaos's protégé, Kaos's widow, or Kaos's girl, not that I minded, because it was true. He was the only man I've ever loved, he gave me my start, and I owe everything I am to him. Kaos is the reason that I will never settle down again. No one could ever possibly fill his shoes. He wasn't perfect, but he was perfect for me. And after about a year or so, I began to receive props for my skills until finally my name began to carry weight on its own.

Today I'm planning on advancing to a whole new level. The Winter Music Conference is the granddaddy of all music forums. There are seminars on mixing and production, on equipment; there are artist showcases of some up-and-coming artists and some tried-and-true legends in the house- and dance-music scenes, and there are a million parties. Over the years, hip-hop has had more of a presence at the conference. In the past dance music has been more of the focus, but I plan on changing that. The highlight of the conference is the DJ battles. They're a chance to show and prove who's got the tightest skills. And I know that I'm among the best of the best, so I plan on winning.

I finish my breakfast, walk into my studio, and look through my equipment bags and cases. Everything is in its place. I fool around on my turntables, just to get loosened up and in the mood. I don't want to overpractice; I just want to take the edge off so my hands aren't shaky when it's time for me to compete. I play a bunch of classic rap songs that get me amped: "C.R.E.A.M." by Wu-Tang, "Oh Yeah" by Foxy Brown, and the "Quiet Storm" remix by Mobb Deep and Lil' Kim. And when I'm feeling the vibe of the streets through the music, once my pulse is racing and that feeling that I'm the baddest bitch in the world washes over me, I shut off my set-up and head to the bathroom to get my wardrobe and makeup together.

I'm a bundle of nerves by the time I make it to Wyndham Miami Beach where the competition is being held poolside. The venue is packed, but I don't speak to anyone when I get there. I'm in the zone, prepping myself with a little liquid courage. I pour out just a splash from the jigger before I down a double shot of Jack. Then I pour a bit of brew out of the evergreen-tinted glass bottle of Heineken and watch the froth foam and bubble on the hot asphalt before chugging half of it down. Respect due to the brother who ain't here, my baby Kaos. He would be so proud.

I pull out a picture from my back pocket. I keep it with me at all times; it's my good luck charm, a picture of me, Kaos, and Jam Master Jay of Run-DMC taken in New York at the Scratch DJ Academy that Jam Master Jay founded. Kaos and I were there so I could learn some tips to improve my technique from the Jam Master himself. I pour out a little beer for Jay and think to myself that it's a fucking shame that he had to die such a senseless death—that both of them had to die such senseless deaths. I rub the laminated surface of the snapshot, wishing that Kaos was still here with me. He's the first person that ever believed that I could make it as a DJ, and no matter how much time goes by, I still miss him so much. But I know that he's watching every second, and that keeps me from getting sad—most of the time. I picture him up in heaven, lining up angels and seraphim and cherubim, bragging how good his baby girl is and passing around a huge cup of holy wine, and that makes me smile.

I've entered both the beat matching and scratching contests, and I'm one of only a handful of females invited to compete. I am the only sister. I rub my hands together because I see that as a plus: I'll definitely stand out, and when I reveal the few tricks I have up my sleeve, I know that it will be a long time before people stop talking about me. When it's all said and done, everyone will know my name.

The contest begins, and round after round of DJs give it their best. Some of them are nice, but not as nice as me.

"Next up, we have Miami's own Ms. Bobbi," the emcee announces when it's my turn. There's applause and a few people are chanting my name in support, but I block it all out. All I can hear is the thumping of my heart as I step up to the ones and twos and prepare to do my thing. I swear I hear Kaos's voice saying, "I love you, baby girl. Now kill these motherfuckers," so that's what I do.

In my allotted two minutes, I cut, scratch, transform, juggle beats, and put on one hell of a performance. But what really wins the crowd over is when I simultaneously work the turntables, manipulating the fuck out of New Edition's "Cool It Now" so that all you hear is the name Bobbi scratched over and over again as I remove my shirt to reveal my 34Ds covered in so many Austrian crystals that my boobs look like two giant disco balls. It's a new take on an old trick. Guys come out of their shirts in battles all the time, but none of them have the assets that I do. I end things with the line from the song that says "if I love the girl, who cares who you like," and the crowd's response tells me all I need to know. No matter how the voting goes, I'll be the people's champ. I go through the beat matching competition in a haze, but it doesn't affect my performance. Once again I throw down.

"Fuck yeah!" I scream when my name is announced as the winner of the 2006 Winter Music Conference DJ Spin-Off for both categories, an unprecedented victory. Some people cheer, a lot boo, but I don't give a fuck. Victory is mine.

# CHAPTER TWO

## *April 2006*

I'M CHILLING AT THE PAWN SHOP, AN ECLECTIC NIGHTCLUB IN Miami's Design District that is a haven for locals and a spot most tourists don't know about because they don't realize that there is more to life in Miami than South Beach. Most tourists are still shook over the carjackings of the '90s all these years later, and if they don't see the signs bearing a sun logo designating that they are in a tourist-friendly area, they freak out. I guess that it's better safe than sorry, though, because one wrong turn in the Design District will send you straight to Overtown and Liberty City, two areas that even locals tread with care.

I'm a South Beach girl all the way. Most of my life revolves around that strip of land between 1st and Alton Road, and I rarely venture west of Biscayne Boulevard, unless of course I'm going shopping. But now that I am the Winter Music Conference DJ champ, I go any- and everywhere that I can when I'm not working, although I'm almost always working now. I've got to get out there and network, because I've got big plans for my career.

People treat me like a star now, and it's only been a couple of weeks since my win. As far as I see it, though, I've always been a star, these people are just late. I get the VIP treatment, and I'm ushered to a table even though I'm rolling solo, the way I always do when I go out to kick it. I promptly order a bottle of JD and I'm told that my "friends," a group of girls sitting at a table across the room, are buying. I scribble a thank-you note on a napkin and ask the waitress to take it over to them and to invite them over for a drink when the bottle comes. But I hope they decline the offer.

I don't have many female friends. They always bring drama and not much else to the table. Female friends will smile in your face and fuck your man behind your back. Your so-called girls will tell you that your hair looks good when really your weave tracks are showing. And don't even trust what comes out of a female's mouth when you ask her which outfit looks best when you're going out. She's going to tell you the one that looks worse so she can be the best looking. Women will lie and tell you that you look cute and let you walk around with your skirt unknowingly tucked into the top of your panty hose.

I know that socializing is good for business, so of course I'm friendly to just about everyone, but I keep that shit real. It is what it is. Acquaintances and associates are not the same things as friends. I'm never at a loss for acquaintances, especially not now, but truth be told there are times when I miss having friends. Kaos was not just my man, but my best friend, and just as difficult as it has been to replace him as my romantic partner, it's been equally difficult to find a friend that I can trust the way I trusted him. So until I find that special person, my boy Jack Daniels and I will kick it. He never lies to me and he never lets me down, which is why I keep him by my side almost all the time.

I look out onto the dance floor from my perch in the VIP section that overlooks the psychedelically lit dance floor. The "friends" who bought me the bottle are out there doing their damnedest to produce their own version of a girl-on-girl porno, dry humping and grinding against each other in such a way that I'm embarrassed for them. They think it's cute, but it isn't. It's as pathetic and desperate an attempt for attention as ripping off your shirt in a *Girls Gone Wild* video. I'm all for being sexy; I love being naked as much as the next chick, probably more. But when I show *my* shit, I'm getting paid. I raise the bottle of Jack Daniels that has been delivered, pour out a little liquor, and take a hearty swig. When I put the bottle down there's a guy standing in front of me.

"Hey, aren't you that DJ chick?" he asks me.

"The name is Ms. Bobbi," I say. "But yeah, I'm that DJ chick." The guy who's joined me is tall, built like Adonis, and looks like a thugged out Ashton Kutcher if you can imagine that. He's got that look that Kevin Federline is going for but gets all wrong: the edgy, street, but still fashionable vibe. He's not my usual type, but he's pretty fucking hot. He's the type of guy that should be an underwear model or something. I'm usually not down for the swirl; I love black men. But I'm all for equal opportunity. Besides, Mr. Natty Dreadlocks had been a disappointment, so I figure that branching out into the spectrum might yield a higher probability of sexual satisfaction. After all, it's what's inside (his underwear) that counts.

"My name is Cut," he says.

"Oh yeah? Well, nice to meet you, Cut. Where are you from?" I ask him.

"Up top," he says, referring to New York.

"Where about up top?" I ask. If there's something I like better than a dread, it's a native New Yorker. But it depends on what borough he's from. I don't want some corny Wall Street guy, even if he commutes from Brooklyn. Matter of fact, I don't want a guy from Brooklyn if he's from Park Slope or Fort Greene. And Queens is out of the question; I may make an exception if it's Queensbridge that he's repping and he's really, really fine. When it comes to guys from NYC, there are only a few acceptable points of origin: South Bronx, Harlem, or BK, but only the rough parts like Bed-Stuy or Brownsville. I need that rugged toughness that guys from those areas almost always inherently have.

"I'm from the boogie down. You know this," he says, popping his collar.

"Well, where about in the boogie down?" I ask. There are some pretty nice houses in the Bronx, for all I know he could be a bougie little rich boy.

"Patterson Houses," he tells me. I can hear KRS-One in my head singing South Bronx, South, South Bronx. Winner!

"Where you from?" he asks.

"The Chi," I tell him.

"West Side?" he asks. I want to pop him in his mouth for asking me if I'm from the West Side. That's an insult to a South Sider; the West Side is where the *real* Chicago hood is. I know I've got that tough chick vibe going on, and I might look a little rough around the edges, but not that damn rough.

"South," I say, turning up my nose. "You boricua?" I ask, already knowing the answer. I can tell from the way he pronounces certain words that he's from PR. I love Puerto Rican men, and although Cut is more Ricky Martin than Daddy Yankee, I can see he has some flavor. He's definitely not a pasty, pale, Marc Anthony type, thank God. I just hope he's straight, because you know what they say about Ricky.

"*Ya tu sabes*," he says.

"Nice," I say. "Well then, now that we have the formalities out of the way, Cut, can we?"

"Can we what?"

"Can we cut?" I ask.

"It's like that?"

"It's like that," I say, taking another swig from the bottle. I hand it to him and he takes a sip.

"Damn, girl," he says with a grimace from the strong taste of the whiskey. "Damn."

"I'm going to take that as a yes," I say, and I take the bottle with one hand, and his hand with the other.

I don't feel like taking Cut to my place, and even though I'll fuck a stranger (with protection of course), I won't go to one's house. So we hop into my Range, I put in a Marc Anthony CD (hey, I didn't say I didn't like the man's music, I just don't think he's sexy), and we get busy.

Cut was just what I needed. He had a decent sized dick, and he knew how to work it. There was no kissing, no licking and sucking, barely any foreplay. I wasn't in the mood for all that. I just wanted to bust a nut, and that's exactly what I did, three times.

After Cut and I handle our business, he asks me if it's cool to smoke in my truck, and I tell him yeah. He pulls out a bag of weed and rolls a couple of joints. He lights one, and as it is dangling from his lips he says, "This is for now." He places the other joint in my palm and says, "That one's for later." He gives me his number and tells me if I ever want to hook up, to fuck or just to get some weed, to holler at him. I plan on it, until he starts telling me that he's a DJ too, and starts in on how maybe we can get together so that I can give him some pointers. I nod and say cool, but it's not cool. There ain't no way I'm about to give away any of the tricks of my trade to anyone. Not even for a fine ass Puerto Rican with some good dick and some good weed.

A COUPLE OF DAYS LATER I'M OFF TO NEW YORK TO DO SOME appearances on BET. I appear on *Rap City*, where I spin in the Bassment with Mad Linx, who is cool, but I've gotta admit that I miss Big Tigger. I am also a judge for Freestyle Friday on *106th and Park*, but I really miss the hell outta Free and AJ. I always wanted to be on the show so I could find out where Free gets all her cute shoes and where on earth she finds jeans that fit in the waist but still accommodate her ass, because with all the wagon I'm draggin', I need to know. My tailoring bills can get kind of steep. I also wanted to see up close and personal just what the hell AJ was wearing on his head: you know, those braid/dread things that hang from the back of his head like he's the Predator or something. He's got such a cute face, but someone needs to tell him that those shitlocks he rocks do absolutely nothing for him.

The BET appearances go very well. Everyone gives me my props and no one patronizes me, which I find refreshing. But the real fun time in New York happens after my work is done and I'm hard at play. I go to the 40/40 Club to kick it at a party hosted by an up-and-coming starlet named Bianca.

Bianca has just posed for the cover of *Vanity Fair*, quite the coup for a Puerto Rican and an Indo-Jamaican. Bianca has gotten rave reviews for her portrayal of a crackhead turned nun in some independent movie directed by the latest flavor-of-the-month NYU film school dropout who is being touted as a boy genius that will undoubtedly change the face of modern cinema. What people don't seem to realize is that Bianca wasn't acting like a crackhead—she *is* a crackhead!

Bianca's fingertips are nearly brown from holding a smoldering hot pipe, and she's got to weigh about ninety-two pounds soaking wet. She twitches, jerks, and rambles when she speaks about incoherent nonsense, but everyone loves her. Go figure. I never can understand what the bigwigs in Hollywood and New York are thinking when they decide that some mediocre talent with a nice rack or a famous parent is the next big thing. But people are drawn to Bianca and just about every A-list celebrity that you can think of is in attendance at the soiree.

One guest in particular has garnered all my attention, Adwele Olatunji, a rookie for the New York Rush. Adwele is seven foot four and fresh from Africa. He looks a lot like that brother from the movie *Amistad*, and I really want to "give him his free." His skin is so smooth and ebony that I just want to reach out and touch him all over. Every inch of his luscious body is muscled and powerful. He is delicious.

Adwele doesn't drink or smoke. He doesn't swear. And his eyes don't roam all over my body even though my leather pants and corset don't leave much to the imagination. Adwele likes to dance though, and when his body grazes against mine, I almost come on the spot. He moves with the grace of a gazelle and the ferocity of a lion. The sexual tension between us is so thick it seems like the entire club can feel it.

"Do you want to get out of here so we can talk?" he asks me in his heavily accented voice.

"I'd love to," I tell him.

So we go to the Hotel Gansevoort and get a room, and can you believe it? Brother really wants to talk! I mean really, who goes to a hotel to talk? I flirt, I'm suggestive, but he doesn't get the hint. And just as I am getting so frustrated that I figure I ought to just tackle him, rip his clothes off, and pop his dick in my mouth because surely he'd take *that* hint, he asks me if I've heard the good news of Jesus Christ. That's right; he's a Jehovah's Witness. There will be no sweaty tribal sex. I won't hear the drums of the Congo as he brings me to climax after climax. My body will not be reunited with the motherland.

"Too many times," I tell him, and I leave him there in the room.

PARTY AND BULLSHIT AND PARTY AND BULLSHIT. THAT'S MY LIFE in Miami; it ain't just a song by Biggie. But I'm not complaining one bit. I love the life I live and I live the life I love. I can't imagine getting dressed at the crack of dawn to go work in corporate America, and I feel sorry for the poor slobs that do it every day. In my opinion corporate America is the devil. Think about it. Only in corporate America are the so-called values that politicians are always stressing that Americans lack totally ignored: Fuck your family. The corporation is your family. Your kid gets sick and you want to take off to stay at home with him or go to the doctor? Not their problem. Need some time to decompress because your blood pressure is sky high due to some office politics? Fuck you. Do it outside of the forty-plus hours you're scheduled to be at work, because the "team" can't function without you and we all know that there is no I in team.

They hire you because you're bright, creative, and talented, but if you flex any of that muscle without being told to do so, crack goes the whip; now get back into the box, you fucking gimp. And to top it off, you get to look just like everyone else in a gray, blue, or black suit. How fucking original. So you put up with that shit because what's the alternative? You work or you starve. And in the end, you're lucky if you get a gold watch because more than likely some of the higher-ups have made off with the pension fund and they won't serve a single day of prison time for robbing people of their entire lives, even if the matter goes to trial. That's why I will never, ever work a nine-to-five job in my life. I won't even date a so-called corporate thug. You know, a guy from the hood who has made it to the boardroom. There's usually too much corporate and not enough thug. Those kinds of guys just don't take the time to stop and enjoy life, which is way too short to be spent stuck in some office tossing a bunch of buzzwords back and forth to mask the fact that you don't know what the fuck you're doing.

But since my win at the Winter Music Conference, I know that I'm going to have to start adopting more of a corporate mentality if I want to really blow up. Because I want to be more than Miami's hottest DJ; I want to be the world's hottest DJ. I'm after world domination, a total global takeover. So after thinking about things, I've realized that I need to maximize my exposure and diversify. I had hoped that the Winter Music Conference wins would garner the attention needed to acquire a sponsorship from an equipment company, but that hasn't happened yet, probably because my style can't be easily categorized. How can these companies sell me if they can't label me?

I'm not just a house DJ, or just a hip-hop DJ, or just a reggae DJ; I love all three genres. I won't fucking touch techno but I throw in rock, punk, metal, and pop into my mixes whenever I can. Still, I definitely can't be categorized as a rock DJ or a pop DJ. I thought that having universal appeal would help me, but it hasn't. It has gotten me fans from all walks of life, but it hasn't translated into dollars yet. I've debated whether or not to hire a manager, but I've decided against it for the time being, because I don't want to give up 15 percent of my money while I do all the work. Besides, no one knows me or can sell me better than myself, so I've decided that I'm going to knock down some doors, bust through some ceilings, and get things done my way.

"I want to see George, and I know he's here, because I saw his car. So don't give me any more of your bullshit," I tell the girl at Opium Garden when I go there to show the manager a proposal I've created. I want to pitch a new hip-hop night featuring myself and also bringing in some of the nation's hottest female DJs, and I want to boot the current promoters out of their spot. Not only do I want to DJ, I want a cut of the door *and* the bar. A healthy one. I don't want to rent the venue on some off night and pay some exorbitant fee and just get paid from the door revenue. That shit's too hard. I want Saturdays. Saturdays haven't been poppin' in Miami for a minute.

The secretary is a total bitch and she's coming up with all kinds of excuses as to why I can't see him, and not only that, but she's demanding that I leave. I don't take no for an answer. Especially not from people with no power.

"He's in a meeting, a very important one, and he can't be disturbed," she says in a snooty voice. "You won't be able to see him today so you may as well just leave and come back some other time."

"Is he in there with Jesus?" I ask her.

"No," she says curtly.

"Then tell him Ms. Bobbi is here. He knows me. I'm here to do him a favor," I say.

"Looks like you're the one who needs a favor," she says under her breath, but I hear that shit and I don't like it one bit. I want to smack the shit out of her for getting out of pocket, but it wouldn't do me any good to hurt an employee when I'm trying to hustle up a job. She's a nobody, a gate-keeper, but she's no pit bull. I know I can get around her and if I can't, I may as well hang it up and try another profession.

Instead of letting her get the best of me, I stroll right past her and head to George's office.

"Where do you think you're going?" she asks me, and has the nerve to grab me by the arm.

"You'll be on your way to the hospital if you don't get your hands off me," I tell her. She knows she can't stop me; I'm playing the gangsta girl role to the fullest and she has no idea that it's an act. I'm not a punk. If I have to fight, I can throw bows with the best of them, but I'm a lover not a fighter; it's not like I'm going to pull out a gat or a shank. But she has no idea, and since I'm dressed like a chola in a white wifebeater, tight jeans, Converse Chuck Taylor All Stars, and a fedora cocked jauntily to the side, she buys it. She follows behind me helplessly as I turn the knob and enter the office.

"I tried to stop her but she insisted that she knew you and just barged in. I can call the police," she says to George meekly, but he laughs at the suggestion.

"Ms. Bobbi," George says with a smile. "What the fuck are you up to? Being a troublemaker, I see."

"Trouble is my middle name," I tell him. "Sorry to interrupt your meeting, George, really. I just wanted you to know that I was here and that I need to talk to you. Your gatekeeper wasn't going to give you the message and we both know it. Ain't that right, hall monitor?" I look at the secretary and she slinks out of the office.

"No problem, Bobbi," he says. "We were just about to go grab a bite to eat. Have you met Eric Milon?" he asks me.

"No, I haven't, but I know who you are." I extend my hand and shake Mr. Milon's. "It's a pleasure to meet you, Mr. Milon," I say.

"Please, call me Eric," he tells me. I can't believe my luck. Eric's presence is the best thing that I could have hoped for. Eric is one-third of the Milon Brothers, the owners of South

Beach's trifecta of premium nightclubs: Mansion, Prive, and the Opium Garden. There will be no excuses of "I need to ask my boss" from George. I'll get either a yes or a no today.

I go on to tell them the purpose of my ambush. I whip out the proposal I've crafted that tracks the projected earnings and presents a strong case for them to take this project on, along with my ever-expanding press kit. Hey, I never said I was stupid and didn't know how to do the whole corporate thing; I just don't want to do it for a living. But I know that in order to win over real businessmen, which George and Eric are, I've got to come at them hard and on their level, if not a level higher than theirs. They seem a little hesitant, but having been in sales, I know that every no they give me is just another opportunity for me to convince them to say yes.

It's a hard sell. I hear a lot of excuses, but after a lot of negotiating we come to an agreement. My dad always told me that compromise is when both sides of a negotiation are equally dissatisfied. I don't get the percentage I wanted of the bar, but I do get a percentage, which was the biggest roadblock. We also come to the agreement that the event will be held at Mansion rather than Opium Garden, which is a little disappointing to me because Opium is the prettier club. But I think to myself that once I show and prove that I can be a bomb-ass promoter as well as a bomb-ass DJ, I can write my own ticket in the future.

I turn Mansion out consistently. Every week my set gets better and better. And every week I fly in another banging female DJ to spin with me. The crowds are ridiculous, and the money is really nice, plus my name is hotter than ever. Saturday nights at Mansion are the place to be if you want to hear the best in hip-hop, R&B, reggae, reggaeton, and such.

Memorial Day weekend I partner with Missy Elliot as my celebrity guest host, and I've got Beverly Bond and DJ Shortee coming in. It's a very important night and I know I'm going to make a ton of money. I make phone calls on my way to the club, just to make sure that everything is running smoothly. I talk to both of the DJ's managers; both Beverly and Shortee have made it into town and settled into their hotel rooms, and they'll be sure to leave early in order to make it to the venue on time. I also chat with the VIP hostess, who assures me that she's going to milk the patrons for all they're worth and charge a grip for expedited entry.

I light up and take a puff of a super fat joint of potent weed called "Northern Lights" from Alaska. It's the good shit, so I only need a couple of tokes to feel a nice buzz, but it makes my truck stink to high heaven. The night air is charged with electricity; I can sense there's going to be adventure, as corny as that sounds, because I've always been a little clairvoyant. I can usually sense when something important is going to happen. I think it's a part of the reason why I'm so confident. Mother says that many of the Toussaint women had "the blessing and the curse of sight" as she refers to it. Mother always claims to know exactly what I'm up to because of it, but she's usually just trying to manipulate me into confessing something. But sometimes she's dead on the money, and when she is, it's creepy. I just wish that I had more control of whatever it is because maybe I'd be able to pick some winning lottery numbers! Unfortunately, the feelings and visions that I get for myself aren't always as clear as I'd like; things almost always have to play themselves out a bit before I can connect the dots. Although I've seen things as clear as a bell for other people, I can't see shit for myself. I guess that's why it's a blessing and a curse.

When I hit the Washington Avenue strip, it's packed and traffic is slowed down to a snail's pace. I see that my street team—a group of model-pretty chicks wearing matching T-shirts and booty shorts and handing out flyers—is on their job. They wave at me as I pass them on the street and crawl through the maze of cars.

I extinguish my joint and spray some odor-neutralizing air freshener as I pull up in front of Mansion. The line for the valet is a little long but I'm able to boguard my way to the front without much of a problem. Then I see *him*, and my world stops. It's only for a split second, but there's a definite glitch in the matrix. Standing next to the weekend doorman, Rico, is a burly bouncer who immediately captures my attention. I know that this man can't possibly be my Kaos. But the second I laid eyes on him, I could feel Kaos. His presence is so strong around me that it sends a chill through my body as if I'd been touched by a hand from the grave. I can't tell exactly what it is about this man that reminds me so much of Kaos—they don't look anything alike—but there is an inexplicable connection.

I eye the roach of the joint that I'd been smoking in the ashtray and close it shut. I shake my head and tell myself that it's just my mind playing tricks on me because of the weed. This is what I tell myself, but I know that there's more to it than that; I can feel it in my bones. I have a serious case of cottonmouth as I watch the two of them approach my truck.

"What's up, Ms. Bobbi," Rico says to me as I step out of the Range Rover.

"Hey, Rico. How is it tonight?" I ask him, giving him a Hollywood hug and a kiss on each cheek. I can't take my eyes off the bouncer. He's eyeing me as well, but his face is stone and he says nothing.

"Packed!" he says. "You ready to do your thing?"

"Aren't I always?" I ask him, grinning. I pop the trunk and

the bouncer steps around to the back and pulls out the large aluminum case that holds my equipment.

"Is this all she has?" the bouncer asks Rico, even though I'm standing right there. I remove my house keys from my key chain before I hand it over to the valet.

"Yeah, that's it," I tell the bouncer. "I use my laptop to spin." I extend my hand, hoping that my palms aren't all gross and sweaty, and introduce myself. "I'm Ms. Bobbi, the DJ. Damn you're fine," I say with a coquettish smile. I wouldn't mind getting to know him better.

"Yeah, I know. I'm Q," he says, devoid of any emotion, his dark brown eyes meeting mine directly while shaking my hand. His hands are soft and his nails are neatly groomed, but his grip is firm and powerful. Confidence oozes from every pore in his body.

"Do you know that you're fine or do you know that I'm the DJ?" I quip flirtatiously.

"Both," he says. He closes the trunk and walks quickly toward the club's entrance. I watch the muscles in his ass and thighs flex and dance beneath the fabric of his pants as he walks away. I can't believe this dude just played me like that, but I can't help but think that even though his attitude sucks, he's got a magnificent ass. I've always been a sucker for a nice, big, juicy ass and chiseled thighs. But despite his good looks and his vague similarity to Kaos, I immediately dislike Q. Not only did he practically ignore me, but I get the distinct feeling that he's rushing me from the way he's standing impatiently and obviously irritated at the door. Someone must have told him wrong because he obviously doesn't realize that no one rushes Ms. Bobbi. I hate when other people say this, but doesn't he know who I am?

I forget about Q and focus on myself. I walk slowly through the velvet ropes and down the red carpet that leads to the club. That red carpet stroll is just as important to me as it is to a Hollywood starlet on her way to the Oscars, and what I'm wearing, or not wearing, is just as important to me as it is to Charlize Theron or Nicole Kidman or Halle Berry. After all, part of my notoriety now is due to the fact that I spin in outfits outrageous enough to make a stripper blush. I'm such an exhibitionist that I won't even begin to deny it; I get off on people staring at me and desiring me. Hell, I provoke it on every possible occasion.

I can hear people whispering about me as I chat briefly with the door hostess and a couple of the doormen who are deciding which hopefuls have what it takes to get in quickly and which ones have to wait who knows how long in line *and* pay a hefty admission price. It's not that I have anything important to say. I just want to make sure that everyone sees who's about to turn the club out. I pivot as if I'm at the end of a runway in Bryant Park during New York Fashion Week. I'm going to make sure that this is a night to remember.

I've got on a "bra" made of pink, green, and clear Swarovski crystals that are glued in an abstract pattern across my breasts with liquid latex. My pink leather shorts barely cover my ass, but they look so hot with my matching pink stiletto boots that come up to my mid-thigh. My sandy colored hair, which is somewhere between curly and kinky, is teased to the outer limits and held fast on both sides with pink and green rhinestone clips in a funky faux hawk. My eyes are made up dramatically with glittery eye shadow, tiny pink rhinestones, and ultraglam false eyelashes made of mink. It's over the top, but that's the point. I decide that the grueling daily workouts I've endured with my sadistic personal trainer, Palmero, were well worth the pain as the men look at me with lust and the women stare at me with envy.

When I get good and ready I meet Q at the door. He holds

it open for me and escorts me inside and upstairs to the DJ booth. Then he walks away without saying a word. *How rude*, I think. I know bouncers aren't necessarily supposed to be *friendly* to the clientele, but he could at least be cordial.

"Bye, Q. It was nice meeting you too," I yell sarcastically at his back. I don't think he hears me over the music, but he turns around and flashes me a peace sign and a wink before disappearing down the stairs and into the crowd. I feel my heart flutter a little bit because he's so damn sexy, but I ignore the feeling. Q hasn't given me my props, and it is really too bad for him because if he had, he could have had some pussy.

I give my opening act, DJ Money T, a wave and he gives me a nod. I know that's as good as I'm going to get from him, but I don't really care. Money T isn't even on my level; he's a hater. The only reason he has this gig is because he's a tenacious little fucker and at least to my face he shows me respect. He's cute too, and lots of women like him. He has a strong fan base and I'm not stupid enough to get rid of him when he pulls bodies in. He will never admit that he's intimidated by me and jealous. But we both know the truth. My skills on the turntables are lovely, and I will put that shit to the test anytime, anyplace. But at least Money T isn't as bad as some guys who refuse to work with me at all. Dumb asses! They let their egos get in the way of their careers, and I don't understand that, but as far as I'm concerned, they can kiss my pretty ass.

My favorite waitress, Blaze, cheerfully greets me before handing me a Heineken and a shot of Jack. "You look outrageous!" she squeals. "Knock 'em dead, girlfriend."

"Thanks, Mama," I say appreciatively, then slip her a ten spot. I don't have to pay for drinks, but by hooking Blaze up every now and then, she always takes real good care of me.

Money T ends his set and steps away from the decks. I perform the ritualistic splash of whiskey and brew into a trash can for Kaos. Then I hook my laptop and the turntables up to my Serato Scratch Live Box, the interface that connects my computer to the sound system, and pull out the vinyl control platters. Some DJs are purists and say that traditional vinyl is the only way. But I disagree. I think a good DJ can spin with vinyl or CDs or a laptop. Hell, I can rock a club with eight-track cassettes if need be. My few high-tech tools enable me to do the same thing I would have to carry a million crates to do, and I'm too cute to be lugging that stuff around.

I scan the crowd. They're young, upscale, and definitely ready to get crunk. The VIP sections are filled with socialites that want to dance on the tables so badly I can see it in their eyes. There are a few athletes in the house, and a couple of rappers. There are a few dope boys and kingpins in the house trying to outdo one another and see who can buy the most bottles and cop the most honeys. I make mental notes on who to check on when I'm done. As always, I'm in the mood for a little fun.

There are wall-to-wall bodies, and as usual, there are a ton of beautiful women, the South Beach trademark. I cue up the first two tracks of my set and exhale. I signal to my lighting guy that I'm ready to begin my set.

There's the sound of an explosion and then the room goes dark. Sirens blare as red and blue police lights perched atop speakers flood the room with bright flashes of light. Smoke swirls around the crowd's legs and multicolored lasers dance about, making designs on the walls before spelling out Ms. Bobbi on the wall behind me. A spotlight shines down on me and my pulse races wildly as people begin to hoot and applaud. The crystals on my chest pick up the lights and make me shine as bright as a Fourth of July sparkler, as smoke billows from either side of me and I begin to execute the cutting and scratching tricks I'm known for.

I start out with some songs that are sure to please the ladies. They go wild as I play "Queen Bitch" by Lil' Kim. One advantage to being a woman in the game is that I know what women like to hear. And once you get the women on the dance floor having a good time shaking their asses, the men are sure to follow. I mean really, how sexy is it to watch a bunch of hard legs two-stepping with each other? But when you have a bunch of girls dancing with each other, it's a totally different story. I see Money T roll his eyes as he stands off to the side, observing the way things should be done. *Watch and learn*, I say to myself.

Miami seems to be made up of about 60 percent transplanted or vacationing New Yorkers, so I yell out, "Is Brooklyn in the house?" The crowd yells "without a doubt" in response and I play Notorious B.I.G.'s "Big Poppa." I throw in Jay-Z and Foxy Brown's "Ain't No Nigga" and watch the women all sway and shimmy to the classic duet. Brooklyn is definitely in the house. I play around, segueing from B.I.G. to Jigga and back again, and the result is hotter than the Biggie duets album. Then I create a lyrical battle between Foxy and Kim, switching back and forth between their songs so that it sounds like they're challenging and answering each other. I ask, "Is Queens in the house?" Then I add some Nas joints and a little Mobb Deep into the brew. I ask the sea of writhing bodies, "Where's Miami?" When I play Trick and Trina's "Take It to the House," all the Miami girls start popping their asses and dropping to the floor. I know that I have the crowd right where I want them, in the palm of my hand.

My set lasts three hours. I was scheduled to play two, but an encore was demanded. For me DJ'ing is about making people happy and making sure that they have the best time possible, and I don't stop until I know my mission is accomplished. Shortee is up next and, after her, Beverly Bond will close things out. I'm restless and not ready to go home just yet so I sit in the VIP section and order a bottle of Cristal from Blaze. Why not celebrate, right?

I go speak to Missy and we chop it up for a little while and then I return to my table when I see my champagne arrive. I spot Q, and I swear that he's staring at me, but when I smile at him he simply turns away. Fuck him! I pop the bottle open myself, letting a little of the foam spill over onto the floor before pouring myself a glass of bubbly. That way I don't have to pour any out for Kaos because it costs too much to just dump. I'm not sitting there for more than five minutes before I'm joined by a model and a rising actor who's in town shooting his first movie; they come to congratulate me on my set.

They're a little on the strange side, and I get the distinct feeling that they're trying to initiate a threesome, but I'm not really interested. The model is beautiful, but so thin that she's borderline anorexic. I want to feed her, not fuck her. And the actor is clearly geeking off coke, and I'm in no mood to babysit a tweaker. I refrain from saying much, hoping that they'll get the point and go away, but no such luck. They just sit there chattering away, guzzling my champagne and getting on my nerves. I glance around, debating if the scene was worth any more of my time when a man seated alone on a banquette starts flirting with me.

I drink in the sight of this man. He's about five foot ten, a little short for my taste, and appears to be in his mid to late forties, a little old for my taste. Generally, I don't like anything old but money, but something about this guy intrigues me. Maybe it's the fact that the crowd is young, hip-hop, and overwhelmingly black, and he is none of those things. I can't help but wonder what he's doing here and if he feels out of place. He certainly looks comfortable and confident, and that adds to his allure.

He has high cheekbones, a crop of dark wavy hair, piercing green eyes, and he's in all black, Armani I assume, from the excellent cut and the way the fabric drapes over his lean frame. He reminds me of an even more fly version of Bono, the lead singer of U2. Very sexy indeed! I return his flirtatious glances, seductively trailing my finger around the rim of my champagne glass. He smiles. I smile back.

"Excuse me, but I see someone I must talk to. Have a good night." I pour the rest of the champagne in my glass leaving the bony babe and her guy, and head toward the mystery man.

"Hello," I say as seductively as possible, slightly arching my back so that he'll take notice of my breasts.

"Hello, Ms. Bobbi," the mystery man replies in a thick accent. "You were incredible tonight," he says.

"So you know who I am?" I ask, grinning. I absolutely love to be recognized, even if it's right after I step down from the DJ booth. It lets me know that people are paying attention.

"Naturally. I came here just to see you," he tells me.

"Well, now that you've seen me, what are you planning on doing?" I ask. No sense in wasting time. I'm feeling really horny; I usually do after a set because DJ'ing is like sex to me—sensual, hot, and passionate. I want this beautiful stranger in my bed, not just standing in front of me.

"I have lots of plans for you, Ms. Bobbi. But for now, I'd like to take you to breakfast," he replies, smiling. His teeth are a little crooked, but oddly, that adds to his appeal.

"Before or after we sleep together?" I ask him bluntly. I love shocking my victims before I go in for the kill. I wonder if that makes me a sexual predator.

He chokes a little bit on a piece of ice he'd been chewing. "You mean I have a choice?"

"Not really," I tell him. "You can come with me to my place, where I guarantee you I will blow your mind and then fix *you* breakfast, or you can catch me at my next gig just like everyone else."

"Are you always this aggressive?" he asks.

"Only when I'm trying to get what I want," I tell him.

"Well, what do you want from me?" he asks me.

"Everything, and then some," I say. I grab him by the hand and lead him out of the club.

I take him to my home, hoping I won't regret it. We get to my place in no time flat, him following behind me to my small Ocean Drive condo in a canary yellow Lamborghini Murcielago. *We're balling like that?*, I muse with a smile of approval. The car alone makes me wet; it's like a hard cock with wheels. But I wonder if he's overcompensating for a lack of manpower in the bedroom.

As soon as I shut and lock the door behind him, I grab a handful of his thick, soft hair and kiss his full pink lips. I never kiss guys; I guess that it's the whore in me, but kissing really is too intimate to do with strangers. But I want to be intimate with this guy. I don't know if I'm feeling out of sorts from being reminded of Kaos earlier, or if I'm stinging from Q's rejection. Maybe I'm just tired of empty sex and I want to feel intimate with someone, not just sexual, even if it's just for one night and even if it's all pretend. Whatever it is, he's a good kisser, and I can feel his body respond instantly. We stand in the alcove, our mouths pressed together for what feels like hours, before I take him into the bedroom.

"Wait a minute," he gasps in between kisses.

"What?" I moan.

"You don't even know my name," he says.

Apparently my reputation as a slut does not precede me. "So what," I tell him, and begin to kiss his neck as I unbutton his shirt.

"Don't you want to?" he asks.

I look him dead in his hypnotic green eyes. "Maybe I will later. But right now, I want to feel you inside of me. Now can you get with that or not?" He stares back at me, as if deciding what to do. Then he pushes me roughly onto the bed, loosens his tie, and rips his shirt open before descending upon me.

We make out for a while longer, frantically removing our clothing and grinding our pelvises together like a couple of high-school kids. Groaning, I flip him over on his back like a wrestler and straddle him. I reach into the nightstand and pull out a condom. In a swift motion I rip open the package and place the rubber into my mouth. As I pull out his cock and slip the condom on with my lips, I feel his body tense and then relax. Oh, hell no! I sit up in disbelief. This man is older, but I can't believe that he's gotten off already.

"Did you come?" I ask him.

"Yes," he says.

I sit there momentarily dazed. I knew that I was good, but not that good.

"It is not a problem," he says matter of factly. "Do you have more condoms?" he asks.

"Well, yes but," I begin. He grins at me and then motions toward his crotch with a nod. Although he'd climaxed, his penis is still at full attention. He won't need any time to rest or recuperate; he is rearing and ready to go.

I reach into the nightstand drawer again, extracting a roll of six condoms. I dangle them in the air and with a sly grin ask, "Will this be enough?"

"Maybe," my new friend answers, "or maybe not."

Ah, music to my ears!

WHAT CAN I SAY ABOUT THE SEX? IT WAS MIND-BLOWING! I have what I think of as an insatiable appetite for all things carnal, but the man who shared my bed made sure I was fully satisfied. He was more than I could have hoped for, a very pleasant surprise.

"So what's your name?" I ask him after our marathon sex session. We're sitting in my bed, sharing a joint.

"Do you make a habit of smoking with gentlemen you don't know?" he kids.

"You're no gentleman," I tease back.

"Well, Ms. Bobbi, you are right about that," he says with a little laugh. He looks at me with those amazing emerald eyes. "Hello, gorgeous," he says, then smoothes my hair back from my face and kisses me on my forehead. "Allow me to introduce myself. My name is Mikhail Petrov," he says.

"Get the fuck out of here!" I say, rising to my knees on the bed. "You've got to be kidding!"

"I sure hope not. I had on his underwear most of the night," he says grinning.

"As in Mikhail Petrov, the new owner of Babylon?" I ask him.

Babylon had been one of my favorite clubs. Located on 6th and Washington, the club had been shut down for about six months, after the original owner died of a heroin overdose. His wife got everything he owned, which included the club and two very posh restaurants. Having no interest in running his businesses, she decided to sell them. Then rumors started circulating that a group of Russians came down from New York and bought everything for $15 million. In cash! The words *mafia* and *organized crime* had been circulating too. True enough, those words were used to describe just about everyone in Miami, from street gangs to the government, but I can't help but wonder if the man I'd just screwed seven ways to Sunday was a Russian mobster.

"One of the new owners, yes," he says.

"Wow. I thought you would be older," is all I can manage to say. I settle back in the bed and take a deep drag of the joint.

"I am older," he says. I emit a small, stiff laugh. I'm not sure if it's Mikhail or the weed that has me so nervous, but I'm starting to get paranoid. It isn't like I haven't been around my share of dope boys, hustlers, and pimps. And I love the thugs. But the things I've heard about Russian organized crime send a chill through my body. They aren't like Folks, or Disciples, or Latin Kings, or even MS-13s. I've heard that even the Italian mob is scared of the Russians! They're rumored to be the most powerful and most brutal of all the so-called ethnic mobs. I sit there trying to act normal, but even Stevie Wonder could see that the vibe has changed dramatically. I've gone from being sensual and aggressive to acting all weird, a combination of horny and scared and I don't know if I want to kick him out or jump his bones. I fidget. I twirl my hair. I can't stop clearing my throat.

"Why don't you go ahead and ask me what you want to ask me?" Mikhail props his weight onto one elbow and faces me. He looks amused. Amused is good. It's better than angry. "Then I can ask you what I want to ask you."

"Ask you what?" I stammer and avoid Mikhail's piercing stare.

"If the rumors are true, if I'm a part of the dreaded Russian mafia," Mikhail says, wiggling his fingers in the air and making a noise like a ghost and then he laughs. "I'm foreign, I'm not dumb. I own a television, and a radio, and I read. I know what people are saying about me," he says.

"I haven't heard any rumors," I lie and regret it instantly. Of course I've heard the rumors. Everyone on the scene has heard them.

"You're a horrible liar," he says, ruffling my hair like I'm a child and kissing me on the forehead again. "And you're a horrible actress. Everyone on the South Beach scene wants to know about the Russian mobsters who bought Babylon."

Fuck it then. I'm busted. "Okay, I admit it. I may have heard a peep or two."

"Peep, peep," Mikhail says and tweaks my nipples. I laugh and then I get serious.

"Well, are you? Are you in the Russian mafia? Are you some ruthless, cold-hearted killer?" I ask.

"I am no killer," Mikhail says. "This I can assure you." Mikhail reaches for his pants and for a second I panic because I think he's going to put his pants on and walk out the door. But I don't want him to leave. I want to know everything about him. And I want to fuck him again. But he doesn't put on his pants and he doesn't leave. He pulls a pack of clove cigarettes out of the pocket and throws the pants back on the floor.

"You didn't really answer my whole question," I reply. I extend my hand for a cigarette. Mikhail hands me one.

"I know," he says, wiggling his eyebrows devilishly. He laughs and cups my chin in his hand. He kisses me softly, then gazes at me. Damn those green eyes! I'm weak. I look into them, and I can't think straight.

"I mean, what is the Russian mafia anyway?" Mikhail asks.

Oh, hell yeah, he's in it. He's definitely in the mafia. He's about to get all semantic with me and try to run me in circles with some game.

"I'm from the South Side of Chicago. I know a gangster

when I see one. I don't care how much you try to clean it up."
I take a puff of the clove and blow smoke circles.

"Is that right?" he asks.

"Yep," I tell him.

"Bobbi, this is something that I think you will be able to understand. I'm sorry to disappoint you but a lot of people jump to conclusions about me just because I am Russian. It's as simple as that. If a bunch of us who have made it try to help each other out and build a legacy for our families, our people, our country, people say we're a gang. The same thing happens to successful black men, does it not? Racial profiling, stereotypes . . . people are afraid of what they don't know or understand. Some people always want to think the worst, no matter what," he says, and I nod my head to show that I feel him because he does have a point.

"I am educated. I have an economics degree from the University of Lvov. I am an international businessman. I happen to be very ruthless when it comes to business. I didn't get rich by being nice. For that I have no apologies. Like you, I am who I am," he says, puffing his clove.

I wonder how straight Mikhail is being with me. I have yet to meet a hustler, a gangster, or a criminal of any kind that has readily admitted to what he does. The people who are always yapping off at the mouth usually don't have shit and haven't done shit. Posers. The ones with something to lose, the smart ones anyway, lie like a motherfucker. After all, we'd just met and he had no obligation to tell me anything. *What difference does it make anyway?*, I tell myself. *It's just sex. It isn't like he's my boyfriend. His business is his business.*

"Okay, I feel you," I say. "I'm sorry if I offended you. Really, I am. I wasn't brought up to jump to conclusions about people," I tell him. I realize that it's not a totally true statement; my mother has always encouraged me to jump to conclusions about people based on appearances, but I don't go into all that with him. Instead I ask, "Now, what do you want to ask me?"

"Well, the reason I came to see you tonight was to ask you to consider becoming a resident DJ at Babylon."

"Well, I'm not just a DJ, I'm a promoter," I tell him.

"Even better. I want you to bring the same event you do at Mansion to Babylon. We open in a few months and I want you to come on board as a part of the team."

"Word?" I ask. Talk about luck. I get the fuck of a lifetime and a tight gig at the same time and I wasn't even trying. I knew being a slut could pay off.

"Yes," he says, "word."

I laugh at his contrived attempt to sound cool.

"Why me?" I ask.

"I've been following your career for a while now. You're a star in the making."

"DJs don't become stars," I tell him. "Not really. They become known."

"That's before you came along. Besides, you've got more up your sleeve, don't you?"

"I'm not wearing sleeves," I tell him. "I'm naked." Mikhail kisses my shoulders and runs his tongue down the side of my arm.

"You sure are," he says. "But you've got a plan. You're not going to play records all your life, are you?"

"Why not?" I ask. Then I laugh. "Yeah, Mikhail, I have plans," I inform him.

"Care to share?"

"Eventually."

"So you think you would want to work for me? I am, after all, a very dangerous man." He crooks his eyebrow at me.

"I laugh in the face of danger," I say and laugh in his face.

Mikhail kisses me and then looks at me with a serious expression.

"Well, do you feel bad about sleeping with your new boss?" he asks.

"No. It's not like I knew who you were before I seduced you. And you're not my boss yet. Besides, who says I'm going to continue sleeping with you?"

"Aren't you?" he asks.

I say nothing, I just slide beneath the sheet and take Mikhail into my mouth.

# CHAPTER THREE

*June 2006*

DAYS GO BY AND NO WORD FROM MIKHAIL PETROV. NOT a peep. I wonder what the fuck his problem is. It's not like I expected a relationship from the guy, but he made some pretty lofty promises; I did expect him to call so we could at least talk business. When I hadn't heard from him after a week I decided to do a little reconnaissance so I could see what he's really about. Maybe this guy I slept with wasn't even the real Mikhail Petrov. It dawned on me that maybe he was some sicko in a rental car who got off on pretending to be someone else. In Miami, anything is possible!

I go online and google him; the first thing I do is an image search. The guy I had the one-nighter with was definitely Mikhail Petrov. So what was the deal with the disappearing act? Did he reconsider hiring me? Or worse, did I get played? I search some more, and up pops a lot of boring shit about company takeovers, mergers, and acquisitions. Standard businessman shit. Not one peep about mob ties. Not even a peep about associating with mobsters. Maybe he was on the up and up, at least about the mafia stuff. But as far as I was concerned he was full of shit about everything else.

Mikhail had already gotten the pussy so he didn't have to lie about wanting me to spin at Babylon. Maybe he wanted to string me along and secure some future pussy. I don't know what else his motives could have been for telling me he wanted to hire me, because he certainly doesn't act like he wants to. Maybe I'm being too antsy; Mikhail's a busy man and I'm sure Babylon is only a part of his vast empire. So I will give him a little time, but only a little. Guys like him think the world revolves around them and people bend over backwards to give them what they want. But Mr. Mikhail Petrov is in for a surprise.

I GO TO NIKKI BEACH CLUB ON A SUNDAY NIGHT AND AS USUAL, people are dying to get inside. Once again Q is at the door. What is his deal? All of a sudden he's everywhere. And he still isn't friendly. I speak to him, and he barely acknowledges my presence. He just gives me a little nod and continues to stare forward with all the seriousness of one of Louis Farrakhan's security force, the Fruits of Islam. Once again, I've been igged by this nobody. He must be gay or something, because no man in his right mind would turn away from me. But whatever it is, it's his problem. A guy is one thing I will never chase.

The men clamoring for entrée are schmoozing and attempting to bribe doormen, discreetly pressing bills damp with sweat into the gatekeepers' palms. Young women are exploiting their flesh by wearing the skimpiest outfits they can find, and craning their necks so that their flawless young faces can be seen, expediting their entrance. People fight for recognition, not wanting to be seen waiting to get into a party, the ultimate sign of not being in the loop on South Beach. Adding to the fervor, Jamie Foxx is in to celebrate the multiplatinum success of his album, *Unpredictable*. Lucky for me I'm on the list, and I sail in. I'm pissed that I'm not DJ'ing; who's better than me, right? But I look on the bright side; I can actually kick back and have fun. There's champagne everywhere, women are throwing themselves at Jamie, and he's charming everyone in sight, enjoying himself to the fullest. It's the party of the year.

I first met Jamie when he came down to shoot *Any Given Sunday* years ago. I opened for Miami favorite and Terror Squad's DJ Khaled at a party he threw while Jamie was shooting *Miami Vice*. I know a million women who'd kill to be hanging out with this super talented movie star with a tight ass body, a beautiful voice, an Academy Award, and all the perks that come with that. But no matter how hard I try, I can't really get into the swing of things. Sure, on the outside, I appear to be the same fun-loving, outrageous Ms. Bobbi, but inside I'm in turmoil. Even though I thought I'd gotten Mikhail out of my mind, I find myself thinking about him all the time. My body even experiences aftershocks when I reminisce about the way we felt together.

This isn't like me at all; I never, ever wait for a man to call me. And I don't get sprung just because the sex is good. I'm not that girl. Just to make sure I don't become that girl, I have a rule: I never take phone numbers. I let guys come to me. But here I am like a dork hoping that I run into him, crossing my fingers in hopes of him dropping by my place although I detest unannounced visitors, or looking for flowers even though guys hardly ever have flowers delivered these days.

Then I snap out of it. Here I am, the famous Ms. Bobbi, well, *almost* famous, and I'm sitting around thinking about some short Russian guy, instead of having a blast chilling with Jamie Foxx and his friends. The best of everything is on the house, and I get to kick it instead of having to work and miss all the fun, and here I am tripping! I should be mixing and mingling with the celebrities since, in a way, I'm one too. I should be networking and having a good time, so that's what I decide to do.

More champagne is delivered. Jamie looks at me with an impish grin, shakes his bottle, and pops the top. Champagne sprays all over me, but I don't care. Normally I'd be ready to beat somebody's ass to the white meat if they did that to me. I'm not a fucking video girl so I don't get off on champagne showers. But instead, I get him back, spraying him with bubbly until his white linen shirt is soaked and transparent. Before I can say boo, groupies are flanked around him, offering to help dry him off. One woman damn near licks the champagne right off him. Groupies! I ignore them, fill my champagne glass with Cristal, gulp it down, and then refill it again. I'm on a mission. I have libation so all I need is to meet some people, maybe even find a fine, muscular body to play with after the party, and I'll be good to go.

Now Jamie, although I find him attractive, isn't my cup of tea. I've gone out with comedians before, and it's cool for about fifteen minutes, but the jokes don't stop. In the worst cases, it's like an improv show that won't end. No thank you! And there aren't any vibes between anyone in his crew and me, which suits me fine because I prefer alpha males and not peripheral flunkies. But tonight I'm in a carnal mood, and *someone* is going to satisfy my desires.

Luckily, I don't have to look too far. Strolling up to the cabana we're chilling in comes platinum rapper and all-around honey, Bentley. Bingo! Bentley is young and fine and paid. He has body, style, and a flow out of this world. Over the past few years, he's taken the rap world by storm and has also been tied off and on again with his label mate, the model turned rapper, Dez. But at the moment I don't care who he's with because he looks even better in person than he does on TV. We can talk a little business and then have a little fun.

"Jamie, man, you always have all the ladies! I guess an Oscar will do that for you, huh?" Bentley says. Bentley and I lock eyes and I feel my nipples get hard.

Jamie introduces us.

"It's a pleasure to meet you," I say, standing to shake his hand. I never sit when I shake someone's hand. It gives them the false illusion of power, and I'm going to be the one in total control. Bentley is the chosen one. "Want to join me for a drink?" I ask him, making room for him on the banquette and motioning for him to take a seat next to me.

"Sure," he says, sitting down. I pour him a glass of champagne.

"I love your music," I tell him as I hand him the glass. "Cheers!" I say, just because everyone and their mother says "salud," and I hold up my glass in a toast.

"Uh, cheers," he says as he clinks the rim of his glass with mine. "So you're the Ms. Bobbi I keep hearing about, huh?" he asks.

"Lies, all lies!" I joke. I smile and ask Bentley, "So I take it you haven't seen me perform?"

"No, but I've heard you put on quite a show," he says, smiling back.

"Well, let's just say I know my way around a deck. I'm the best. You should try me out." I toss my hair and let my hand trail from his shoulder down his arm. No sense beating around the bush.

"Do you spin vinyl or CDs?" he asks.

I turn up the heat a little. "Mostly I use my laptop. But I

can spin anything. I love to get really hands-on, you know? You ought to see how I handle those big, black, twelve inches. Once I get them in my hands, it's magic." I lick my lips and purse them slightly in what I like to call my "sexy mouth." I want him to visualize what my lips are going to do to him.

"Hmmm," is all he says while absentmindedly stroking his goatee. Then he stands up and chats with some woman who has the nerve to just walk over and interrupt our whole groove.

*No—this Negro didn't play me!* I think, getting vexed.

The woman moves on and Bentley sits back down. "My agent," he says. He helps himself to another glass of champagne. "You know, a lot of females in the game that I know don't like you," he finally says.

"Excuse me?" I ask. I know I sound stank, but he's tripping.

"You know, female producers and DJs—they say that you make it harder for them because you're always naked," he continues. "They don't want it to be about looks, they want it to be about skills."

"It *is* about skills. I make it *harder* for them because I'm *better* than them," I say firmly.

Now, I know what you're thinking. You're thinking that I'm a hypocrite because I want to be taken seriously as a DJ, I've got all these big dreams, but I want to sleep with industry guys and perform half-naked. And I have the audacity to expect a man to know which lines to walk when, and not cross those lines. You're damn straight I do. I'm not a hypocrite, I'm just a brat that wants everything her way. And as I already told you, I'm a slut. It's not going to change; I'm never going to be a one-man woman. But more than that, I'm a feminist. Not one of those hairy-armpit, man-hating, rhetoric-spouting feminists that is always on the attack, but I truly believe that women can do damn near anything a man can, and men just need to get with the program.

"I embrace and exploit my sexuality on *my own* terms. Just because I work in a male-dominated field does not mean I have to look and act like a man, and those chicks who say I make it harder for them can kiss my pretty ass. They're just mad because they don't have it like me," I tell him.

"Well, I do think you make it harder for them," he says. "And you make it harder for brothers like me too." Bentley flashes a wicked grin and leans in so close to me that I can smell the Altoid he has in his mouth. It's a cinnamon one and I want to taste it on his lips. "Do you want to feel how hard you make it for me?" he asks.

He smiles and places my hand on his inner thigh. I slide it up to his crotch and squeeze gently. I'm sure the look in my eyes speaks volumes. And then wouldn't you know it, just when things are about to get hot with Bentley, and after two weeks of being M.I.A., here comes Mikhail's short ass with some big blonde glamazon with huge silicone boobs and fishy-looking, collagen-injected lips. I know her boobs have to be fake because they jut out from her chest like twin rockets and do not bounce or jiggle, even though she's clearly not wearing a bra underneath her cheap scrap of a dress.

"Hello, Bobbi," he says to me.

"Ms. Bobbi," I say, correcting him. "Hello."

"I thought we were beyond formalities, Bobbi," he says with a crooked grin. I smile a fake-ass smile.

"Mikhail Petrov, meet Bentley. Bentley, meet Mikhail Petrov," I say in a voice that screams *you peasants bore me!* I'm determined not to let Mikhail know that I'm affected by his appearance with some blonde bimbo. I turn my attention back to Bentley, stroking his thigh and nestling in closer, determined to beat Mikhail at his own game. I want Bentley and me to look as cozy as Mikhail and his skank.

"I'm a fan of your music," Mikhail says to Bentley. Bentley nearly knocks me over as he stands to shake Mikhail's hand. He pumps it up and down, but the whole time his eyes are glued to the cheap blonde.

"I just bought Babylon. You've had a party there before, but when I reopen I'd love to have another event for you," Mikhail says. No he isn't turning this into a networking session with Bentley when we still have unfinished business!

"No doubt," Bentley tells him, giving him some dap. "I like that spot. I've got a lot of good memories there."

The blonde tosses her hair in what is clearly an attention-seeking move.

"My apologies," Mikhail says, taking the bait. "This is Misty Blue." Mikhail introduces us to his date. She sure has some nerve to choose a classic soul song by Dorothy Moore to name herself after. I figure she's probably some wannabe singer who thinks she's the next Teena Marie.

"I know," Bentley says, smiling. "I'm a fan!" He shakes her hand and is beaming at her like she's some kind of royalty.

My neck snaps back so fast it feels like I have whiplash. "Hmph! A fan of *what*?" I ask sarcastically, curling my upper lip in disgust. Who the hell is this bitch that Bentley knows who she is? He hasn't even seen me perform, but he's a fan of her work? She was cute if you liked the plastic look, but she wasn't all that.

"I'm an actress," Misty answers in a breathy Marilyn Monroe–type voice that I know is fake, because nobody *really* talks like that. "In adult films," she adds. It figures. Now, I know I can't talk about anybody being a ho, and I'm not even mad at her for her choice of work. I mean, if that's all the talent she has, then oh well. I am, however, pissed that she's hogging all the attention from both Mikhail and Bentley.

"You mean a porn star?" I say with a sneer.

"Well, yes," she says with a giggle.

"Well, Bentley, it seems like she's just your speed," I say. Bentley's girl Dez had been involved in a scandal over a sex video she made when she was still underage. It was in all the tabloids and word on the streets was that the tape had always been a bone of contention in their relationship. I know the comment is a low blow, but I don't care. I am not about to allow myself to be upstaged by some freak who is probably an idiot to boot.

"Perhaps, but Misty is all mine for the evening," Mikhail says with a laugh. He extends his fist and he and Bentley give each other a pound. I give Mikhail a look that could send him straight to his grave, and I'm hoping that it does.

"That's right, Mikey!" Misty coos in Mikhail's ear.

"Mikey?" I cluck.

"That's my nickname for him," Misty explains. I want to strangle her because she says this to me as if *I'm* too slow to understand, like I'm one of her dimwit buddies. "His name is sooo hard for me to say." All I can do is shake my head. If that's what he wants, then more power to him.

"Well, it was good seeing you again, *Ms.* Bobbi," Mikhail says, winking at me. "We've certainly got a lot to talk about. Let's do lunch or something?"

"Yeah sure. Buh-bye, *Mikey.*" I give a phony smile and nod, and wave the two of them off. What I really want to do is slowly and painfully choke the life out of *Mikey*, and pull Misty's hair out by the roots.

"I'll give you a call soon," he says. "Don't disappear on me," he says as he and Misty walk away arm in arm. *That asshole!* Mikhail has something that I want and he knows it, and not only does he know it, it seems like he's going to make me play games to get it. Well, if it's games he wants, it's games he'll get, but I'll be the winner. I want that residency at Babylon: it's the perfect spot for me to take my career to the next level, and I'm going to get it.

I sit there fuming while Bentley looks at me smiling.

"Why is it that pretty girls are always so insecure?" he asks me.

"Man, fuck you," I say bitterly. I'm already feeling shitty enough, I'll be damned if I sit there and let him rub my face in my humiliation.

"I was hoping you would. But you being jealous that the Russian you're fucking is fucking around with Misty Blue isn't helping things," he says with a grin.

"First of all, I'm not fucking Mikhail," I lie. "We're supposed to be working on a business deal, but I haven't heard from him in, like, almost a month." I toss my hair and try to make everything seem casual.

"Sure you are," he says sarcastically. "I didn't expect you to be the type of chick that was into white guys," he continues.

"Fuck you," I repeat. I've had enough of Bentley. I just want to go home.

"You mad now?" he asks.

"Excuse me!" I say, trying to wriggle my way past him.

"Sit down," he says kind of forcefully, which turns me on. I know I can't get past him so I plop back down on the banquette. He just sits there smiling at me. Damn him! He's so fine and I'm so horny. I turn my head away from him. I feel his hand on my knee, and although my body is begging for more, I sit there pretending to be unaffected. But that doesn't last long. Pretty soon, Bentley's hand is far beneath my skirt, unobstructed by the fact that I don't wear underwear, and I can't stifle the moan that escapes my lips as he begins to stroke my clit.

"You're feisty, aren't you?" he whispers in my ear. "I like feisty women." I squirm beneath his touch, but my face maintains its calm demeanor.

"Look at your stubborn ass," he teases me. "You want to sit there like this isn't even getting to you, but you know it feels good, doesn't it? You like the way I play with that pussy?"

"Yes sir," I say as I nod to the beat of Gwen Stefani's "Holla Back Girl." I open my legs wider to accommodate him. The rush I get is amazing. I know I shouldn't be doing what I'm doing for a myriad of reasons, but it feels too good to stop. I can't hold back any longer. It's exquisite torture. So I put my champagne glass down and wave my hand in the air, bouncing and rocking to the beat to cover up the fact that I'm grinding against Bentley's hand. He throws his head back and laughs as I come against his hand singing "Ooh, that's my shit! That's my shit!" with no one the wiser.

There's no reason for me to go home with Bentley. He knows that I'm digging on Mikhail, no matter how much I try to hide it. And I know he has Dez and probably an army of groupies that I don't want to join. Maybe one day we'll hook up if fate allows it. But for the moment, I have everything I need.

# CHAPTER FOUR

*June 2006*

THE NEXT MORNING MY PHONE RINGS BRIGHT AND EARLY, jarring me out of my slumber. I don't answer it though; I can't imagine who could possibly be calling me before noon because everyone knows I work nights. The early bird might catch the worm but in my eyes, there's nothing that can be done before noon that can't be done after noon so this little bird is going to catch some more z's. I figure it can't be anyone that I want to talk to, so I pull the pillow over my head and try to get back to sleep, but the phone rings again! The only person who would be so persistently irritating is my mother, but only if she has a damned good reason like the death or illness of a relative, so I reach over and check the caller ID on the nightstand to see if it's her. It reads *Unknown*. I hate blocked phone calls so I am definitely not going to answer. I turn off the ringer so that I won't be disturbed again, and settle between the sheets.

Just as I'm about to drift off, a loud buzz goes off in the far corner of the room. I left my BlackBerry on vibrate, and now it's buzzing away on top of my dresser. Whoever wants to reach me doesn't seem like they're going to stop trying anytime soon, so I kick the covers aside and stomp over to my PDA to see what the big emergency is. A number with a 305 area code is listed under missed calls, but I don't recognize it. I check the voice mail.

"Hello, Ms. Bobbi. Rise and shine, sleeping beauty. This is Mikhail. I'd love for you to join me for breakfast to discuss our business matter. Please call me at 305-555-9111." Bullshit. I know that the only reason he's calling so early is to see if I'm sleeping alone. I debate whether or not to fuck with him and pretend that Bentley is here just to see how much he's really about business. I decide to call and be cool and detached; I'll be professional.

I dial the number he left, and he picks up on the first ring.

"Hello, may I please speak with Mikhail?" I ask, although I know it's him.

"Hello, Ms. Bobbi. Sorry to wake you," he says.

"No you aren't," I say, cutting him off.

"Okay, so I'm not," he admits. "Did you get my message?"

"Yes," I reply.

"Well, is this a good time? If you're preoccupied, perhaps we can meet at another time," he suggests.

"If I were preoccupied I wouldn't have called you at all," I say. *Kinda like you did with me,* I think.

"Well, if you have company . . ." Mikhail says.

"That's not really your interest or concern," I say.

"And why is that?" he says.

"Look, Mikhail, I don't want what's happened in the past between us to get in the way of business. So going forward, let's just keep this relationship on a professional level, okay?"

"Hmm, and I was looking forward to having so much fun mixing business and pleasure," he says. He doesn't believe that's what I want; I can hear it in his voice. I don't believe myself either. But I'm going to make him work if he wants any part of this pussy again.

"I'll bet," I say.

"Is this about Misty?" he asks me.

"Is what about Misty?" I ask, pretending to be innocent. "What are you talking about?"

"I'm talking about your change of heart," he tells me. "You're so cold. We both know that you're hotter than that."

"How do you know it's not about Bentley?" I ask. *You want hot? Feel the burn,* I think. *I know you're jealous.*

"Misty and I are just friends," Mikhail says. I wonder if he's going to react to my insinuation about Bentley, but he doesn't. There's just dead air buzzing in my ear. Bastard!

"So would you care to join me for breakfast?" he finally asks. "To talk business, of course."

I look at the clock. It's 9:30 AM. I've only slept for about four hours.

"What time?" I ask.

"In about an hour," he says. "It's a perfect day, and I was going to have the chef prepare something on my ship. Meet me at the marina?"

My ears perk up. A chef-prepared meal on a yacht would be tight. I know it's a yacht because he'd said his ship and not his boat, and there is a big difference. My curiosity is getting the better of me so I accept his invitation. Suddenly energized, I pop out of bed and into the shower. Then I wrestle my thick hair into a smooth bun at the nape of my neck. I keep my makeup simple, just a couple coats of mascara and some red lipstick, and throw on a sexy black monokini, a one piece swimsuit with the same effect as a bikini. From the rear view it looks like any other Brazilian-cut bikini. But in the front, the top and bottom are connected by a wide band of rhinestones. I put on a black skirt, diamond studs, two black enamel cuff bracelets, and simple black high-heeled sandals. Black Chanel shades complete the look. Not your typical breakfast outfit, but I'm not a typical girl.

I walk leisurely over to the Miami Beach Marina on Alton Road, glad that the morning sun's rays aren't very intense. It really is the perfect day to go boating. When I reach the marina, I look into my handbag to find my cell phone so I can call Mikhail, but before I can do it I see him walking down a narrow walkway leading from what has to be a three-hundred-foot yacht!

I grew up around money. I've spent countless summers at the Inkwell on Martha's Vineyard and a few at the Hamptons, and I've seen some pretty great yachts, but Mikhail's ship is *phenomenal*. This is no weekender or cruiser; this is a mega-yacht. But it isn't the size that makes it so breathtaking, it's the details. Even from a distance, I can see that there are rich details that make the yacht ultra luxe. He's put a lot of time and money into the ship; he's proud as hell and it's written all over his face.

I stare at the ship. The railings look like they're made of gold, not brass like most ships. And everything is so fucking shiny! It just screams, "I'm rich, bitch!" I can't wait to get on board and inspect things.

"Hello, Ms. Bobbi," Mikhail says, greeting me with a hug and a kiss on both cheeks.

"Hi, Mikey," I tease him.

"So you're jealous of Misty, aren't you?" he asks.

"No way! I just thought it was funny," I say.

"Sure," he says and leads me toward the magnificent vessel.

"Welcome aboard *Krizia*," he says, opening his arms dramatically as we walk aboard the most beautiful ship I've ever seen.

"Daaaaaaaayum!" I drawl as I twirl around on the ship's deck. "How big is this thing?" I ask.

"Only two hundred and eighty feet," Mikhail says. "Come, I will take you on a tour."

Mikhail leads me through *Krizia*, which has eighteen staterooms and an onboard crew of thirty-six, including a masseuse, a personal trainer, and a nurse. There's everything imaginable on this ship. There's a play area for children that has swings, a sandbox, and a jungle gym. There's a beauty salon and spa where a Swedish esthetician and a British hairdresser are on call. The workout room rivals any Bally's and it even has a swimming pool if dipping in the ocean isn't your thing. But if the ocean is your thing, there are Jet Skis, wave runners, water skis, scuba gear, and a sailing dinghy. *Krizia* even has a business center for those who need to work and play—complete with an executive assistant if you need one.

But the *pièce de résistance* is Mikhail's quarters. This guy has got to get a ton of pussy, because the master suite is resplendent. There's a bedroom with a California king-sized bed, a huge plasma screen television, and panoramic views that Mikhail reveals by pressing a remote control button that draws back the heavy silk curtains. There's a separate sitting area, decorated in a warm, earthy palette composed of creamy beiges, lustrous golds, and rich browns. The shiny wood floors are covered with fabulous rugs that look like they're handmade, and Indian or Moroccan. There's even a baby grand piano. The sofa, loveseat, chair, and ottoman are crafted in suede the color of hot chocolate. I know it's suede and not ultrasuede because I rub the upholstery just to make sure. I know that's kind of ghetto, but I can't help myself! When I was growing up I used to touch the fur coats of the women in church to see if they were real too, mainly because it drove my mother bananas when she saw me do it; my "no class" behavior reminded her of when women would find reasons to pat and rub the lustrous furs draping her shoulders during conversation. She was convinced that people were inspecting their quality and authenticity and she was so insulted that someone would even dare think she'd wear faux fur.

I sit down at the piano and tickle the ivories. "This is a great piano. It's in absolutely perfect pitch," I tell Mikhail as I play a few bars of Alicia Keys's "Fallin'." "And it's so responsive."

"Thank you. It is a handcrafted Steinberg, made from the finest wood in Europe. It is rumored that the soundboard is made of wood from the same forest that Strativari hand cut for his violins," he tells me.

"Uh, okay," I say, and continue to play. Mikhail sounds like a piano salesman.

"I didn't know you could play the piano," he says as he strolls toward me.

"How could you?" I ask him.

"Oh, I have my ways of finding things out," he says chuckling.

"Is that right?" I ask, arching my eyebrow in suspicion. I have the feeling that Mikhail gets off on making people think he's some mysterious tough guy one minute and a perfect gentleman the next. I can dig it though; it's always good to keep people guessing.

"You remind me of a Russian Donald Trump," I tell him. I can see that he doesn't take that as a compliment by the way he twists his face up.

"You think I'm that tacky?" he asks.

"No," I say quickly. But this boat, the car, the hanging out with porn stars . . . it just screams that he's trying to get attention and be noticed. He wants people to bow down and kiss his ring, but I won't be the one. I'll tell him what he wants to hear so I can seal this gig, but that's it. I'm not going to be sloppy seconds to a porn star or some on-demand pussy for this guy just because he's rich. My family has money—though not this much by any means—and it isn't my first time at the ball.

"No, you're not tacky," I tell him. "But you are flashy. Not gaudy either—I mean, everything you have here is really very nice, but you're so obvious," I say. "You're screaming."

"I thought it was all about the bling-bling these days," he says and I crack up.

"First of all, no one even says *bling-bling* anymore," I manage to say through my laughter. Mikhail doesn't think it's so funny—at least, he's not laughing.

"Well, what do they say now?" he asks.

"Just *bling,* or *shine* I guess, or *floss,* something, just not *bling-bling.* Never mind. It's not that important and I know what you mean. You just remind me of a rapper or something. Like you've been hanging with Diddy too much."

"What's wrong with that?" he asks. "Diddy's a great guy."

"Nothing's wrong with him," I say and continue to play the piano. I play a classical-sounding version of "Mo Money, Mo Problems."

"You're good," he says.

"Yep," I tell him. "My mom made me take lessons all my life." I pound out some Beethoven with a very serious expression and dramatic aplomb. "I always knew I wanted to do something in music ever since I was a little girl. I wanted to go to school to learn recording engineering and sound for films, but my parents weren't having it. The only acceptable musical career in Mother's eyes would have been concert pianist, but that's not exactly my style. I've always wanted to be a rock star, but I have the worst voice on earth. Ain't that a bitch? I mean, it's so bad I couldn't even sing punk! I'd get booed off the stage," I say laughing. "But if I could sing, Alicia Keys, eat your heart out!"

I stop playing the piano and look up at Mikhail. He's smiling at me and shaking his head. He walks over and sits on the bench beside me. Then, out of nowhere, he grabs the back of my head and kisses me hard. I don't know if I should kiss him back or slap him, because after all, we're supposed to be strictly business. I pull away but he holds my face in his hands. I feel uncomfortable under his penetrating stare but I can't look away.

"You are an amazing woman, Bobbi," he says. "You're better than any rock star." I can't help but blush even though I know it's game.

"I bet you say that to all the girls," I tease.

"No, I don't," Mikhail says. There's an awkward silence as we sit on the piano bench looking at each other. The silence is broken by the sound of his cell phone ringing. He leaves me hanging and stands up to answer it.

"Da?" Mikhail says some things in Russian that I can't understand and hangs up the phone. He turns to me. "Are you ready to eat?" he asks.

"I could nibble on something," I say, then giggle because my mind is surely in the gutter. Food is the last thing I want to nibble on.

"Great. Let's join my friends on deck. Come," he says. I follow him up a spiral staircase to the deck where breakfast is being served. Actually, breakfast is an understatement. There are two huge buffet tables lined up along the side of the deck and covered with all kinds of food, from your standard American breakfast fare such as waffles and sausage to carved roast beef, ahi tuna, and salmon filets. There's also a large dining table, elaborately set with fine china, crystal, and flatware and decorated with a massive centerpiece that consists of a candle in a hurricane holder surrounded by a spray of tropical flowers.

Seated at the table is a couple: a very tall, muscular man with the same wavy hair and verdant eyes as Mikhail, and a woman so gorgeous and glamorous that I immediately feel ugly. So you *know* she's fine!

"Ms. Bobbi, I would like you to meet my cousin and business partner, Dimitri Yurkovic, and his girlfriend, Amara de Laurenti." Mikhail presents the striking couple to me.

"Ah, finally I get to meet the famous Ms. Bobbi," Dimitri says, smiling as he shakes my hand vigorously. "You are even more beautiful than your picture or my cousin give you credit for." Then Dimitri kisses my hand and looks me over from head to toe.

"I am sooo not famous," I tell him, and I wish that I was just being humble rather than telling the truth. "I just know a couple of people and I'm good at what I do."

"Maybe you're not famous yet, but you will be one day," Mikhail says and gives me a wink.

Amara rises from her chair, all six feet of her. Since I only stand at five feet four inches, she makes me feel like a midget. And although I am curvy and thick in all the right places, Amara makes me look like a twelve-year-old boy. She's the type of woman that my father refers to as a stallion or a brickhouse. She's absolutely beautiful, her skin is the color of caramel, she has hazel eyes, and her long silky hair perfectly frames her gorgeous face.

"Ay, Ms. Bobbi, baby," Amara screeches in a high-pitched voice, grabbing me firmly by the shoulders and kissing me on both cheeks. "You are my favorite DJ! Mikhail and Dimitri play your, how do you say again, oh yes, your mix tape all the time. I loved it when I heard it, and when they showed me your picture and I saw that you were a beautiful woman, I said

to myself, 'Amara, baby, this Ms. Bobbi is your new favorite.'
I am so happy to meet you, baby," she rambles a mile a minute. I can barely understand her because of her thick accent.

"Thanks, Amara. It's nice to meet you," I tell her. I can't
really think of anything else to say. Amara links her arm
through mine and guides me to the buffet. Mikhail waves at
us, then he and Dimitri disappear around a corner. I shoot
daggers at his back with my eyes. I think it's pretty rude to
invite someone to breakfast and then not even bother to
entertain them. I don't appreciate being dumped off on one
of his friends I don't even know. Besides, how can I get what
I want if he's not around?

"Come, I will fix you a plate, Ms. Bobbi," she says, snapping me out of my thoughts. She picks up a plate and begins
to pile on mounds of ripe, juicy cantaloupe, watermelon, and
honeydew.

"You don't have to do that," I say, attempting to take the
plate away from her. "And please, just call me Bobbi."

"I insist, Bobbi," she says.

"This certainly is a lot of food," I tell her, hoping that she
will get the hint and stop piling it on. "When Mikhail invited me to breakfast he didn't mention that he was going
to offer lunch, dinner, and dessert."

"Don't you know why he did all this, baby?" Amara asks.
Then she winks and tosses the shiny, heavy hair that drapes
her face and says, "It's because he didn't know what kind of
food you liked, so he had them cook a bit of everything. He
wanted to make you happy, baby. Someone's got his sights set
on you." She laughs and snaps her fingers, dancing about and
singing, "Someone's got his sights set on you, on you." Amara
is a bizarre woman, but amusing. She continues to load my
plate with all kinds of things. Not even a Sumo wrestler would
eat so much food! A part of me wants to scream, *Don't you know*

*there are millions of starving people in the world? You do realize that this is enough to feed a small country, don't you?* But another part of me is sickly flattered by the display if it is for my benefit.

When one plate gets full, Amara just hands it to a butler named Fabio, of all things, who lines the plates up on the long banquet table. So when Amara finally feels that she's sufficiently provided me with all the food there is to offer, she takes me over to a bar that has not only every spirit known to mankind, but a wine rack and a refrigerator filled to the brim with fine wines and champagnes.

"Your champagne, baby? We have it all. Brut? Sec? Demi-sec?" she asks allowing me to choose my poison.

"Got any Krug?" I ask. Since Mikhail seems to be in a "waste not, want not" mood, I think to myself, *Why not go for the gold?*

"We've got Clos du Mesnil, 1995," she says. "It's the best."

Amara fills two champagne glasses with bubbly, then raises hers toward the sun.

"Here's to you Ms. . . . I mean Bobbi," she winks at me and tilts her head back, gulping the contents of her champagne glass all at once. "Finally someone who is not such an utter bore around here. Mikhail has the worst taste in female companionship." I wonder just how many companions Mikhail has brought around. I wonder even more how many he's lured here under the guise of taking care of business. Amara refills her glass and pulls out our seats.

To call Amara eccentric would be an understatement. She talks to me nonstop about people I don't know and then asks me what I think; before I can answer, she's on to the next thing. She punctuates her sentences with finger snaps and flamenco claps and spontaneously breaks out into the samba. She's very touchy-feely; she has no problem with hugging me, kissing me on the cheek, clasping my hand, all things I really have to know someone to let them get away with doing. But I can tell that she's really just trying to be nice, so I don't say anything or pull away like I usually would with someone so in my grill.

Amara calls me *baby* practically every other word, and she flips her hair so much I'm afraid that her neck is going to snap off at any minute. She does all this while nibbling off my plate and downing Krug like it's water. We are on the second bottle within twenty minutes, and I know that it runs around $800 a pop. I also know that I shouldn't be drinking so much considering that it isn't even noon, but that's never stopped me before, and I think it's rude to turn down champagne, especially such a good year. Furthermore, it is probably very hard to be subjected to too much direct and focused contact with Amara de Laurenti without first numbing the senses with some kind of mind-altering substance.

"So are you going to Greece with us?" Amara asks.

"Uh, not that I know of," I tell her.

"I thought Mikhail was bringing you. Oh shit!" she says, pronouncing the word *shit* like *sheet*. "Did I let the cat out of the bag? He was supposed to ask you, baby," she informs me.

"Mikhail and I are supposed to talk about me spinning at Babylon, not going to Greece," I say.

"But I know he is planning to invite you. I heard the whole thing with my own ears. Granted I was eavesdropping, but I distinctly heard Mikhail say to Dimitri that he was going to bring the lady DJ with him on the cruise. We always go to Greece in the summer. Everyone's going to be there; you have to come."

"Maybe he hasn't gotten around to it yet because he's nowhere to be found. It doesn't matter though. I'm not here to talk about any vacation; I'm here to discuss my career," I tell Amara.

"He's just shy, baby. He really likes you. I know he's going to ask. You should come, baby. It will definitely be good for your career if you do. It's going to be so fabulous, baby," she says. Before I can ask Amara what she means by "good for my career," she's on her feet and screeching.

"Ah, here they are now. Mikhail, you cretin! How dare you ignore this fascinating creature and walk around with boring Dimitri, baby, ah?" Amara scolds Mikhail and playfully slaps him on the arm.

"Amara, be good," Dimitri says, swatting her on the bottom.

"Baby, I am always good," Amara says with a toss of her luxurious, sun-streaked hair. "Anyway, Mikhail, are you bring-ing Bobbi with us to Greece? You said she was coming, but you never asked her. I thought you were going to ask her. I am so bored of you two boys. I need a friend here," Amara says with no room for anyone to get a word in edgewise. She puts her hands on her hips and taps her foot looking from Dimitri to Mikhail.

"Amara, have you been eavesdropping again?" Dimitri asks her.

"Yes, baby," she says. "It was an accident. If I had a friend around, I would have better things to do than to listen in on your boring conversations."

"Ah, Mikhail, I thought you were going to bring her, no?" Dimitri says to Mikhail. "We will party, party, party!" he exclaims, smiling at me. "Have you been abroad before?" Dimitri starts dancing and Amara joins him.

"Yes," I tell them, looking at them as if they've lost their minds. I've been to London and to Paris but those were both school-sponsored activities, nothing sophisticated or any-thing. I had fun staying in hostels and meeting lots of young and fun-loving people, but I never met anyone like them.

Dimitri and Amara are disco dancing to a groove of their own, moving and shaking as if there is actually music playing. Hell, they are on a planet all their own.

"Ah yes, Mikhail, baby! She is the perfect person to come with us, no? Did you show her the sound system? The disco? Baby, have you seen the disco?" Amara asks as she and Dimitri switch to what I think is supposed to be the tango. What the hell kind of circus is this? I sit there unsure of what to say or how to react. Mikhail steps in and saves me.

"Bobbi, why don't you step into the business center with me? We have an important matter to discuss." It's about time! I look over my shoulder as I follow Mikhail, and Amara winks at me. "Say yes, baby," she shouts before Dimitri picks her up and twirls her around in a circle.

"YOUR FRIENDS ARE INTERESTING," I TELL MIKHAIL.

"Ah yes, my young cousin's girlfriend has a real passion for life," he says, adding, "and a very big mouth."

I take a seat in the office and look around at the walls that are adorned with what looks like some old and expensive art. "I do want you to come to Greece. I had been planning on surprising you. But I am aware that you're here to talk business, that you want things between us to remain strictly professional. That's what you want, right?"

I nod yes. It isn't the whole truth. I find Mikhail sexy as hell, and I already know what he's capable of in the bedroom. Plus he intrigues me to no end. He's so mysterious and I'm fascinated by the world that I imagine he lives in. I don't want to keep things professional. I want it all.

"Well, then, let me make this simple and get to the point. As we discussed before, I want you to be one of the resident

DJs at Babylon. I also would love it if you could re-create the magic you've brought to Mansion at my club."

I want to scream yes, but I keep my cool.

"Go on," I say.

"I want you to be the face of my new club. You have the 'it' factor, star quality. You make people notice you, and once they notice you, you make them fall in love." Mikhail smiles at me when he says this.

"Well, thank you for all the nice things you've said," I say.

"I sense a *but* coming on," Mikhail says.

"Well, yes. Let me get this straight. You want me to go to Greece *and* you want me to be a resident and promoter at Babylon, but you want to keep things professional?"

"Yes," he says.

I don't buy it. "Do you make a habit of taking all your resident DJs to Greece?"

"Actually, yes I do," he says. "As Amara may have told you, I go to the Mediterranean every summer. I love music, I love to entertain, and I throw a lot of parties. I like to travel with the best. I *am* inviting you to Greece as the onboard DJ, because you're the best. We're going to all the major destinations in Europe: Ibiza, Saint Tropez, perhaps even Monaco."

"So you want me to come on board as a part of the staff?" I ask him.

"Not exactly," he admits. "Bobbi, I really like you. I want you to work with me, but make no mistake, I also want *you*."

"I'm not for sale," I say.

"Rich girls usually aren't," he says.

"Who's a rich girl?" I ask him. I wonder what he thinks he knows.

"You are," he says.

"You got it wrong, buddy," I tell him.

"Oh, I know a lot about you, Ms. Bobbi Hayes. I know

that you're from Chicago and that you aren't as street as you make yourself out to be. I know that your father is a big shot lawyer and your grandfather is a famous civil rights leader. You're not as mysterious as you think," he says.

"First of all, I don't try to be street or mysterious. I'm from the South Side of Chicago. I am what I am," I tell him.

"And you probably grew up in a mansion," he says back with a hint of sarcasm in his voice, "and with servants. So why the act?"

"There is no act," I say. Here we go again, another person with preconceived notions of what I should be like. "It's possible to live in a mansion and still be a down-to-earth, around-the-way girl. Believe me. When are people going to realize that with me, what they see is what they get? Just because I'm not walking around with a damn tiara on my head and carrying around a little yapping mutt doesn't mean I'm not being true to myself," I tell him. I've had this conversation a million times before and it irks me every time. "You don't hear me out here yelling gangsta gangsta, do you? No, you don't. Yes, I lived in a mansion. Yes, we had people who helped run our home, but I never refer to them as servants. I'm no snob. It seems like you want me to be just like the rest of the world expects me to be, but I'm not. I don't judge people for not having money and I don't want to be judged because people think I have it."

"Yes, but you have to admit that having money makes your life easier," he says.

"The hell it does," I tell him. I'm not going to go into my life story and tell him about girls who didn't like me and wanted to jump me because I wore cute clothes, or boys who only wanted to kick it with me because they thought I was a meal ticket. That was a long time ago. I'm over it. Kind of. "Besides, I wouldn't know because I don't really have any money," I tell him.

"You aren't hungry," he says.

"That depends on your perspective. I'm hungry because I want to be a success at what I do. I have ambition and drive. No, I'm not worried about what's for dinner. I mean, I'm eating. But my parents cut me off years ago. Everything I have, everything you see me with, is all mine. I've worked for everything I've got."

"Really?" Mikhail asks, like he doesn't believe me.

"Really," I tell him. "Is it hard to believe? It isn't like I'm living in the lap of luxury. I'm comfortable, and I'm fine with that."

"You're happy being . . . comfortable?" Mikhail asks, like I shouldn't be. "You'd rather be comfortable than have it all?"

"I didn't say that. Of course I want it all. But I want it all on my own terms. I don't mind working hard to achieve my goals. I like to hustle."

"I think you'll change your mind about that," he says knowingly.

"Oh you do, do you? And why, may I ask, is that?" I ask.

"Oh, I have my reasons," he says cryptically.

"Well, whatever," I tell him. "God blesses the child that's got his own. I'm proud of the things I've managed to get on my own, prouder than anything else. I have a nice condo, I have a Range Rover, and I'm able to pay for those things with the money I make spinning. I get to do exactly what I want and I love my job, and not a lot of people can say that. My parents have the money. I'm just your average Jane."

"There's nothing average about you," Mikhail says. I grin but say nothing. "That's why I want you to accept my offer."

"Which one?" I ask. "The residency or the cruise?"

"There is only one offer," he says.

"So you want to play hardball, huh?" I ask him.

"Always."

"So how much does this offer pay?" I ask.

"I thought you didn't care about money," he teases.

"I don't care about my parents' money. I never said I don't care about mine."

Mikhail grins at me. He puts his hands together and swivels a bit in his chair. He's trying to figure me out. I can always tell when someone is doing that.

"Let's just say that you won't be dissatisfied."

"And let me guess, is sleeping with you a requisite of the job?" I ask.

"No," he says. "You can do that if you want to, though. I will not try to stop you. But you can have your own quarters if you like."

"What if I want to do both?" I ask. "What if I want to fuck you and have my own room?" I ask.

"You can have it," he says. "Is that what you want?" he asks.

I don't answer his question. Instead I step out of my skirt, climb on top of the desk, and kiss him. He removes my bathing suit and spreads my legs. Then he kneels to the ground and unbuckles my sandals. He slips my shoes off and begins sucking on my toes, which tickles a little bit, but feels really good. He kisses his way around my ankles, up my calves, across my thighs, and stops just short of my dripping wet pussy. He looks up at me, his green eyes full of yearning before he dives in, engulfing my clit in his mouth and swirling his tongue around it. I grab a handful of his thick, wavy hair as I arch my back in pleasure. I kick all sorts of papers and cups holding pens and envelope openers off the desk when I come, pulling his hair and moaning his name as my orgasm drains my body of all energy.

But Mikhail is far from finished. He reaches in the desk drawer, pulls out a condom, and slips one on. And instead of a quick nut Mikhail is long-lasting and nonstop. He twists my limbs like a pretzel, taking me in every possible position in every corner of the room. He pounds me on top of the desk, I ride him in his swiveling chair, and he hits it while standing up against the wall. Somehow we end up by the window and my breasts are pressed up against the glass.

"Look at the ocean. It's beautiful, isn't it?" he asks as he fucks me doggy style.

"Yes," I scream while reaching around to massage his scrotum.

"This is nothing compared to what you will see. I'll give you fame. I'll give you the job of your dreams on our return, I'll give you anything you want in this world," Mikhail pants in my ear.

"For now, just give me the dick," I moan, bucking and thrashing. I'm so turned on and moving around so much that our bodies are soaking wet, especially between my legs.

"Come away with me," Mikhail says, slapping my ass and biting my neck.

I'm so close to the brink of ecstasy again, and all it will take to send me over is a few more strokes. Mikhail teases me. He enters me a millimeter at a time.

"Does it feel good?" he asks. I can barely speak. He slaps me on the ass again, this time harder, adding a yank to my hair.

"Answer me," he commands, but I don't say a thing. Not because it doesn't feel divine, but because I want him to slap my ass one more time, just one more good whack and I'm there.

"Are you going to come?" he asks. Mikhail spanks my ass so hard that my eyes water.

So I say the only thing a girl in my position can say:

"Oh yes!"

# CHAPTER FIVE

W HEN I ACCEPT MIKHAIL'S OFFER, I DON'T REALIZE HOW much my life is about to change. I see the gig as just another job and Mikhail as just another fling. That is, until I see just how much money is on the line. Mikhail doesn't lie; I am very, very satisfied with my compensation. He pays me the sum of $150,000 to be his official summer cruise DJ. In cash. No bullshit! He slides a briefcase with stacks of money wrapped in paper bands over to me, pops the lock, and flashes the cash. I look as hypnotized as John Travolta did in *Pulp Fiction* when he opened the mysterious briefcase containing whatever it was that people were dying and killing each other over. I swear that the money glows, it has a bright gold aura to it, and I can hear a choir of angels sing as I ogle the bills before snapping the case shut and holding it tightly on my lap.

I know you're probably thinking that because my family is wealthy $150,000 should mean nothing to me. But it does. Like a true rich kid, I've lived a life of credit; I charged whatever I wanted and someone in an office somewhere paid the bills. My parents never even got on my case about my spending either, no matter how much I spent. I never had much cash in my personal accounts because of that. I didn't need it. My "real" money was in my trust fund and Mother and Daddy supplied all my needs. Poor me, right? Well, before you go judging me, let me just tell you that if you're never trusted with any money, you can't possibly learn how to manage it. My parents did me a great disservice, because when they first cut me off I went into so much debt I thought I'd never find my way out. So I'm just like anyone else; when I see a hundred and fifty grand in cash just for me, it feels damn good. I know a hundred and fifty g's isn't exactly equivalent to hitting the lottery, but it's nothing to sneeze at, especially for what can only add up to a few hours of work a week, and especially with the luxurious working environment.

Mikhail tells me I can expect to make at least $10,000 to $15,000 a week and probably more, working as a resident and promoter at Babylon; we're "seeing how things go." When he first ran the number by me, I asked if he was adding an extra zero by mistake. His answer was that if it were any other DJ, it would be a mistake, but that he wanted me and would pay top dollar to get me. I know that I'm nice on the turntables and everything, but I'm pretty sure that a part of the reason that I'm making so much is because I'm fucking him. Some folks (like Mother) might say that makes me a high-priced ho. You know what I say to that? Kiss my pretty ass. Correction: kiss my pretty *rich* ass! I already told you I'm a slut and that isn't going to change.

On top of all the money, Mikhail also says that he'll leave my schedule flexible if I need to travel, and that I'll have more freedom than I would working at any other club on the beach. I'll definitely travel on occasion, but part of the reason this whole setup appeals to me is because I can stay put. I've traveled so much over the past couple of years that I just want to chill for a while. Besides, why go anywhere? I live in Miami, the greatest fucking city in the world. Fuck what people say about New York and LA and Vegas. Nothing beats Miami.

When I do the math in my head I realize that I'll make at least a half mil in the next year. That's bananas! No DJ makes that kind of money, but then again, no club owner is like Mikhail Petrov, there's no club like Babylon, and we all know that there's no DJ like Ms. Bobbi! Mikhail told me that he's willing to spare no expense to have the best club in the world, and he doesn't care if it's well into the millions! Yes, my deal is so sweet that it seems too good to be true. But I know that what Mikhail is going to pay me is just a drop in the bucket for him if he's willing to pump millions into such a fickle business as the club scene. He must anticipate making a shitload of money when the club opens.

As I sign my name on the dotted line, I hope that I'm not signing my soul over to the devil. I am a preacher's grandkid, and I was raised in the church, so I think I'm pretty knowledgeable about how the devil operates. "The devil is a liar!" my grandfather always says. "He's a trickster and a slickster! He'll offer you the world, but he can't really give you anything but a one-way ticket to hellfire and damnation and eternal misery." But come on! Who's gonna turn down that kind of cash? Would you? Besides, as a preacher's grandkid, I also know that God hasn't given me the spirit of fear, and no weapon formed against me can prosper. So I say a little prayer and get ready to embark on this new phase in my life.

I decide to call Dad to let him know about my new business venture. Maybe he'll be proud of how much money I'm making even if it isn't being made practicing law, plus I want someone to know my whereabouts. I am going to Europe after all, and I'm not sure how long I'll be gone. I don't owe anyone any explanations but I do want to show a little consideration. After all, what if something happens while I'm away?

I call my dad at the office, but he isn't in. I try his cell, but he doesn't answer. Begrudgingly I dial my parents' home. *Please pick up, Dad*, I pray silently. *I do not want to talk to Mother!* No such luck. The phone rings a couple of times and I am greeted by Mother's voice on the other end.

"Mother, it's me. Is Dad there?" I ask, without even saying hello. But I already know that he isn't there. Think about it. If you were married to a shrew like my mom, would you hang around?

"He's not here, Roberta," she says. My mother's voice is as sweet as Alaga syrup, but masks more bitterness than bad vinegar. I hate being called Roberta; it sounds so matronly. She knows this. But if I say anything slick about it, she'll act all hurt and accuse me of attacking her. I can hear her whining now. "Why are you disrespecting me just because I called you by your given name? You should be proud of that name." Then she'll go crying to my dad, whenever he makes his way home, about what a horrible child I am. I know her tricks. Ten seconds on the phone and she's already trying, and succeeding, to get on my nerves. I sit there quietly, trying to figure out what to do next. Send a fax? An e-mail? I *really* do not want to talk to her.

"What do you want?" she barks. "You know I hate it when people just sit on the phone and don't say anything." Yes, I do know, which is the reason why I did it.

"Look, I'm going to Europe for a while, about two or three months," I tell her.

"Well, which one is it, Roberta? Will it be two months or three months?"

"I'm not sure. I just wanted to let you know. My cell will

work there if you need to reach me. Or you can send an e-mail because I have a BlackBerry," I blurt out quickly. I'm hoping that I can speed this call along without a lecture or any insults being fired back and forth, as is usually the case when I talk to Mother.

"Why are you speaking a mile a minute? You're obviously up to no good. Don't lie to me, Roberta. You know that I have the gift of sight. *Je suis une Toussaint*. I'll see right through any of your lies," she says. Oh Lord! She's getting Creole on me! Then she sighs, "Honestly, Roberta, I don't know why you can't get your life together."

"My life *is* together," I inform her. "I'm going to Europe to work."

"So the topless DJ'ing hasn't worked and now you're going to go for the gusto and become a full-out strip dancer," she drawls sarcastically, her Southern accent particularly heavy. "Are you going to dance the cooch in some tawdry burlesque cabaret in some godforsaken country?"

"Oh, Mother, no one even says strip dancer," I tell her. "And for your information, I'm not going to go dance the cooch, whatever that is. I'm going to Europe to DJ. And I'm not exactly topless. Sometimes I wear feathers," I say, just to piss her off. "I'm the guest of Mikhail Petrov. I'll be the official DJ on his luxury yacht. And he's paying me a hundred and fifty thou," I say.

"A hundred and fifty thou what?" she sniffs.

"A hundred and fifty thousand dollars, Mother." I want to see what smart remark she can come up with in response to that.

"So is this man the Russian version of the sultan of Brunei? Are you going as some kind of hooker?" Good old Mother, she's as quick-witted and negative as ever.

"Please, Mother, don't be vulgar," I say, affecting her tone.

"It's all on the up-and-up. He's my new employer, the one who'll be paying me close to a half million dollars a year to be the resident DJ and promoter at his new megaclub. It's going to be the biggest and best club on all of South Beach."

She's quiet for a second, and it's a second I'm grateful for, because she starts in on me as soon as it is over. "I'm sure you slept your way into the job."

"What are you talking about, Mother?"

"You might not think I know what kind of person you are, but I do. I've always known. You've had a problem keeping your legs closed for a long time. You're a slut. Your ways are whorish. You are not a lady, you're a tramp. You always have been, and you always will be. I don't know where you get it from," she says.

"Ask Dad," I tell her. As respected as my father is, I know he keeps girlfriends. I come by my whorish ways honestly, and that's what she can't stand. She knows Dad isn't faithful, but she would prefer to live in denial. She'd never divorce him anyway. She likes his name as much as she likes his money. Dad won't divorce her because he'd rather spend his money on women my age than give half of it to her.

"You're disgusting. You're a hateful child. But your attempts at hurting me won't work. You are the focus of this conversation, Roberta, you and *your* whorish ways. Leave your father out of this. You think that because you toss around the amount of money you're getting paid, I won't see this situation for what it is? I *know* you're sleeping with this new boss of yours," she spits. "You can't tell me otherwise."

I hang up the phone. There's no sense in me sitting there and being verbally abused. Sure, what she's saying is partially true. I *am* sleeping with my boss. But the point is I don't have to. I want to. Nothing is going to change with my mother anyway. I wanted someone to know where I was going and I accomplished that. And since my mother voiced her displeasure, she's made the trip all the more appealing to me.

THE DAY THAT I SET SAIL, A LIMO COMES TO FETCH ME, AND I kick back for the quarter mile drive to the marina. I promptly open the bottle of Gentleman's Jack in the wet bar, pour a glass, and mix it with a little OJ. I toast myself and drink it down quickly since the ride is so short.

When I reach the yacht, I find an entire stateroom filled with goodies just for me. There are clothes, shoes, handbags, some gorgeous jewelry, both real and costume—you name it, all in my sizes and suiting my taste. It's just like a scene out of my favorite movie *Casino,* when Sam blesses Ginger with a chinchilla coat and all the jewelry she could ever dream of wearing. Mikhail has clearly put some thought into these purchases, because there isn't a single item there that doesn't scream Ms. Bobbi. Everything is just my style: unique, original, and outrageous. I ask Mikhail if this is just another perk for being a valued employee, but he simply laughs and leads me up on deck where we meet Amara and Dimitri.

"I told you, baby," Amara says when she sees me, laughing heartily. "When I eavesdrop I do it right. I knew he was going to invite you."

When we set sail, a loud foghorn blows, and Amara and I prance about singing the theme song to *The Love Boat.* When we finish our duet, Amara gives me a huge hug and kisses me on both cheeks. "I'm so happy you said yes, baby. I guarantee you're going to have the time of your life. Just you wait and see," she enthuses as she clasps my hands in hers. I notice a fat rock on her ring finger. It's at least five or six carats. My eyes bug out and I raise my brows at her.

"Is Dimitri your fiancé?" I ask her.

"Ay, baby, no!" she says, holding her ring up to the heavens so it sparkles in the sun. "He'd have to do much better than this trinket if he wanted me to marry him! This is just a friendship bauble."

As materialistic as I claim not to be, I realize that I'm very happy that I have friends like that, and I'm anticipating some trinkets of my own.

OUR FIRST STOP IS NASSAU. MIKHAIL, DIMITRI, AMARA, AND I go shopping as soon as we get off the ship, where I load up on perfume and gold bangles. I also get some handbags and gear from Fendi. Fendi has never really been my cup of tea, it's so '80s in my opinion, but it's Mikhail's dime, and the selection in the boutique is so much different than what I see hoodrats in the States rocking.

Mikhail seems to enjoy the shopping as much as I do. If my eyes light up when I see something, he just buys it; he doesn't even wait to see if I really *want* it. I tell him that he's being way too generous, but he keeps insisting, which is good, because I don't really mean it when I tell him the gifts are too much. A nagging voice in my head keeps telling me that nothing in life is free, and that if it seems too good to be true it probably is, but I shut it out. After all, I am going to be working on this cruise and the no-holds-barred shopping is too much fun to resist.

Amara has no such qualms or reservations; she exudes an air of entitlement. She knows that she deserves the best things in life, and when she sees them, she just makes her desires known and Dimitri foots the bill. Their relationship seems so free, natural and easy, unlike Mikhail and me. We're going into this wrong, mixing business with pleasure and playing games. Someone is destined to end up hurt. But I'm determined it won't be me.

After Nassau, we sail to the Turks and Caicos Islands and hang out there for a couple of days. It's absolutely gorgeous! The crystal waters are excellent for scuba diving and snorkeling, and I get a chance to see and touch all kinds of fish, and even a giant sea turtle. I feel like I'm in the middle of *Finding Nemo*, in awe of the blue tang, angelfish, giant manta rays, and dolphins. I also try my hand at parasailing, which I will never do again because it frankly scared the shit out of me, and I Jet Ski until my thighs are sore.

The time I spend with Mikhail in what I regard as paradise on earth is wonderful. Traveling on someone else's dime is always cool, though. Mikhail is considerate and adventurous, and willing to partake in just about any activity I want to do. He makes being around him fun. Not to mention it's heaven being able to indulge in just about anything I can imagine, from food and drink to pampering.

The staff waits on me hand and foot, even though technically I'm one of them. I don't resort to yelling at them and verbally abusing them the way I see Amara do frequently, but I do pick up the habit of snapping my fingers at them. It sucks because my mother does that and I hate it, but now I know what a power trip it is to snap my fingers and have whatever I want at my tips in a matter of minutes. But the snapping isn't the only thing that is changing about me. The way I think about a lot of shit is changing. I can't deny it. What surprises me is how quickly it's all happening; what surprises me more is that I am not putting up a fight.

I don't recognize myself anymore. I'm already caught up in my own hype. I'm becoming everything I said I'd never be. Materialistic. Shallow. I'm committing a great sin. I'm becoming an idolater. A lover of the world. Before all this, nothing gave me a bigger high than playing my music. But this glamorous life is starting to feel real good, and the high it produces is running a close second. When it isn't forced on me, couture fashion feels good against my skin. Once my adversary, money has become my friend, and now that I have it, I'm never letting go. I have decided to embrace excess. The lavish life is definitely for me. Kimora better watch her back because there is a new queen of fabulosity on the scene.

My old life is over, because now I have the best of both worlds. This is my game and I'm playing by my own rules. I get to do what I love and I'm making a gang of money for it. I get to kick it on a whole new level, a level that most people only dream of. But this isn't a dream; it's my life, my new life. Meet the new and improved Ms. Bobbi. I am so over anything regular. From now on, it's absolutely nothing but the best.

Even though I'm not about to commit to Mikhail, I am so done with run-of-the-mill hotboys that I pick up at my gigs back in Miami. There's no way that I can go back to bullshit. And everything that isn't this is bullshit. Mikhail is the real deal. He isn't a hotboy, he is pure fire. Ghetto celebrities just aren't going to cut it for me anymore, and the way Mikhail is living, he makes everybody I've ever kicked it with, no matter how rich and famous, seem like a peasant. He has style, class, looks, swagger, and the money to set shit off lovely.

I've never met anyone quite like Mikhail Petrov, and I doubt that I ever will. But although he's fly, there is one thing competing with him: my memories of Kaos. And no amount of money and no gift can ever give Mikhail the edge over his competition. There was something so indescribable, so beautiful about the way we were in love. I've moved on, yes, but a part of me will never be able to let that go. Ever. So it doesn't matter that I'm here with another man, and it doesn't matter how many new lives I begin. I still think of Kaos all the time.

I still dream of him. Probably now more than ever. I still feel him every time I step up to a deck and do a set, because if it hadn't been for him, none of this would be happening. I wouldn't be the DJ that I am. But then, if he hadn't died, I wouldn't be here on this ship. Hell, maybe I would; maybe Kaos would be the DJ and I'd be along for the ride. There's no way to know.

What gets to me the most, what keeps me awake some nights, what makes me feel that there's a sliver of ice in my heart that will never melt, and what causes the pain that I do anything in my power to numb, even self-destructive shit, is the fact that his death is my fault. Because I warned him. At least, I tried to warn him about that damn bike. Maybe I didn't try hard enough. It wasn't that he wasn't a great biker; he was. He always drove carefully. Hell, I used to ride with him, and I loved it. Then one night I had a dream that the street opened up and swallowed him whole, and I knew. I knew something bad would happen to him on that motorcycle. He laughed at me. They say God has a reason for everything, but what reason did he have for taking my love away from me? Not even the good Reverend Dr. Robert Hayes Sr. can tell me that.

Don't get me wrong. I'm happy. Life is really good. And the smell of success is so sweet. But Kaos's love was sweeter. Money can't even replicate that feeling. But it helps, even though nothing will ever bring him back.

WHEN WE SET SAIL FOR EUROPE, THERE'S NOTHING BUT THE Atlantic Ocean for a few days. It's kind of scary sitting on a deck and just seeing nothing but water all day and all night. I wonder what would happen if we got lost or ran out of gas or broke down. And my crazy ass can't get the theme to

*Titanic* out of my head, even though Celine Dion is my least favorite singer. How does the captain know where the hell he is going anyway? And what if someone on board goes crazy and tries to kill us all? Who would rescue us? I've seen scary movies with plots like that, and you know the black person is always the first to die in a scary movie. So I'm limiting my time looking at the sea to a minimum, because it makes me too paranoid.

Mikhail and Dimitri hole themselves up in the business center for hours. It seems that I hardly even see Mikhail, which is crazy as hell because we're on the same ship! And when he is around, his cell phone is glued to his ear, or he's fiddling around on his Palm Pilot, or he's pecking away at his laptop. So I spend most of my time with Amara, which is cool because Amara is fascinating.

Amara has impeccable taste and always looks fabulous, seemingly without any effort. She wears nothing but the best, but what she wears never screams that she's trying to impress. Amara doesn't like to stay put in one place for long, so her clothes are never fussy and complicated but rather free and easy like herself, which, when you think about it, is probably the best way to go for someone so statuesque. Her hair hangs long, loose, and straight to the middle of her back, and is a combination of various shades of brown due to constant sunshine and sea water. She never wears it up or pulled back. She wears a lot of jewelry, but it's classy and never gaudy, and as for makeup, although she certainly doesn't need it at all, she seems to always have it on. She is always camera ready, and I have no idea how she does it. I think I'm pretty, but my good looks don't come naturally. There's a lot of work, thought, warpaint, and chemicals that go into making me look good.

As stunning as she is, Amara's appeal is more than skin deep. She's been everywhere, she knows everyone, and she's done everything. She was born to a wealthy family in Brazil that, she reluctantly admitted, owned a sugarcane plantation. She thought I'd be insulted that her family once owned slaves, and she was right; I didn't like to hear that she was associated with a plantation of any kind. But since I don't want people to judge me based on my family, I decide to extend her the same courtesy.

She went to school in the English countryside, and when she finished, her life consisted of shopping and partying and pretty much nothing else. She tells me that her brothers run the business, that she has a trust, and that she gets her money from the business and her family. They don't really expect her to do anything but be Amara. She's free and happy and genuine, and I want to be her so bad.

"You don't want to be like me, baby," she tells me when I share my admiration of her hedonistic lifestyle with her. From the way she says it, part nervous and part sad, I know that there's a lot more to that statement and a lot more to Amara than meets the eye. I'm instantly curious.

"Why is that?" I ask her.

Amara smiles and chuckles softly. "No one should ever try to be like someone else, ah?" She goes on in that way of hers that is somewhere between making a statement and asking a question.

"Mmm," I say, raising my eyebrow at her. Amara is hiding something. "Is that it?"

"Yes. Comparison is the source of unhappiness," she says wisely, and I know it to be true, but I wish she would tell that to my family. They are always comparing me to other people.

"Oh, okay," I say, not believing her. Amara and I sit in awkward silence for a moment.

"You are suspicious of me, no?" she asks.

"I like you, Amara," I tell her.

"I like you too, but you have suspicions about me," she replies.

"Well, I know there's plenty about you that you aren't telling," I say.

Amara smiles widely and clasps my hands. "What makes you think that?" she asks.

"Just a hunch," I say. "But it's cool. A woman is entitled to her secrets."

"This is what I like about you. You're smart," she says. "And you are right. A woman must have her secrets. But a woman must have her confidantes, no?"

"No doubt."

Amara looks around to see if any of the staff is present. We're alone. She speaks in a conspiratorial whisper.

"Can you keep a secret, baby?" she asks. "Will you be my confidante?"

"Of course," I say. I love gossip, the juicier the better. I can't wait to hear what she has to share.

"I tell Dimitri that I am from a wealthy family. But let's just say I bend the truth a little."

"Word?" I whisper back. "You're not rich?" She's a good actress because there isn't anyone around who could guess that she isn't from the manor born.

"Well, I am now, baby," she says with a laugh.

"But what about the sugarcane plantation?" I ask.

"A lie."

"What about the school in the English countryside?" I ask.

"I read about one in a book," she says.

"I can't believe it," I tell her.

"Is my secret safe with you?" she asks me.

"Of course. I'm no snitch," I tell her. "But what's the real deal?"

"I'm from a small village outside Sao Antonio," she whispers. "I have learned from a very young age how to use my feminine wiles to get what I want. For me, it is a matter of survival. I watched my mother work for rich people her whole life. She almost worked her way into the grave. She got me a job scrubbing floors and doing housework for a family near the home where she worked. The man of the house took one look at this *bunda*," she says pointing to her perfectly round ass, "and I never had to scrub floors again. Neither has my mother."

"Damn, that's like a Spanish-language soap opera," I tell her.

"Yes it is, baby. Where do you think my mother got the idea to send me to work for a rich family? I've never done well in school." Amara laughs and raises her eyebrow at me.

"You go, girl," I tell her. I ain't mad at her. "So how did you meet Dimitri?" I ask.

"I met Dimitri three years ago in Monaco," she says. "I was there with my Italian lover, Antonio. Antonio was a bastard. He was filthy rich and very good-looking, so sometimes I would forget what a bastard he was. But he had a habit of drinking too much and then wanting to make love, and I could not forget about that. I detest a sloppy drunk man, baby. I will not share my bed with one. But he would drink and think he was more irresistible than Casanova. This caused a lot of friction between us and I had made it up in my mind that I was going to leave him, but I was going to enjoy myself in Monaco first and then catch up with my friends in Saint Tropez. I think he could sense that I was going to leave him, and he became very bitter about losing my favor, baby. You know that the men, they can not resist Amara." She tosses her hair and laughs.

"One night, Antonio and I were at a casino playing baccarat, and he starts to call me all kinds of filthy names. Baby, it was awful. And he slapped me, right there in front of everybody. I was mortified. I was going to scratch his eyes out, when out of nowhere comes Dimitri. He's dressed in a fine tuxedo, baby. You should have seen him, it was so fabulous. He grabs Antonio by the face and slams him to the floor. There's a moment of silence, and everybody is sitting there with their mouths open wondering what is going to happen next," Amara continues. She's sitting so close to me that if I moved an inch we'd be French-kissing.

"Girl, what did he do?" I ask.

"Nothing. He just raised his hand, and out pop two guys who pick Antonio up and carry him out of the casino. Then Dimitri straightens himself out, adjusts his tie, and smooths his hair, and buys me a bottle of champagne. We spent hours talking, and when it was all said and done, I had my things moved out of the suite with Antonio and into the suite that Dimitri was in. We've been together ever since."

"Well, what happened to Antonio?" I ask.

"I don't know, baby. I don't care really. No one has seen him, but it's probably because he's too embarrassed to show his face. That or he drank himself to death," Amara says.

We sit there cruising and sunning, not saying a word.

"I have a question I've been dying to ask you, baby," Amara says suddenly.

"Go ahead," I tell her.

"Well, why would you choose to date a guy like Mikhail?" she asks.

"Why wouldn't I want to date Mikhail? He's rich as hell. He's sexy. He can help my career."

"Yes, but you come from money, you can date any man you want. Why would you get caught up with a man like him? Why would you risk your safe, secure life to be with a gangster if you don't have to?"

"Gangster?" I ask. "Mikhail isn't a gangster, Amara. He's a businessman."

"I have known this man for years," Amara tells me. "I know what I know, and I know what he is." She asks me, "What has Mikhail told you about his business?"

"Nothing much really. We haven't discussed it in detail," I say.

"What is it you think that he does?" she asks.

"He works with a bunch of Russian guys. And he's the new owner of Babylon. That's pretty much all I know and that's all that concerns me. If this is about those mafia rumors, I already talked to him about that."

Amara looks at me with deep seriousness. "How do you know they are rumors?" she asks. "You know, there's always a shred of truth to every rumor."

"He said he wasn't in the mafia," I say.

"And you believed that?" she asks, looking like she couldn't believe what had come out of my mouth.

"Shouldn't I?" I ask her.

"Oh, baby, I know you're smarter than that," she says.

"Okay," I admit. "I know that even if he were in the mafia, he probably would deny it; he wouldn't admit it. But if he were really in the mafia, a gangster as you put it, would he be free to live like this? Wouldn't the feds or somebody be on to him? They don't let people get this large. Big Brother has too many eyes for him to be on this level and not get locked up."

"What if Big Brother is just watching and waiting? What if Big Brother is on to the whole thing and is just waiting for the right moment? Or what if Big Brother is in on the whole thing and making money from it?" Amara asks.

"Is that the case?" I ask her. "I mean, you say that like you know something."

"I don't know anything for certain," she says. "I just know the world. Usually, nothing is as it seems."

Well, she's right about that! I know Amara has a point, but I don't want to admit it. I want to enjoy this lifestyle guilt free, and I can't do that if I know that Mikhail is a part of some notorious crime consortium.

"Come on, Amara," I say, waving my arm at our luxurious surroundings. "This doesn't exactly scream mafia, does it?"

"Well, what do you think screams mafia?" she asks with a laugh.

"Well, for starters, he's not tacky at all. He's classy. And all the mafia guys I've ever seen—and remember I'm from Chicago so I've seen plenty—were pretty cheesy. You know, gold chains and open shirts, clothes that are out of style and don't fit right. They were greasy; you could see them a mile away. You know, real Guidos."

"Guidos?" Amara asks.

"Yeah, you know. Gosh, this is so horrible I can't believe I'm saying this. Okay, there are African Americans, and there are niggers. One group works hard, tries to live right, while the other group mooches off the system and commits crime. Well, just like we have divisions for black folks, other people have their little sects too. Like for instance, there are Cubans and then there are Cubanosos. Cubans ran from Castro; Cubanosos are the folks Castro sent over to America to mess things up for us. Then there are Italian Americans, and there are Guidos. Get it? In every ethnic group there are the people who try to live a decent life, who have values and work hard to get ahead. Then there's the lower-class type," I tell her, "the kind of people who are looking for an easy way out, who don't want to work and want everything handed to them. They have no class, no style, they're just out to look rich, get rich, or die trying, and they don't care who they hurt in the process."

"Careful, Bobbi, you're starting to sound like an elitist," she says.

"Oh God," I say, rolling my eyes. I sound like my mother and that doesn't sit well with me. I also realize that what I said may have offended Amara on top of the fact that I sounded like a closed-minded moron.

"You know I didn't mean that the way it sounded," I tell her.

"I know, baby," she says and smiles at me. "I know exactly what you mean. But Bobbi, you mean to tell me that you bought the legitimate businessman bullshit?" she asks. I am comfortable in my denial, so I nod yes.

"No one can make this much money legally," Amara says with a laugh. "Name me one person, one family with this much wealth, and I'll show you a crook, baby."

I sit there trying to think of someone. Amara cuts to the chase. I want to prove her wrong, but I can't.

"Baby, look, don't waste your time. Maybe there are legitimate people with this much money, but not these guys. Mikhail and Dimitri are not businessmen. Not the way you think. They work along with a group of other men. There are thirteen of them all together. They're all filthy rich and their corporations are somehow tied together."

"What kinds of corporations?" I ask her.

"I don't know what kind they are; I just know that there are a lot of them and they are worth a fortune. They use them to launder the money, no doubt. You'll meet the Apostles soon enough," Amara told me, "and then you can come to your own conclusions."

"The Apostles?" I asked her.

"Oh, that's just what I call them. They follow Mikhail about like he's Jesus or something. Mikhail is—how do you say?—a Teflon Don. Nothing sticks to him. He's got so much money and so many people in his pockets, nothing will ever happen to them." Amara is so cavalier about it all.

"Aren't you afraid? Doesn't it scare you?" I ask her.

"Not as much as being poor does," she says.

FOR MOST OF THE AFTERNOON THAT FOLLOWS, I THINK ABOUT the conversation I had with Amara. I believe what she says. She has more reason to be forthcoming than Mikhail, but what was Amara's purpose in revealing all this to me? Why did she tell me the truth about herself? Maybe Amara considers us friends and she doesn't want to lie to me. Or is she watching my back? Perhaps she's trying to scare me in an attempt to run me off to protect her turf. Who knows?

What I do know is that Mikhail is not the innocent victim of gossip that he's portraying himself to be. He's shady. *But what is the harm in taking a little trip?* I ask myself. It's a question I already know the answer to. Plenty! Back when I was in high school, one of my classmates, Tricia, disappeared. She had gone on a "little trip" to New Orleans to visit her boyfriend, who happened to be a drug dealer. No one ever heard from her again. There was a huge search for her; search parties canvassed the area, put up flyers, and her mother put in an impassioned plea for information on her daughter with the media. When Tricia's body was found, she was nearly decapitated, and the autopsy showed that she'd been raped repeatedly, tortured, stabbed, and shot. It turns out that some goons kidnapped Tricia and her dope-boy at the airport because of some beef or other over turf or product or what have you.

*I won't end up like Tricia,* I reassure myself. Her boyfriend was probably small-time. Those are the kinds of hustlers that get caught up in those kinds of messes, right? Mikhail is different, right? Besides, he may not even be a drug dealer. I know he's shady, but I don't know exactly what he's into. Maybe he's into some Enron type of shit, which is really fucked up, but it shouldn't affect me. I mean, it won't put my life in danger. And if he is some prick who's ripping off people's pensions, then he deserves to get used by me.

The voices argue back and forth in my head. I feel like one of those cartoons when there's an angel on one shoulder and a devil on the other.

*He's in the Russian mafia,* the angel tells me. *He's probably into far worse than Tricia's boyfriend. Run! Now!*

*Maybe he's in the Russian mafia, but if that's the case, the less you know the better. Besides, he's more careful. He's smarter. He wouldn't have all this if he was into taking stupid risks,* the little devil tells me.

My grandfather used to say that the devil wanted my soul more than other people's because of my lineage, because I came from "a good Christian family." We were *anointed*. It's a greater coup for him to reel me in. Satan gets to thumb his nose at God when he lures one of his children into a life of evil. Right now, God is raining tears from heaven for me, because the devil is winning. The devil replaces the fears and wariness that God and his angels have planted in my head and heart with twisted logic.

*It's not like I'm going to marry Mikhail or have his children. I'll get in, get the money and the power, and get out. Mikhail will probably grow bored with me before anything bad happens.*

*Why are you doing this?* I hear my angel say, though her voice is getting fainter. *You don't need that much money. You're not a material girl. Are possessions worth your life? Your soul?*

It won't get that far. Everybody bends the rules to get ahead, everybody that has anything. I may not be as worldly as Amara, but I'm not naïve and I know how Miami works. People grease the palms of building and zoning inspectors, or pay a little extra to expedite a liquor license's processing. And I'm no stranger to the club scene; I know that a lot of club owners and promoters and the like have some pretty nefarious reputations. The way I see it, no matter where I work or who I work for, chances are I'll be working with someone at least a *little* crooked. Better a guy like Mikhail than some foolish amateur who thinks that the game is like a movie and learned everything about the streets from a rap song.

I'm sure the rest of the world works the same way. This is an opportunity. I get a chance to be something different, someone special. I'm not about to look this gift horse in the mouth. Besides, Amara seems to be doing just fine with Dimitri. I don't see her shaking in her Christian Louboutins.

Still, I know that I'm probably playing with fire. But what would you expect a rebel like me to do? Play it safe? Play by the rules? I don't think so. Anyway, I know what I'm doing and I have everything under control. I'm not some naïve high-school girl, I'm Ms. Bobbi! This is business, and sometimes you have to get your hands a little dirty if you want results.

WE'RE GETTING PRETTY CLOSE TO OUR DESTINATION AND Mikhail decides to have an extravagant surf and turf dinner consisting of gigantic, spicy, peel-and-eat prawns, boiled Maine lobster and Alaskan king crabs with drawn butter, and filet Oscar grilled to perfection. There's plenty of salad, potatoes, rice, pasta, veggies, and bread to accompany the meal, as well as vodka for the guys and champagne for the women. After we dine like pigs and are full of liquor, we play dominoes. The funny thing about slapping bones is that it's universal. I guess because numbers are the same no matter where you go. And I learn that shit talking while playing dominoes is universal as well, because Dimitri runs his mouth and runs us off the table.

After dominoes, we go to the disco, and I play some old school hip-hop and deep Chicago house for them. It's hilarious watching them dance all crazy and off-beat to Public Enemy and KRS-One, rapping along with the lyrics of the handful of songs they know, like "Fight the Power" and "Criminal Minded."

"When we reopen Babylon, Ms. Bobbi, you are going to be a megastar!" Mikhail says in my ear while wrapping his muscular arms around my waist. He's slipped into the DJ booth while Amara and Dimitri are busy making out on a large sofa that sits just off the dance floor. The disco is laid out very similar to the nightclub B.E.D. in Miami, with four canopied beds that are recessed from the mirrored walls. If Babylon is done up half as nicely as the ship's disco, the club is going to be tight.

"Is that right?" I ask him, turning around and planting a kiss on his lips. "That's hefty talk."

"That's real talk, Bobbi. The club is going to be the most fabulous thing on South Beach that anyone has ever seen. It is going to be my best venue yet. You see, the nightclubs that I own . . ." he says.

"Clubs? You own more than one?" I ask him curiously.

"I have an interest in several clubs all over the world. New York, Budapest, Amsterdam, Stockholm. They are just a small part of my empire, but they're my favorite. I work hard, and I play hard. You are going to be a very big part of Babylon, hopefully a big part of more than one of my clubs, and a very big part of my life. I want so much more than sex from you, Bobbi; I want something long term. I hope you know that," Mikhail tells me, his green eyes transfixed with mine.

"I do now," I say, grinning. This has to be game, but I'm enjoying it.

"I'm serious, Bobbi. You are a very special woman. You're classy. You have a sharp mind. You have a way with people. You're talented. And you're very, very sexy," he says, palming my ass and squeezing a handful. "You're amazing."

I had believed until this point that Mikhail was in this thing with me just for kicks. And Bentley had called one thing right the night of our encounter: I've never been in a relationship with a white man. And as hard as it is to believe considering how big of a slut I am, I've never even slept with one before now. It's not that I'm prejudiced. I just hadn't gotten around to it. I sure as hell never expected a filthy rich white man, one who was probably a billionaire, or at least a megamillionaire, telling me that he wanted more than a roll in the hay. I don't care what background I come from, guys like Mikhail like supermodels, blondes, and women like Amara, not around-the-way black chicks like me. There has to be a catch.

"Want to go to the cabin?" I ask him. I plan on doing some sexual espionage: I'm going to fuck his brains out and then probe him. Plus, Amara and Dimitri are getting pretty intense over on the couch and I don't want to stick around for what comes next. Amara has already stripped down to her LaPerla's and Dimitri is buck naked. I like them, but I don't really want to know them like that. Still, I can't help but notice that Dimitri is hung like a horse, just like his cousin. Whoever started the rumor that white men were less endowed had obviously never bedded a Russian!

"No," he says to me. I turn to face him.

"Don't you want me?" I ask.

"I always want you. There hasn't been a time that I've been in your presence when I didn't want you. I want you right here, right now."

"What about Amara and Dimitri?" I ask.

"What about them?" Mikhail begins to tweak my nipples through my blouse.

"Uh, I really care about you too but I'm not into the group thing," I stammer. I am certainly not a prude, and I've been with women before and probably will be again. I've even partaken in a little group sex in the past, back when I first moved to Miami and had a tad bit of a cocaine habit. (Blow makes you do some crazy things, which is why I forced myself to stop.) And although Amara is alluring to say the least, I just don't want to take it there. I don't want to taint what is starting to feel like one of the first pure friendships I've had in ages. Amara may be on the shady side, but up till now she's been pretty honest with me, which is more than I can say for most women. Besides, we're going to be together on this ship for who knows how long, and I don't want the trip to become some nonstop orgy. My face must be transparent to my thoughts, because Mikhail laughs and shakes his head.

"Oh no, I was not suggesting an orgy," he explains. "What I had in mind was a bit different. I would never share you with another man, especially not my cousin. I could never bear to watch what I feel is now mine with another man."

"What you feel is yours?" I ask.

"Bobbi, let's cut the bullshit. The games have been fun, but we both want more than games. Stop fighting the inevitable. You belong to me," he tells me.

"And where do you belong?" I ask him.

"I belong to you," he says. "We have something special. We can do anything together."

"What is it that you want to do?"

"I want to experience the sensation of watching two beautiful women watching each other make love." I'm going to need a little more convincing because this doesn't sound sexy to me. It sounds homoerotic and we *are* on our way to Greece.

Before you know it, there will be sweaty, entangled bodies everywhere, a total freak fest. I'm freaky, but not that freaky. I'm not going to be a part of doing two cousins, or two cousins doing each other.

"Look at Amara," Mikhail commands in a forceful voice. Dimitri is behind her, kissing her neck and fondling her breasts. He removes her bra then slides her panties off her ass and down her legs, grazing her body with his lips. Amara and I make eye contact. This is embarrassing, but I don't look away. She smiles at me and winks as Dimitri laps eagerly at her backside. From the distance I'm standing, I can't tell if he is licking her pussy or her ass, but whatever Dimitri is doing, Amara is enjoying. She arches her back, spreads her butt cheeks, and Dimitri dives in, slurping loudly. This is as raunchy as the alleged R. Kelly sex tape, when the "maybe" R. Kelly allegedly has that chick (the grown one) on a chair and is tossing the hell out of her salad. Amara wiggles her ass like she's dancing a sensual samba and moans as Dimitri ravishes her body.

"Relax," Mikhail purrs in my ear. "Enjoy."

I feel the tension ease from my body as Mikhail's hands roam over my curves, removing my clothing.

"Wait," I tell Mikhail. I cue up a few songs by Prince. If there's one thing I can't stand to do, that's have sex with no soundtrack.

I kiss Mikhail deeply as the sounds of "When 2 R in Love" fill the room. He leads me out of the DJ booth to one of the canopied beds, and I lie down. Mikhail spreads my legs wide and begins to taste me.

"Does that feel good?" Amara asks me as Dimitri works her from behind.

I look up to answer her and that's when I notice it. Dimitri is more tatted up than Tupac, Travis Barker, or a neo-Nazi! When I say he is inked, I mean it. His entire chest and back is covered. Everything is done in an indigo color, and the images run the gamut from what looks like a Russian castle branded across his chest to barbed wire around his forearm to cats, skulls, and snakes. In all the time we had been on the ship, I'd never seen Dimitri shirtless. He always wore classy clothes, like linen suits and crisp dress shirts. And he didn't swim or Jet Ski so I'd never seen him in swimming trunks. All the tats just seem so out of character for Dimitri. He's pretty conservative, and even his casual clothes give off an air of polished sophistication. I'm stunned, still I answer, "Yes, it does."

I continue to stare as Amara caresses her own breasts, and then moves her hand between her legs. Dimitri grabs a handful of her luxurious mane with one hand and slaps Amara's ass with the other.

"Oh, baby, Dimitri is sooo good," she shrieks as Dimitri pumps away. Eventually I lose fascination with Dimitri's tats and Amara; Mikhail is doing an excellent job distracting me. I moan and writhe as Mikhail licks me, bringing me to the brink of orgasm.

"Don't stop, baby!" I gasp, pulling his head back toward me.

Mikhail stands up and removes his clothing. I tear at his clothing to help speed up the process. His erection jutts out, and I can see his hardness throbbing with anticipation.

"Bobbi, I don't want to get a condom, I want to feel all of you," he says in my ear as he lies down on top of me. I know what Mikhail wants, he wants the raw dog: unprotected sex. His dick is an inch away from entering me. He teases me with the tip of his penis, which is driving me crazy. My head is screaming *Don't do it!* but my body is saying *Now!*

I should tell him that people in hell want ice water, or that you can't always get what you want and make him get a rubber, but I don't. I know better, but I'm so caught up in the moment that I go against my better judgment.

"Okay, baby," I say, with only a tinge of hesitation.

Mikhail thrusts himself inside me, and I'm lost in the sensation. I lock my legs around his back and thrust my pelvis against him, trying to get more and more of him inside me. Mikhail stops thrusting altogether and through clenched teeth says, "Be still." I do as I'm told, but my breath is coming in rapid gasps, causing my body to move spastically. Mikhail waits for me to calm down, then begins to flex and pulse his cock inside me. He makes his dick jump and twitch until I'm screaming at the top of my lungs, oblivious to anyone or anything.

I moan as he tosses me onto my stomach like I'm a rag doll and begins to forcefully thrust himself inside me from behind. I go crazy, throwing my ass against his body until I reach another climax. Amara follows suit, muttering in Portuguese as she comes, before finishing Dimitri off orally. Mikhail holds me by the hair, forcing me to watch the whole thing. Well, he doesn't really have to *force* me. It's like looking at a live porno.

"Come for me, baby," I plead because I can't take much more.

"Where do you me want to come?" he asks. I'm going to answer him, but he asks me a question before I can respond.

"Can I come inside you?" he asks me.

"No!" I reply, quickly.

"It's okay," he says, grabbing my hips firmly.

"I don't want to get pregnant," I manage to utter.

"Bobbi, I love you!" Mikhail shouts. "I'm about to come. Let me come inside you," he says. Dumbstruck by the fact that Mikhail has just told me that he loves me, I'm unable to speak.

And then it's too late.

# CHAPTER SIX

THE NEXT MORNING I WAKE UP EARLY BUT I DON'T OPEN MY eyes. I hear Mikhail talking on his cell phone, and my curiosity gets the best of me, so I eavesdrop while I play possum.

"Yes, I miss you," he says. "Of course I do. I think of you often . . . You know why things must be this way, I do not wish to explain them again . . . I'm going to go now . . . No . . . No, I will see you when I return to Miami. You just concentrate on the tasks on hand. You have a lot of work to do. Yes, I love you too. Good-bye." *Who does he love too?*, I wonder as he disconnects the call and then comes to my bedside. I want to sit up and ask him who he was talking to; after all, he professed his love to me the night before. But I don't; the time isn't right. I continue to pretend that I'm sleeping.

Mikhail gently kisses my forehead, eyelids, and the tip of my nose before planting a kiss on my lips. I crack my eyelids open and smile sweetly.

"You even wake up beautiful," Mikhail says to me.

"Mmm, you must need glasses," I murmur.

"I don't need glasses to see that I'm in bed with the most

beautiful and talented woman in the world, and that I'm madly in love," Mikhail says.

"With me?" I ask. I *did* just hear him telling someone else he loved them.

"Of course with you, silly girl."

I grin at Mikhail, because I think he's running game.

"Does that grin mean you love me too?" he asks. Uh-oh. I'm checking for Mikhail, this is certain. But love is another thing. I gave up on love when Kaos died, and I know I'm not ready, or even willing, to go there. But you can't tell a man that kind of thing without hurting his feelings. Even if there may be another woman in the picture. Fuck what they try to act like; men are just as sensitive as women are about these kinds of things. So I just continue to smile. I lift the covers up over my face until only my eyes are showing.

"Maybe," I say slowly and mysteriously before erupting into a fit of giggles. Attagirl. Keep it light.

"Maybe?" He pokes out his bottom lip and folds his arms across his chest like a child.

"Aww, baby," I say soothingly as I stroke his back. And then he turns on me. Before I know it, Mikhail ambushes me, tickling me all over until I think I'm going to wet the bed. Then he kisses me until my head starts spinning. When we finally disengage after what feels like forever, he ruffles my hair and we sit up in bed.

"So who were you on the phone with?" I ask, now that he's off guard. It isn't so much that I care, but my curiosity must be satisfied.

"That was an ex," he says.

"You still love her?" I ask.

"You could say that I love her. But I am not *in love* with her. Not in that way. That, my sweet angel, is reserved only for you," he says with a smile.

"Mikhail, I don't own you. You can do whatever you want, just be honest, okay?" I tell him.

"I am being honest," he says. "And I am precisely where and with whom I want to be. Come, let me show you something." Mikhail leads me to the windows and draws back the curtains. I gasp at what I see. We're docked at a marina that is nestled beside an island with a large, cone-shaped mountain jutting up from the center, with billows of white steam floating around its peak. The water is so blue it doesn't look real, yet it's so clear that I can see the ship and the surrounding cliff side reflected in the water.

"It's gorgeous! This is absolutely breathtaking. Where are we?" I ask him, anxious to get off the ship and get my land legs back.

"The Azores. We are on a little island called Faial not far from Portugal."

"Why is that mountain steaming?" I ask.

"It's not just a mountain, it's a volcano," he answers.

"Active?" I ask, my eyes bugging out.

"Yes, but not in a while."

"Okay," I say hesitantly. The last thing I need is for a volcano to erupt.

"I think you'll be safe," he says, laughing at my cowardice. "We will get something to eat, and walk around a bit," he says.

"Go shopping?" I ask, hopeful. Mikhail laughs heartily.

"There is nowhere to shop here. This island is very undisturbed," he explains.

"You mean boring." I say, correcting him.

"You and Amara are two of a kind. Always wanting to shop and party."

"What else is there?" I ask him, grinning.

"There is more to life than a good time," Mikhail says to me.

"Oh yeah, like what?" I ask him.

"Like having something or someone else to live for. Like belonging to something bigger than you," he says, running his hands through his hair. "Coming from a family like yours, I thought you'd understand that."

"Let's not talk about my family unless you're ready to talk about yours too. You have no idea what it was like growing up in my clan," I tell him.

"I'd love to talk about my family, but I have none left aside from Dimitri. We have been each other's only family for over thirty years. But believe me, Bobbi, I know all about pressure. Not the kind of pressure you speak of, but the pressure to survive. I would have preferred your kind of pressure over the strain of not knowing where my next meal would come from. I wish I didn't know the pressure of waiting in lines for hours for government rations, only to be refused, while corrupt pigs filled their bellies with the hard work and blood of the common man. You see, my sweet angel, Americans live to enjoy. Russians live to endure," Mikhail tells me.

"Damn," is all I can say, because I feel like a complete and total asshole. I guess it's written all over my face, because Mikhail kisses me on the forehead.

"Do not worry. Your spoiled ways do not offend me," he says chuckling. "You could not have known the struggles I have been through, nor would I wish them on a dog, let alone *milaya angelochek moya*, my sweet angel. I do not regret my life. My struggles have made me strong." Then Mikahil swoops me into his arms and twirls me in a circle. "And rich," he continues. "Rich enough to give spoiled little girls beautiful gifts."

Mikhail reaches into his pocket and pulls out a small velvet-covered box.

"What's this?" I ask.

"Open it and find out," he says.

I open the box and gasp. Inside there's an emerald pendant set in gold and attached to a delicate gold chain.

"Do you like it?" he asks.

"Are you kidding? I love it! It's beautiful. But when did you have time to get this?" I ask him, turning around and lifting my hair so he can place it around my neck.

"I am a man of many mysteries," he says.

"You've got that right," I say, admiring the pendant that dangles between my breasts. I turn to face him.

"This is the most beautiful gift I've ever received. I don't know what I could have possibly done to deserve this, but thank you. Really. I'll treasure this forever," I tell him, staring into his eyes.

"I know you will," he says. "And that's why you deserve it. As spoiled as you are, as charmed a life as you have led, you are still somewhat humble underneath it all. You appreciate me; you don't take me for granted. That's why I love you. That is why I am going to open up my world to you."

I blush but it's slightly out of guilt. Mikhail thinks I'm his sweet angel. I do appreciate him, but it isn't as pure as he seems to think. I admire the pendant once again and feel my guilt slip away like mist. The emerald is hypnotic. "You know, this emerald is the same color as your eyes," I say absent-mindedly.

"I know. It's my way of saying I've got my eye on you," he says, grinning.

"Is that all you've got on me?" I ask him.

"Not for long," he says suggestively, as he caresses my breasts through the flimsy silk of my gown. And then Mikhail puts everything he has to give on me, just the way I like it.

Aside from the pendant and the phenomenal lovemaking that follows, the time spent in Faial is pretty uneventful. One thing does stand out in my mind, though, and that's Amara's comment about the emerald when she sees it.

"Mikhail gave you that, baby, no?" she asks while we wait for our food at a local restaurant. Dimitri and Mikhail have gone to the restroom, and we're seated at a table awaiting an Azorean specialty, a stew that has been prepared by putting the ingredients in a cookery vessel and placing it underneath the ground where it is cooked by the island's natural hot springs.

"Of course. I can't afford anything like this on my own," I tell her.

"Bobbi, baby. Nothing in life is free, remember that."

I know that what Amara says is true. Nothing in life is free. I just wonder what price I will ultimately have to pay for everything that's been bestowed upon me.

THE REAL ADVENTURE BEGINS WHEN WE REACH IBIZA. WE AR-rive just as the sun is setting, and we gather on the deck as the ship docks at Marina Botafoch. As dusk draws, the sky is illuminated in a shade of purple, and the entire island seems to be made up of little ivory buildings that are layered and piled up, one on top of the other, causing it to glow like a giant birthday cake. From the sounds of horns, scooters, radios, and laughter, I can tell that there is much fun to be had and I'm anxious to get off the ship. There are tons of people out, mill-ing about the street that runs alongside the harbor.

We slide into a row of luxury yachts, all lined up in ascend-ing order. There are actually a couple of ships that are even larger than Mikhail's. I wonder who they belong to, and what the hell the owners do for a living. If Mikhail's a gangster, these people must be super-thugs.

We go to our suites to get properly dressed for a night of

clubbing. We're going to go to a club called Pacha later on in the evening, but first we're going to have a reception on board for Mikhail and Dimitri's friends. I'm the DJ at this party, which is going to serve as my official overseas debut. When Mikhail first ran the idea by me, I assumed it would be a small gathering since it seemed pretty last minute. But there are over a hundred people on the guest list, including several local promoters, club owners, and other DJs.

I decide to kick it typical Ms. Bobbi style, over the top and outlandish. In need of a little inspiration, I grab the case that contains my makeup, body paint, crystals, beads, sequins, and liquid latex, and head off to Amara's suite. I knock on the door to her stateroom, but there is no response. I can hear Amara speaking heatedly to someone, but can't imagine who. Dimitri and Mikhail are in the business center preparing for the festivities. *Ooh, she's probably going off on one of the staff*, I think to myself. *Let me go rescue this poor soul*. I open the door and pop my head inside.

"You heard me, I want out! I'm tired of this. I just can't do this anymore. I want my life back. This doesn't feel right. This isn't fair to her. She's a good person. There's got to be another way. I've held up my end of the bargain, now I want out!" she's shouting into her cell phone. She must have heard the door or sensed my presence, because she whirls around and faces me. Amara pales like she's seen a ghost.

"I've got to go," she says looking guilty, and disconnects the call.

"Hey, baby! Are you excited about the party tonight?" Amara asks, trying to play things off. I don't know what's going on, but it's definitely something.

"Did I interrupt something? Is this a bad time?" I ask her.

"No, baby, come on in," she says, fiddling with the strap on her sexy high heels.

"Who was that?" I ask. "Are you fooling around on Dimitri with a married man? Dish, girl, tell me what's up," I say with a sly grin.

"Oh, that phone call? That was nothing, baby!" she says.

"Bullshit!" I tell her. "If you're cheating on Dimitri I won't tell. I wouldn't do you like that, girl," I say.

"You got me," she says. "It was a fling and he won't let go. Now let's not talk about it," Amara whispers. "What are you going to wear for the party?"

"That's why I'm here," I say, remembering why I'd come to her room in the first place. I have to figure out a mind-blowing, jaw-dropping getup to rock for the party. But I have no idea where to start.

"I always perform in costume," I say to Amara. I wave the makeup case in the air. "I've got stuff with me, but I just feel like it's been seen and done. I know this sounds crazy, but you wouldn't happen to have anything, any kind of costume, would you? I wasn't expecting to work before I got a chance to check out the scene, you know, see what everybody's into, what's wild and what's ordinary," I say. "I guess I wasn't thinking, huh?"

"You have come to the right place. Amara has some costumes. I think we can come up with something unforgettable. Come," she says dramatically in a throaty voice. We go into her dressing suite, and she starts poking in drawers and sifting through the clothes hanging on padded satin and wooden hangers on the vast racks filled with her ensembles.

"Is this stuff going to fit me?" I whine as she tosses things at me from every direction. "You're way taller than me. Hardly anything you have is going to fit me! I need something fabulous Amara. Not cheesy, okay?"

Amara stops what she is doing. "Amara de Laurenti is never cheesy!" she says. I want to tell her that referring to herself by her full name might be viewed by some people as cheesy, but I keep it to myself. After the mad clothes pull, we begin to narrow down the selection, placing the rejects in one pile and the maybes in another. I say a definitive *no* to the dominatrix getup. It's too damn hot to be all laced up and wearing leather. And I don't even want to think about what Amara was doing when she wore the outfit. Gross! Also in the no pile go the nurse outfit—too cliché—and the French maid costume, for the same reason.

In a maybe pile I place a suede bikini that is accentuated with feathers and beads. I can do a sexy Pocahontas-type deal with that because I have some turquoise and suede-fringed high heels that would go great with it. I also put a corset made of black satin with colorful ribbons lacing it up in the maybe pile. I can potentially make it *Moulin Rouge* funky, but I'm not sure if that idea is really shocking enough.

I pull out a gorgeous piece of turquoise silk, with strands of silver and gold thread woven throughout and embroidered with an intricate pattern of beads and stones. "What's this?" I ask her. "A shawl, a blanket? It's pretty." I feel the quality of the fabric and admire the funky design.

"No, baby, don't be silly. This is a sari; I got it in India. Saris are wonderful, baby. They're all the same size; the secret is in how you wrap them. I have a fishtail petticoat that goes underneath. It may be a little long, but we'll work around it," she explains. "We can make you look like a Bollywood queen," she says, referring to the colorful Indian musical movies.

"That would be kind of obvious," I say. "I love Indian clothes, but just wearing a sari isn't really screaming anything at me. Folks just might think I'm Indian, not in costume. Plus, I don't need any fabric hanging down and getting in my way, and if we wrap this over my shoulder I'm going to be messing with it all night."

"I've got it," she says. "Trust me, baby, you're going to look fabulous."

I put on the petticoat, which drags a bit along the ground, but Amara assures me that it will be okay. Then we wrap the sari around my bottom half, until it has an exotic, mystical, ethereal vibe. I like it, but I wonder what Amara is going to do with the rest of me.

"Let me see your tits," Amara says, her accent making the word tits sound more like *teats*. I giggle because my perky and full boobs are far from the triangular, floppy, puppy-dog-ear-shaped boobs I think of when I hear the word *teats*.

"Are you crazy? What the hell are you up to?"

"Take off the tank top. Don't act like it's a problem because I know how you perform. Besides, I've seen them before, and then some," she says, giving me a wink.

I laugh and take off my top. She draws designs on my bare breasts with liquid eyeliners and colors them in with body paint, then she highlights the designs with eye shadows and pigments, and accents them with crystals and some body glitter. Finally, Amara wraps dozens of strands of pearls and beads around my neck.

"What are your friends like? Do you think they will like me?" I ask her as she fluffs my hair and puts an orchid from a vase above my ear. She takes the flower away from my ear and grabs the rest from the bouquet. Then she pulls out a needle and thread and some hairpins and ribbons. I have no idea what she's up to, but she better not have me looking like some crazy flower child from the '60s!

"They will adore you, baby. You look fucking gorgeous. You just do what you do, and don't worry about them. They'll buy whatever you sell them. They're not that deep," she says, laughing.

Amara's hands get busy wrapping the flowers together with thread and ribbons. She fashions a wreathlike crown and places it on my head in a matter of minutes.

"Damn, girl, this is banging! You've got skills! Is there anything you can't do?" I ask her, admiring my reflection in a lighted full-length mirror. "Do you know jujitsu and how to disarm bombs and stuff too?" I kid.

"Of course," she says, and laughs, but it wouldn't surprise me if she isn't joking at all.

I DECIDE TO GO CHILL IN THE BUSINESS CENTER RATHER THAN mix or mingle with the guests before the party. I need a quiet place to take some time to meditate and get mentally prepared for my set, and for once Mikhail and Dimitri aren't barricaded within. I leave the light off, take a seat in the huge leather chair, close my eyes, and take some deep breaths. Then I get that feeling again; something is going to happen, or there's something I should know. I try to shake it off but I can't. I sit there in the darkness, not moving, waiting for something or someone to clue me in.

*Open the drawer,* I hear a voice inside my head say. I don't really want to do it. I'm not a snoop. I never went through Kaos's things; insecurity isn't my style. Plus I'm afraid of what I might find. I've always believed that if you go looking for trouble, you'll certainly find it.

*Open the drawer,* I hear the voice say again. I'm too compelled not to open the drawer now. I put my hand on the handle and give it a slow pull, and I'm surprised to find it unlocked. I take special care not to disturb anything. There's a bunch of papers all neatly stapled and clipped together, and some manila folders, nothing out of the ordinary except for a brown accordion folder that would be more at home in a file cabinet. I pull it out and look at the labeled tab that reads simply—Q.

The label seems odd, very James Bond, so I peer inside and inspect the contents. I find a manila folder that has a picture of me clipped to the outside. On the side of the manila folder is a label bearing my full name, Roberta Ann Hayes. What the fuck?! I pull out the folder and open it carefully. There before my eyes is a complete dossier. There's all kinds of info about me in here, including a credit report. There's a copy of the deed to my condo, and my DMV records. There are clippings about my family from magazines *and* my freakin' yearbook photo! My heart stops when I see a photo of Kaos and me. We're posed on his motorcycle in front of Wet Willies on Ocean Drive, but we're clearly not posing for whoever snapped this picture. It's taken from a distance, like someone was spying on us.

I close the folder and return it to its place. I've heard of employer background checks, but this is obviously the work of a damn good private eye. I don't know how comfortable I am with the details of my life neatly compacted into a file folder, even if it is business on Mikhail's end. I mean, sure he's filthy fucking rich, and he needs to be careful with who he allows in his inner circle, but I feel a little violated. And that just gives me more justification to snoop further. What's good for the goose, right?

I thumb through the stack of folders to see if there's anything else worth taking a look at, but the rest just looks like a bunch of shipping bills. I open another drawer and see a picture of Mikhail hugged up with a nondescript blond woman. They look pretty intimate even though they are flanked by a group of men, the Apostles, perhaps. But who is the mystery lady? Is this the ex he said he loved during the cell phone conversation I eavesdropped on? Is it some-one he's dating now?

I think I hear footsteps so I replace the folder, close the drawer quickly, and try to look normal. The knob on the door turns and the lights flutter on.

"Bobbi, what are you doing in here? I've been looking all over for you!" Mikhail asks. I can tell he's trying to determine if I was snooping. He's got a suspicious look on his face.

"Nothing. I came in here to look for you but you weren't here. I decided to stay since it was nice and quiet. I just wanted to get my mind right before this performance." This answer seems to satisfy Mikhail because he opens his arms and nods, signaling for me to give him a hug, which I do.

"Are you nervous?" he asks.

"Hell, yeah!"

"Why? You're the best there is," he says reassuringly.

"Thanks," I say.

"Well, my sweet angel, are you ready to rock?" Mikhail asks. I crack up.

"Am I ready to rock?" I ask. "Yeah sure, dude. Rock on!" I say. Then I hold up my hand in the international rocker sign and bang my head back and forth.

"You know what I mean, Bobbi. I'm going to take that as a yes," Mikhail says.

"Let's do this!" I exclaim, as I gather up my "mermaid tail" and follow Mikhail. I've got a lot of questions, things I want to investigate, but for now it will have to wait. I still have that fluttery feeling inside; my heart is pounding. I hope that for once I'll be able to see what lies in the path ahead before something goes wrong. Damn my bogus psychic abilities!

When we reach the deck, Mikhail signals to Amara, the designated hostess for the evening. Amara winks at me and stands on top of a chair. She clinks a champagne glass with a spoon to get everyone's attention.

"All right, babies, get ready. My absolute favorite DJ in the world is about to hit the turntables. She's talented and absolutely fucking gorgeous. And I guarantee that after this, she's going to be your favorite DJ too. So with no further delay, here is Miami's own Ms. Bobbi!" Amara tosses her hair, steps down from her perch on the chair, and begins to scream and clap wildly.

Smoke machines from the disco have been set up along the deck, and one of the butlers cuts them on. Smoke billows as I walk through the crowd and approach the deck. I can hear an audible collective gasp as I pass by. I take a deep breath, say a quick prayer, and think of Kaos. *I'm gonna show them how we roll,* I tell him, wherever he is.

My jitters are gone; I'm in the zone. It's just me and the music now. I cue up Stardust's "Music Sounds Better with You," then I segue into Earth People's "Dance, Dance, Dance." Amara gets on the dance floor and begins dancing all wild and crazy, and the other guests join her. When I put on "Lady" by Modjo, the crowd goes crazy, singing along and clapping, albeit not quite on beat. I decide not to look at the crowd, because all I need is for someone from the rhythmless nation to throw me off. Instead I choose my songs by instinct; I go with my gut.

I spin house for about another hour, then switch to hip-hop, using Missy's "This Is for My People" as my transition record. As much as the crowd enjoys my house set, things really get hyped once I start playing rap. And the more hardcore my selection, the more they seem to get into it.

In total, my debut set lasts close to three hours. As soon as I step down from the decks I'm swarmed with people telling me how fabulous I am. I eat it up like Sunday dinner. Amara's friends speak myriad languages, and even though I don't know what the majority of them are saying, I know that it's complimentary from their smiles, hugs, and kisses. Mikhail rescues me from the throng, telling me that there are some people he wants me to meet.

"First we will do a little business, and then I want you to meet my friends," he says, motioning toward two couples standing together drinking champagne and smoking, and then to a louder, more lively bunch of men who look as if they are having the time of their lives.

The fishtail sari swishes about, and the pearls and necklaces clink together and bounce across my breasts as we head toward the couples. Mikhail points out a few people as we walk along the deck, giving me bits of info about the partygoers.

"That man over there is a British ambassador, the woman he's talking to works for the Dutch consulate." He shows me some more politicos and folks with important-sounding titles before we reach his friends.

Mikhail kisses the women who are too thin and look like they've had too much plastic surgery. One looks like a cat, and the other looks like she's in a constant state of surprise. They don't look happy to be here, but on those faces, I'm not sure what happy would look like anyway. The men are both fat, not very attractive, and have gone way overboard with the spray-on tan. They're as orange as Oompa Loompas, and they stare at my boobs for a very long time before acknowledging me. Mikhail is talking away with them, and hasn't bothered to introduce us. I fold my arms across my chest to end the peep show and give a little cough. The shorter man speaks up.

"Ms. Bobbi, you were absolutely phenomenal. Welcome to Spain! Allow me to introduce myself. I am Marco Delgado, and I can't wait to have you play at my club Mystery here on the island," the pudgy, middle-aged man says in thickly accented English as he chomps on the end of a smelly cigar. "Mikhail, where have you been hiding this gem?" Marco asks him as he slaps him hard on the back.

"She's been in Miami," Mikhail tells him. "But now she is here, and just like a gem, she is very precious, very rare, and very expensive," Mikhail says to Marco, grinning and returning the hearty slap on the back. The two of them look like they're going to knock each other down with all the backslapping they're doing. It definitely has to be a European thing because, in the good old U.S. of A., anybody I know would be ready to go to blows over getting hit in the back so hard.

"Ah yes, but of course. I was thinking ten thousand American," Marco says. "How does that sound?"

*Good as hell*, I think to myself. I can roll with that.

"Come on, my friend . . . Bobbi is a beautiful young woman. She's so exquisite she could walk the runway for that kind of money. That's not enough," Mikhail says.

"Mikhail," I say, interrupting him. I'm not about to let him talk me out of ten g's.

"Just a minute, my sweet angel," he says.

*Ain't this some shit?* I think to myself. Here he is discussing my career like I'm not even here. But before I can object Marco speaks up.

"Okay, how about fifteen thousand?" I shut my mouth quick and let Mikhail do all the talking.

"Make it twenty thousand dollars, my friend, and we've got a deal," Mikhail says.

Marco leers at me again and sucks on the end of his wet, smelly cigar. I'm sure his bulimic girlfriend, or whoever she is, has him convinced that he's one of the most handsome men in the universe, because he stands there as if I should be leering at him in return with lust in my eyes. He winks, clears his throat, makes little facial tics like he's got Tourette's syndrome, and shrugs a bit, as if to say, "Hey, you know you want me." I can't believe it because, for one, he is disgusting, but also, Mikhail is standing right here. I snake my arm through Mikhail's and draw him closer. I make sure my body language screams *I'm taken!*

"You drive a hard bargain, Mikhail," Marco says. "I guess that's why you're so fucking rich, eh, my friend?" Marco returns to the backslapping.

"Ms. Bobbi," Marco says, grasping my hand and planting a slimy kiss on it, "it will be a pleasure working with you. I know you'll enjoy your time here in Ibiza."

"*Mucho gusto,*" I say, telling him in the little bit of Spanish I know that it was nice to meet him. I retrieve my hand and wipe it off discreetly behind my back. I don't want his saliva on me.

"*Tanto gusto,*" he says, telling me it was *very* nice to meet me and winks once more. I think that the women would sneer at me but the Botox injections have their faces so frozen that they can barely move. However their thoughts are all too evident in their eyes. Fuck 'em; I'm making twenty g's for one gig!

"That guy's a piece of work," I say to Mikhail when they're out of earshot.

"You were driving him wild. You're too sexy," he says, kissing me lightly on the lips. "An old pervert like Marco can't handle it."

"Well, didn't that bother you, him ogling me like that?" I ask.

"You wouldn't give that slimeball the time of day," he says. "And he knows better than to take it any further than staring at you. He knows not to cross the line."

"My, my, my, aren't we cocky?" I ask, grazing his crotch. "Oh yes we are," I say.

"We'll have time for that later, dirty girl," Mikhail says, licking his lips.

"Ooh, not even a quickie? Making money makes me horny," I tell him.

"Later, sweet angel; that is, if you have any energy left over. We're going to get this night started now!"

We head to the all-male crowd that's creating a straight up ruckus on the deck. There are a dozen men in total that are making toasts with vodka shots, smoking and laughing. Dimitri is with them, the center of attention, the vodka bottle in his hand refilling shot glasses as soon as they're empty. Mikhail introduces me to each of them. They each kiss my hand and both cheeks when introduced, and they say their full names, which seem to be a mile long. They also state their lines of work, which range from antiquities to wholesale jewels, shipping to armaments. I inspect the men's faces, trying to make a connection between them and the men in the picture I saw earlier. These are undoubtedly the Apostles.

They're all Russian from what I can tell; at least they all speak what sounds like Russian, but their points of origin are spread out across the globe. Some are American and live in Brighton Beach, a section of Brooklyn. A couple of the guys live in Israel, and a couple more live in South America. The rest live in the Ukraine, Hungary, or the Czech Republic. They all call each other *bratva*, and I don't know what that means, but I assume from the way they say it, that it's something like *homie*, or *yo*, or *ak*, or *son*, like black folks call each other. It's clear that they all like each other; they remind me of a fraternity.

And these men can drink! They down shot after shot of vodka, practically forcing me to drink with them, and after each shot they break out into song, clapping and dancing, before the next drink. I can forget about asking this bunch any questions, because it's clear that partying is the only thing on their minds. This revelry goes on for a good hour. By this time I'm good and toasted and you can't tell me that I'm not a Soviet hottie after all the shots I take. I sing along with them in Russian, or in what I think sounds like Russian, and when I can't produce any words that sound like what they are saying I just sing "da, da, da." I mimic their dance, adding my own little flourishes, and I could care less that I probably look like a drunken John Travolta from that scene in *Saturday Night Fever* when he did those swooping kneels and kicks all around the dance floor. The mermaid tail sari gets in the way, so I trip a lot and end up on the floor, but I roll around on the floor like Madonna singing "Like a Virgin," and no one seems to mind.

When Amara eventually joins us, accompanied by a few of her female friends, I'm plastered.

"These guys are such a bore," she says discreetly.

"I love these guys, what are you talking about?" I slur. "I love you too, Amara," I hiccup, giving her a big hug and a sloppy kiss on the cheek. "We understand each other, don't we?" I ask her.

"Sure, baby. I understand they got you drunk," she says, tsking and wagging her finger at me. "Hey, you cretins, you got her wasted," she says to the bunch.

"Lighten up, Amara," Dimitri tells her. "She's having a good time. Aren't you, Bobbi?"

"The fucking best," I say. I break into a rendition of "Back in the USSR" by the Beatles and Mikhail's friends go wild with laughter and join in with me.

"Sailed in, from Miami Beach, didn't get to sleep last night!" I sing while shimmying my boobs. Amara tries to stop me, but I'm unstoppable. Dimitri grabs her and makes her dance along with him. She resists at first, but she can't help herself because after I sing the lyrics the way they originally went (or as close as I can muster), I add my own hip-hop twist and the Apostles love it. They get super crazy as I chant "Where's Moscow? Go Moscow. Where's Georgia? Go Georgia. U-kraine, U-U-Ukraine!" And the drunken posse chants right along with me.

I have no idea why I don't pass out or get sick because I'm surely over the legal limit in all fifty American states. But I'm just getting started. We disembark *Krizia*, and head to Pacha for more revelry. The entourage is huge as we walk the short distance to the club on foot, laughing and singing all the way.

Much of the evening is the same as it had been aboard the ship. I'm introduced to more club owners, playboys, socialites, and a few of my competitors who give me my props, but don't do a good job at hiding their envy when everyone raves about my performance earlier in the evening. I let them hate though; I'm used to it, plus I'm too drunk to make any snappy comments. Besides, I'm experiencing too much of a high, both literal and physical, to engage in petty games. And I'm geeked up at the fact that one of the DJs I most admire, Carl Cox, is spinning.

The people of Ibiza definitely know how to throw a party; each event stimulates the five senses. The smell of the ocean and miles of flower blossoms are always faintly distinguishable in the open-air venues, even through the stench of sweaty bodies and cigarette and cigar smoke. There's premium liquor and excellent food. The sound systems are top-notch and the music is nonstop. In addition to the requisite beautiful people, there are samba dancers, transvestites in drag that dance on stilts, fire breathers, people in full-body costumes like cartoon characters, dry-ice machines that blast the heated dance floor with jets of cold air, and some clubs even have swimming pools inside. Not kiddie pools, but full-length ones.

I dance with Amara, with the wildly dressed club kids who work at the club, with the scantily clad socialites and glamourites, and just have a good time. We party until the sun comes up, then head to an after-hours set. I'm exhausted but too excited to sleep when we finally head back to the yacht at around 10:00 AM.

Upon our return to *Krizia*, I have gigs lined up in not only Ibiza, but Saint Tropez, and Mykonos, each paying the equivalent of twenty thousand American dollars! I can't believe my luck. The great thing about dealing with the ultra-affluent is that they can afford to spare no expense.

"Are you happy, my sweet angel?" Mikhail asks me, as we lay wrapped in each other's arms in bed trying to fall asleep after so much activity.

"Blissfully so," I reply. "I can't believe how much money I'm about to make!"

"I told you that they would love you. The people could not take their eyes off you. You totally enchanted them." Mikhail nuzzles my cheek with his nose. "My friends and business associates also love you. They say they've never had so much fun in their lives," he tells me.

I tell myself that this is the perfect segue to find out more about the Apostles who stayed with us all evening. "Those guys tonight, they all work with you or for you?" I ask.

"We work together. One hand washes the other. We've all known each other forever," he explains.

"What does that word you all kept calling each other, *bratva* . . . what does that mean?" I ask.

"Oh, it's just a Russian thing," he tells me. "Now get some sleep. No more talk of my friends," he says.

"But I like them," I whine. "I just want to know more about them," I admit. "Your friends are my friends now, right?"

"Yes they are. But you know all you need to know about them."

"I guess," I say. I'm too tired to interrogate him, and my mind is fuzzy from all the drinking. Chances are, I wouldn't remember much of anything I could get out of him. My curiosity will have to wait for another time to be satisfied. "Well anyway, I can't believe that I'm getting twenty g's a gig!" I tell him, yawning and wrapping myself in the Pratesi sheets.

"Twenty thousand is spending cash," Mikhail says starting to doze off. "You will see, sweet angel. This is only the beginning . . ."

# CHAPTER SEVEN

*July 2006*

W HEN WE ARRIVE IN SAINT TROPEZ THERE ARE LUXURY
yachts lined along the Quai de Suffren, with topless
beauties glistening with oil, soaking up the sun on decks. A
slow procession of luxury vehicles cruise the streets that line
the harbor and lead to the vast stretches of private beaches
dotted with brightly colored umbrellas and beach chairs. It
makes Miami look like a city for paupers, a feat I never
dreamed was even remotely possible.

But ghetto-fabulous athletes and flashy rappers who spend
all their money on bling and whips like the Cash Money Mil-
lionaires have nothing on the people who are kicking it on
the Côte d'Azur. This is not a place for the hood rich; Saint
Tropez is strictly a playground for the ridiculously wealthy.
You can tell that these people have plenty of euros to throw
around but won't be going bankrupt anytime soon as a result
of their lavish lifestyles.

Amara has warned me about hustlers, con artists, and wan-
nabes who flock to Saint Tropez looking for the ultimate
score, and from the looks of things, I can see why Saint Tropez

is a pimper's paradise. There is just too much money around for it not to be. Someone with game and a good mouthpiece can easily come up here. And from what I can assess, Saint Tropez has usurped Miami as a gold digger's mecca. Everywhere I look there are women who appear to be in their twenties and thirties, strolling arm in arm with men nearly three times their age. It's obvious that they're being given the world from the looks of their clothes and jewels. If you want a sugar daddy, one with means that won't stop, Saint Tropez is the place to find him. But the competition has to be stiff; Saint Tropez has more beautiful people than Miami, if that's possible.

Business booms in France. If working Ibiza put me on the map, then I have to say that working Saint Tropez has blasted me into the stratosphere. I spin at three top venues, Les Caves du Roy, the VIP Room, and the bar at the Byblos Hotel. I receive rousing applause and cries for encores well into the wee hours of the morning. I'm swarmed and bombarded by people after my sets and I love every second of it. I've always had people who enjoy my work, but this is something totally different. These people treat me like I'm a rock star. People always say that the French don't like Americans and that they think we are crass, ignorant, and stupid. But if they have any contempt for Americans, I can't tell from the way everyone I encounter kowtows to me. I'm aware that a lot of people here aren't French—they're vacationing just like me—but I don't care where they're from because men and women alike refer to me as "La Belle Americane," and treat me like royalty.

I work at my most exciting party during the whole cruise in Saint Tropez, a private affair for Jay-Z and Beyoncé aboard their chartered yacht (which, by the way, pales in comparison to Mikhail's ship). The crème de la crème of hip-hop society is present at this party. Aside from Jay-Z and some Def Jam execs, the new singer Rhianna is present, as well as Diddy and Kim Porter. Russell and Kimora Simmons are there together despite their separation; they're taking a family vacation but have left the children with a nanny for the evening. To my pleasant surprise, Bentley is there, accompanied by his girlfriend, Dez, who seems a bit distant and unhappy; she doesn't say much of anything to anyone at the party. She clearly doesn't want to be here. I don't know why she's unhappy, because the party is the shit, and from the account of all the tabloids, Dez has overcome insurmountable odds to reach the level of stardom she's achieved and now she's sitting pretty. She's won awards, her albums have gone multiplatinum, she survived an attempt on her life from some crazy woman, *and* she has Bentley. She seems to have it all, but often some of the most successful people in the world are also the unhappiest people in the world, and I guess she falls into that category.

Bentley flashes me a huge grin and winks when he sees me, and I swear that Dez gives me the stank eye as I step up to the turntables dressed in Brazilian carnival regalia. Does she know that I almost slept with her man? It's doubtful, unless he's said something, but I don't sweat it; I have a job to do and I'm intent on doing it to the best of my ability.

I do the damn thing to death! I know I have officially arrived when all eyes are glued *not* on Beyoncé's famous backside, nor fixated on the exotic Dez, nor staring at any of the other international ballers on board, but all attention is centered on me as I work the turntables. In the words of Biz Markie, "Damn, it feels good to see people up on it!" It's exhilarating when Beyoncé comes up to me after my set, enthusing about how much she likes my style. And when Jigga asks how he can get in touch with my management to talk about possible tour dates for some Def Jam artists, I think I'm going to faint. I just give him my cell phone number and e-mail address and tell him to get in touch with me directly. The thought alone of Jigga and I being on a first-name basis and chatting on our cells makes me feel like the queen bitch of all queen bitches. I know that I have to stop being greedy and cheap and put some serious thought into getting representation soon, because things are definitely looking up.

"I see that you are dating the Russian after all," Bentley hisses at me through a tight smile as he shakes my hand after the set.

"Jealous much?" I ask him, smiling right back. "I see you've got your girl with you too," I say, glancing in Dez's direction. Her famous hazel eyes feel like they're going to bore a hole right through my body. I flash her a broad smile and an enthusiastic wave, in an effort to seem casual and friendly.

"Jealous much?" he quips. That's one of the things that attract me to Bentley the most; he's a big smart-ass, just like me. I know that if we'd met under different circumstances, we could have been a hot couple.

"I'm sitting on top of the world right now, and I'm loving it," I say.

"So is that your way of saying yes, you are jealous?" he asks.

"Well, you know how we feisty stubborn women are. That's all you're gonna get, so take it how you want it," I reply. We share a laugh and then Bentley gives me a great big bear hug.

"You are too much, girl! But honestly, you're tight. You've got skills. I don't think Dez likes you much, though," he says, winking at her and blowing a kiss in her direction. Dez simply rolls her catlike eyes and turns away from him. "Too bad, huh? I think the two of you should team up for a project."

"Damn, what did I do to her?" I ask.

"Nothing. She thinks I'm cheating on her, that's all. She acts like that anytime I'm around a beautiful woman," he explains.

"Well, are you cheating on her?" I ask. The thought of working with Dez is appealing; she's one of the few female rappers I actually like. I'm hoping Bentley is right and we can collaborate, because she's a talented lyricist and I'm sure I can diffuse any negative feelings she thinks she has for me.

"Do you consider finger-fucking sexy DJs at nightclubs cheating?" he asks, with a mischievous glint in his eyes.

"Nah, not really," I say, reminiscing on our interlude with a smile. We just stand there grinning at each other like two dopes. I start singing "Holla Back Girl" and we crack up laughing.

Mikhail must catch our little exchange, because before I can say Moscow, he comes right over, slips an arm proprietarily around my shoulders, and hovers by my side. And not only does he hover, but he gets on my last nerve. When I try to discuss religion with Russell Simmons, Mikhail just *has* to put his two cents in. I'm having a great conversation with Kimora about her adorable little girls and her Baby Phat line, and in pipes Mikhail. I can't say two words without Mikhail completing my sentences or even answering questions for me. I don't like it one bit, and decide to try to nip his behavior in the bud.

"Why are you bugging?" I ask him discreetly as I kiss him on the cheek when we go to sample food at the lavish buffet table.

"I don't know what you mean," he says innocently.

Oh, he wants to play the nut role, does he? I give him a small dose of South Side fire. "I don't need a puppet master pulling my strings," I tell him as I feed him an hors d'oeuvre.

I want to cram it down his throat for being so overbearing but I don't. "Let me speak for myself," I say, slightly agitated. Mikhail's cantankerous mood is starting to interfere with my networking and put a damper on my good time. And although I know that I probably wouldn't even be in this situation if it weren't for him and that I should be grateful for my opportunities, I don't need people thinking that I'm some idiot with a Svengali behind me and no talent. That's where I draw the line. He obviously wants it known that we are an item and he isn't about to let another man get close to me; but I'm not about to change the way I do business because of his insecurities. This is supposedly what he wanted and expected from this trip—to make me a star—and now he's acting like he doesn't want to let me out of his sight.

The wild thing is that he had no problem with that greasy club owner, Marco Delgado, winking and drooling all over me in Ibiza, but now that we're here with my peers in a hip-hop crowd, he wants to get all possessive and jealous. I'm not sure if he's jealous because he thinks I'm going to hook up with someone here, or if he's jealous because I'm getting so much attention.

"I'm sorry, my sweet angel. I was just trying to help," he says innocently, but I know better. He's definitely feeling threatened.

"I know you are trying to help, but I've got this," I tell him. "You don't want people to think I'm stupid, do you? Now chill out, okay? Come on," I say with a smile. "Let's get back to the party." But Mikhail isn't placated.

"Like the way you networked with me?" he snaps. "Are you going to sleep with Bentley so you can work for him?" I look around to see if anyone heard him, and luckily he hasn't drawn any attention from anyone other than Amara, who is totally eavesdropping.

"Is that what this is about? You think I want to fuck some-one here? This is business. Don't be ridiculous," I say, flipping the script on him. I roll my eyes and start to walk away from him. He grabs me roughly by the arm.

"You don't want to fuck him? Or have you fucked him already? I saw you on a date with him, remember?" he says, his voice rising a little.

"That was only business," I tell him.

"It didn't look like it," he says.

"You're one to talk. You were out that same night with Misty!"

Mikhail looks like he's going to say something, but ulti-mately does not respond. He just walks away. Amara is standing next to me in a matter of seconds.

"What was that about?" she asks.

"You were eavesdropping, girl! You know what it was about," I say to her with a laugh.

"Okay, baby, you got me," she says back. "Honestly, I don't know what you've done to Mikhail. I've never seen him so possessive before."

"Well, I don't like it. I don't need a man acting like he owns me. I don't care how much he spends on me," I say. "And now look at him, trying to make me jealous."

Mikhail has shifted gears and is in flirt mode. He's so obvi-ous, flitting about and kissing Kylie Minogue's ass, telling Beyoncé how beautiful and talented she is, and chatting up Naomi Campbell. I ignore him and leave him to his games, but this becomes difficult when none other than Misty Blue shows up.

"Speaking of the devil! What the fuck is she doing here?" I ask Amara.

"Oh, baby! Misty Blue? She's a piece of work, a vapid air-head. She's absolutely vile and repugnant."

"Yes, I know," I say, cutting her off. "But why is she always around?" I ask. I swear Misty is as unwelcome as herpes. There is no cure for her and her ass pops up in the damnedest places and at all the wrong moments. It seems like she's going to be around for life, and she certainly gets passed around.

"Baby, let me tell you something about Misty Blue. She calls herself an actress. She's no actress. She is, how you say? A porn star," she tells me.

"Yeah, I know," I say.

"Yes, baby, but what you probably don't know is that Misty is also a call girl."

"What's the big difference?" I ask.

"Not much, I guess," she says. "They both sleep with men for money. One is legal, one is not. But I just don't like her. She's trouble. Girls like me, we never ask for money. We don't cheapen ourselves. We are treated well because we carry ourselves well. I don't need her around making things difficult, confusing people. Gold diggers aren't hookers but when they see her in this circle, sometimes the men, they don't realize that. They think they can treat us the same way they treat them. Girls like Misty are bad for my business."

I don't care about all that. "Amara, are Mikhail and Misty fucking? Did they ever have a thing?" I remember that Misty is a prostitute. "Oh my God, is he a client?" I ask.

"I doubt it, baby. Mikhail wouldn't fuck her with someone else's cock! He likes to think of himself as a classy guy. That's part of the reason he is attracted to you. You come from a good family, your name means something. And you're talented. He can show you off in any circle he runs in. He can't do the same with Misty."

"Yeah, but his dick doesn't care about all that," I tell her.

"True, but I think theirs is a different kind of relationship than what you're thinking. Misty hangs around Mikhail and he keeps her around because he has rich friends that she can sink her talons into. A girl like Misty can be helpful to a man like Mikhail. And Mikhail can be very helpful to her," Amara explains.

"How?" I ask.

"Say, for instance, Mikhail is trying to work a deal. Maybe things aren't going so good. He has a party, and Misty entertains his business prospect. The prospect is happy and much more agreeable to business. Maybe Misty plants an idea or two in his head. And the guy pays her very well for her services. Mikhail uses plenty of girls like her; she isn't the only one."

"So what is he, a fucking pimp?" I ask, my stomach knotting up in disgust. "This whole thing reminds me of the movie *Foxy Brown*."

Amara just laughs but I don't see what the fuck is so funny. I guarantee that Amara wouldn't be laughing if Misty were draping herself all over Dimitri like a cheap suit.

"Why is she here? Why is she at this party?" I ask. "Is Mikhail working some kind of deal?" I ask Amara.

"Mikhail is always working a deal. Everything is business. Everything," she says.

The last straw comes when Misty plants a big, sloppy, wet kiss dead on Mikhail's mouth. Her dime-store lip gloss is smeared all over his mouth. Oh hell no! I'm about to check this bitch right now. There's no way in hell I'm trying to kiss behind that skeezer. She needs to step off! I leave Amara and confront Misty and Mikhail.

"Hi, Barbie," she giggles, "fancy seeing you here." Misty plays with Mikhail's hair and blows seductively in his ear.

I stand back with my hands on my hips and give her the once-over. My lips are curled into a sneer, and my hands are balled into fists that I'm ready to swing at any time. "It's

Bobbi. *Ms*. Bobbi. I hope that name isn't too difficult for you to pronounce," I reply, my voice dripping with sarcasm. "Besides, why wouldn't I be here? I'm Mikhail's woman," I tell her. I've never claimed Mikhail as my man before, and it sounds strange coming out of my mouth, but Misty needs to know that her days of hanging with Mikhail are over. I'm not sharing my time with Mikhail with some hooker. I step in between Mikhail and Misty and remove her hand from his hair. I'm this close to her, and if she so much as blinks too much I'm going to chin-check her.

"Ooh, lucky girl. Mikey's a stallion in the sack," she replies. Her eyes, covered in too much cheap makeup, challenge me to say something. Be careful what you ask for, tramp!

"Excuse you, bitch?" I ask her. I draw my arm back because I'm about to deliver a blow that could lay out Mike Tyson, but Mikhail grabs my hand before I can land it.

"Now ladies, there, there," Mikhail says.

"There, there my ass," I snap.

"Oops, sorry," Misty says. "I didn't mean to cause any trouble." That bitch is so phony that I waste no time telling her so.

"You phony bitch!" I shout, and then I realize that people are staring. I can't let my temper get the best of me. She wants to provoke me, and I'm not going to give her the satisfaction of making me look like a violent, crazed fool in front of all these people. I crack an equally fake smile and grab her by the hand. I crush her bony fingers with all my might and throw back my head in laughter. "I will toss your ass overboard if I catch you disrespecting me again, you got that?" I say through my teeth. I drop her hand, and her big blue eyes fill with tears.

"Excuse me," she says quickly, before sashaying her sleazy ass over to where Bentley and Dez are seated. Mikhail shoots me a look so heated it could start a fire, but I don't care.

Misty crossed the line, and if Mikhail isn't going to check her, I certainly will. But has Misty learned her lesson about fucking with other women's men? No.

Misty is wedged in between Bentley and Dez, and Bentley looks very uncomfortable, Dez looks like she is going to choke the life out of Misty, and I won't blame her if she does. Hell, I'll join in if some shit pops off, and if Mikhail tries to stop me he can get some too. For a second, Dez and I lock eyes. I mouth to her, "What a bitch!" For the first time that night, Dez cracks a smile. I give her a sympathetic look and a wink. She shakes her head and winks back, in a gesture of solidarity. I guess she realizes that I'm not the enemy, because even if I do have the hots for her guy, I would never pull the crazy shit Misty is trying to pull.

Then all of a sudden, Dez stops smiling and her hand sweeps across Misty's face with a loud crack before Bentley or Misty can do a thing about it. I laugh my ass off. Two men in white tuxedos swoop in. Dez's neck is rolling a mile a minute, and Beyoncé comes to her side. I guess she doesn't like what she hears, because the two men escort Misty away from the scene and Beyoncé stays there talking to Dez. I'm dying of curiosity. I want to know what Misty said that warranted Dez slapping her, but before I can go over there and get my snoop on, Mikhail grabs me by the hand and whispers to me, "Stay out of this." I want to tell him to go fuck himself, because I'm mad that he didn't let me get a crack at Misty, but I let it go.

After the party is over and Mikhail and I are back onboard *Krizia*, he explodes.

"I saw how you were flirting with Bentley. You were dying to go over there after Misty and his girlfriend seemed to have words," he shouts.

"They didn't seem to have words. Dez slapped the shit out

of your friend Misty, and I can only imagine why. I didn't want to go over there to talk to Bentley, I wanted to help Dez whoop that ho's ass," I say.

"You are shameless, you know that? You were blatantly throwing yourself at him, and right in front of his woman," Mikhail says as if he hasn't even heard me.

"Are you taking crazy pills? If anyone was throwing herself at anyone, it was Misty. She threw herself at you and then she threw herself at Bentley. She should stop trying sisters before one day someone really gives her a beatdown."

"Leave Misty out of this. You were throwing yourself at Bentley and you know it."

"Oh please!" I say with a laugh. Mikhail seems like he's just aching for a reason to pick a fight. "I was just being cordial. I know Bentley. We work in the same business. It was a party and I was networking," I say. "We were talking about how to approach Dez about a collaboration, that's all."

"Well, act like it. I will not have you disrespecting me," Mikhail says, grabbing me by the chin roughly. He glares at me, his jaws pulsating from him clenching his teeth.

"What? Like the way you're disrespecting me now?" I ask him, slapping his hand away. "You've got some fucking nerve, mister! Don't put your hands on me! Your porno whore mysteriously shows up here and then has the unmitigated gall to kiss you in front of me and then you get mad at *me*? She sticks her tongue in your mouth, plays with your hair, and blows in your ear, and you're talking about my behavior? Oh, and then to top it all off, she strolls her skanky ass over and sits in between Dez and Bentley. That's some rude shit. You need to check her, not me, because if that isn't disrespect I don't know what is."

My brown eyes lock with his green ones. We stand there staring at each other, breathing heavily. I'm fuming, and for the first time, I don't feel as if I'll melt under his gaze. His eyes are icy and frightening. I'm mad as hell, but I'm also a little afraid. So I back down, and it is never like me to back down in an argument. But something inside tells me to let it go. He's already put his hands on me, and there's no telling what else he's going to do or how he's going to respond. I don't want to provoke him any more. And as shameful as it is, I start thinking about the money and fame he has promised me, and I don't want to risk losing it.

"I'm warning you, Bobbi. Don't even think about being with another man. I won't share you," Mikhail finally says, coldly.

He doesn't give me a chance to say anything; he just turns and walks out of the stateroom, leaving me standing there with my mouth agape.

I plop down on the bed in a state of confusion. What am I doing here? Why am I across the globe with a man I barely know, a man who's into who knows what? I should be packing my shit and hauling ass right now on the first thing smoking back to the States. But I'm not packing. I'm sitting here because I don't want to go. And it's starting to feel like maybe, just maybe, I'm not just afraid of losing out on an opportunity. Maybe I'm afraid of losing Mikhail. Maybe I'm starting to feel something for him, even though he just acted like a plum fool. There's something that keeps me drawn to Mikhail, and I'm not sure what it is. Could it be that all the while I was running game, I got caught up in it?

EVENTUALLY, MIKHAIL COMES BACK TO THE CABIN. I'M STILL sitting in the same spot I'd been in for at least two or three hours.

"I brought you something," he says.

"You can't buy my forgiveness," I say to him, folding my arms across my chest.

"Good, because I didn't buy you anything," he says. I look at him in disbelief. No, he can't buy my forgiveness, but he can try. He could at least say it with flowers, although jewelry would be better. He should be kissing my pretty ass right now after the way he acted.

Mikhail is holding a silver serving platter with a lid on top.

"What's that?" I ask, pointing at it.

"It's something from my country," he explains, removing the lid to reveal a glass of milk and some crisp-looking little cookies. "They're called *khvorost*. They're fried cookies with vodka in them."

"Cookies with vodka?" I ask.

"Sure. They are very popular in Russia. My mother used to make them as a peace offering for me when I was a little boy. She had a very bad temper and sometimes she would take things a little too far. She would get so angry it would frighten me. Sometimes she would even get physical." Mikhail's eyes look soft and distant. "I've made them for you," he tells me. He holds out the tray in front of me like a butler.

I take a cookie from the platter and pop it in my mouth.

"This is delicious," I say, and it's true. The cookie practically melts on my tongue. Mikhail climbs into bed with me.

"My sweet angel, I don't want to hurt you. I love you so much. I just can't bear the thought of you with another man. I'm not used to a woman like you. Women usually do whatever I want without my having to ask. You have a mind of your own. It makes me a little crazy sometimes," he says.

"You don't want me to have a mind of my own?" I ask.

"That is not it at all. I want you to stay just the way you are."

"What about Misty?" I ask him.

"What about her?"

"You let her touch you, you let her kiss you," I say, choking on my words with disgust. "Do you like her just the way she is?"

"Misty is nothing to me. She never has been, and she never will be. I feel sorry for her; she's had a really hard life. And I guess that my sympathy for her has made me allow her to behave in a way that isn't appropriate. I won't let her come between us," he says. "I won't let anyone or anything come between us again, I promise."

"You've got to promise me something else," I tell him.

"Anything."

"You can't ever put your hands on me like that again. I don't like how you were all in my face. You make me think you wanted to hit me, and that's the one thing that I will not stand for."

"I'm sorry, it won't happen again," he says, and seems sincere.

"And will you trust me?" I ask him. "I'm not doing anything to disrespect you. I really care about you. I probably shouldn't, but I do. I'm not going to disrespect you or our relationship, not our personal relationship and not our professional one either. I appreciate what you do for me and how you've let me into your life. But you've got to trust me and give me a little time to let you into my life. You've got to let me be me. Can you do that?" I ask. Mikhail nods yes and kisses me softly.

Mikhail has gotten under my skin. I'm not sure when it happened, but he's there. I want to think that I've just been playing some rich old white guy, getting what I want for my career. But there's more to it than that. Mikhail isn't just some rich old white guy who sits around in seersucker suits, sipping on mint juleps. He's got swagger, and I'm checking for that. It isn't love but I really dig him, and it isn't just because he's doing so much for me. Mikhail has fire and passion, not just for me but for life. When he talks, people listen. People respect him and some even fear him. I'm even a little afraid of him, but that doesn't repel me. It just turns me on. He's clearly a force to be reckoned with. He makes his own rules. He's everything I want to be. And he's crazy about me.

Soon Mikhail's hands are everywhere, but his touch isn't urgent. It's gentle and soft and he doesn't miss any of my pleasure points. Mikhail removes the feathered and sequined bra that I had been wearing as a part of my carnival getup. He kisses me lightly, then his lips move from my mouth to my neck, where he nips and sucks my flesh until I'm squirming. He makes his way down to my shoulder blades and bites gently, driving me wild as his fingertips go to work on my erect nipples. I'm so hot that I have an orgasm as soon as he puts his mouth on one. I've never had anything like that happen to me before. I beg him to give me all of him; I want to feel him inside me so bad.

"Not yet," he says. "I want to taste you."

"I can't take it," I say.

"You can and you will take it," he replies. His tone has changed; he's no longer sweet and soft, he's a little more aggressive.

"Do you trust me, Bobbi?" Mikhail asks. I'm panting and moaning so hard, I don't answer. But the truth is I don't want to answer because I don't trust him.

"I want to do something to you," he says. "But you have to trust me. Will you let me do it?" he asks. I nod yes.

Make-up sex is always intense; you always forget what it is you were mad about, and I'm craving that intensity. Mikhail stands up and removes his belt. He lays me down on the bed and raises my arms above my head. Mikhail looks me in the eyes and asks, "Do you want me?" I nod in the affirmative.

"Say it," he says.

"I want you," I tell him. He wraps the belt around my wrists several times and fastens it tightly. My arms tingle and I wince a little. I'm kind of afraid because being tied up is something I've never done before, but it's just adding fuel to the fire of my desire. I think to myself that this is sick, that it can't be healthy. I think only perverts are into bondage. But I guess that makes me a pervert because I want to do this.

Mikhail spreads my legs a little and strokes the fishnet hose that cover my skin. I'm wearing a feathered and sequined pair of booty shorts that just cover my ass over the fishnets, but no underwear. As he pulls the shorts off, he licks his lips at the sight of my pussy peeking through the holes of the fishnets. Mikhail spreads my legs wider and begins flicking his tongue over my clit through the hose. I gasp as he grabs the stockings with his teeth and begins ripping and clawing at the thin material. He sensually rips and pulls the stockings apart and uses them to tie my ankles together. Mikhail bends and twists my limbs to give him the desired access to my pussy and ass. He licks and sucks it all and then looks up at me as he slips a finger in my ass and wiggles it around.

"You like that, don't you?" he asks.

"Yes," I moan.

"You like it up the ass, don't you?"

"Yes."

"Can I fuck you in the ass, Bobbi?" Mikhail asks.

"Yes," I tell him. Anal is no stranger to my sexual repertoire. I know a lot of women think it's nasty and they won't do it, but the truth is I love it. I'm just freaky like that.

Mikhail starts speaking in Russian as he pushes himself inside of me.

"Tell me what it means," I ask, as I arch my back in order to pull him deeper inside.

"*Ya tebya lyublyu*, I love you," he says, thrusting in sync with his words. "I am the happiest man in the world since I met you," he says, slapping my ass. His hand reaches around to my front and he manipulates my clit with his fingers while he slips his thumb inside my pussy. I come almost instantly and Mikhail comes soon after. He unties me and we take a shower together. Mikhail kisses me the whole time and tells me he loves me over and over again.

"You belong to me, Bobbi," he says as we snuggle in bed afterward.

"Mikhail . . ." I say. He cuts me off.

"You don't need any other man. I can give you more than any man you know."

"Mikhail, why me?" I ask. "What makes me so special that you've just got to have me? Why have you gone through so much trouble for me?" I know that men hate questions like that, but I need to know what his angle is. Mikhail is clearly sprung, but the jealousy, the control issues, I wonder if what I've seen is just the tip of the iceberg.

"Because I love you. You're beautiful and smart. You have talent, and I love making love to you. I've never met anyone like you. You come from a good family, you were raised with honor, yet you don't act like a socialite. You don't act like the world owes you something. Socialite women are so boring, but you are exciting. You make me feel young and alive. Your whole agenda isn't about how much of my money you can spend so that you can go to lunch or have tea with your girl-friends and compare what you have. And I think we believe in the same things."

"You don't know what I believe in," I tell him. Because even I don't know anymore.

MIKHAIL AND I DON'T DISCUSS THE ARGUMENT WE HAD OVER Misty and Bentley again, but it isn't the last argument we have. It's just the first in what turns out to be a string of confrontations. Mikhail isn't handling my growing fame very well, and he gets jealous over the littlest things. He is keeping me on a very short leash, and it's making me very testy. I verbally attack him with the ferocity of a mad dog. And what does Mikhail do? He provokes me further. A kinky pattern arises. We argue and yell and then we fuck like animals, always involving some kind of bondage or some form of domination and submission.

I come to realize that the roller coaster is what gets Mikhail off. Mikhail enjoys keeping me in a state of confusion, making things unpredictable, and trying to control every aspect of my life. Everything is a power game for him, and I don't think that Mikhail knows what it's like to be anything other than the alpha dog, the pack leader. He tries to assert his control over my appearance by buying me clothes. He controls where I go because I'm on his ship. He controls my career by getting me gigs and making sure that they pay too much for me to turn them down. And he controls my body with pleasure. And pain.

Mikhail is a sadist. He likes to inflict pain, both mental and physical. In my case, he likes to mix his forms of punishment. Mikhail calls me names; he taunts and pushes and shoves and insults me. He doesn't do this to hurt me; it isn't done in a violent manner. I believe that Mikhail does this for the strong reaction it provokes. He picks and probes and irritates me until I explode. My anger is what makes him hard, and when I cry or scream or do something very dramatic he gets really, really aroused and the sex that follows is always very, very rough. It incites my anger, my fear, and my passion, and he loves it. He wants me to wonder what he'll do next, just as he enjoys trying to figure out what I'm going to do next. It makes him hot.

Our sex life can only be described as primal or animalistic. Mikhail likes for me to slap him and claw his back while we fuck. He likes to choke me until I feel like I'm about to pass out. And I have to admit that I like it too—a lot. I'm so used to doing the using and abusing, being the one that calls all the shots, but Mikhail is the one man that I've come across who won't let me walk all over him, and doesn't punk out like a bitch when I turn up the heat. He matches my fire degree by degree. And that's what scares me more than who he is and what he does. I'm afraid of the fire between us. Because anything that burns this hot has to eventually burn out. And then what happens?

# CHAPTER EIGHT

*Mykonos, Greece*

**M**YKONOS IS UNBELIEVABLE. NOT ONLY IS IT ABSOLUTELY gorgeous, but I swear that everyone that we meet is a shipping heir, which means they're disgustingly rich. I hear it so much that I start to wonder if *shipping heir* is what people call themselves as some kind of code when they're drug dealers, kind of like owning a barbershop or a car wash in the hood.

As much as I'm enjoying the high life, I have to admit I am starting to grow bored. I miss America, I miss Miami, and I miss South Beach. I miss hearing people argue over whether Cubans get more preferential treatment than Haitians, and if the clubs on the beach are racist, or if the only color they see is green. I miss pink houses, and eating *arepas* from vendors on Calle Ocho, and hurricane watches. I want to rock a crowd with familiar faces, and see folks with dreads and braids and grills, driving Escalades and tricked-out classic Oldsmobiles.

Amara notices that there's something different about me. "Whatsamatta, baby? You don't seem like yourself," she asks me while Mikhail and Dimitri are on the ship of one of the Apostles having a lunch meeting.

"Nothing's the matter, I'm just bored. This is fun, but I want my life back. This is Mikhail's life," I tell her.

"Maybe, but it will soon be your life. If Dimitri was going to propose, I'd be anxious to plan my wedding," she says.

"What are you talking about, Amara? Mikhail hasn't proposed. I'm just going to be the resident DJ at Babylon," I say.

"Aaaaaaaayyyyyyyy!" she screams, scaring the shit out of me.

"What the hell is wrong with you?" I ask.

"I did it again. You didn't know?"

"Know what?"

"I have something to tell you, but you've got to promise not to tell anyone that I told you," she says.

"Okay," I tell her.

"Make sure to act surprised later or they will know I told you. Everyone knows I can't keep a secret," she says.

"Then tell me already!" I say.

"Mikhail is going to ask you to marry him," she squeals.

"You're kidding, right?" I ask her.

"No, not at all."

"Amara, how do you know this?" I ask. I think she has her facts mixed up.

"How do you think I know? I was eavesdropping, of course," she says.

"You've got to be the nosiest, snoopiest chick I've ever known," I say, shaking my head.

"Hey, it's how I stay on top," she says. "I have to always, always stay two steps ahead. If I don't, how will I know when I'm about to be replaced or if I'm being cheated on? I have to protect my investments," she says.

"What investments?" I ask.

"My relationships. The way I see it, I only have a few years before I have to start thinking more seriously about my future. I must play my cards right so that I can land a husband when I need to," she says.

"Somehow, Amara, I don't think you'll have a problem finding a husband when you want one," I tell her.

"Well, better to be safe than sorry," she says. "But enough about that. Aren't you excited? You've landed the richest husband a girl could wish to marry. You'll have so much money, baby!" she says, her eyes gleaming.

"I'll get excited when I know it's true—maybe," I tell her. "Marriage is such a big step. We don't really know each other. Plus one morning I heard him tell his ex on his cell phone that he missed and loved her. I even saw a picture of him all hugged up with some blonde woman. Even though Mikhail says he's in love with me, and he's possessive as hell, I don't think I'm the only one."

"I'm sure it's nothing, baby. Mikhail knows lots of blondes, and he is a European. They're more loving than Americans," Amara says with a wave of her hand.

"Amara, Mikhail is Russian. They aren't exactly the most affectionate people," I reply.

"Pish posh, baby. Mikhail is crazy about you. And remember, I'm never wrong. Remember, I told you that Mikhail was going to invite you on this cruise, didn't I?"

"Well, yes," I say.

"And I told you that he was in love with you, which he is. Just you wait and see, baby. Just you wait and see," Amara says.

I'm dumbfounded. Why on earth would Mikhail want to marry me? We're having fun, sure, but till death do us part? Amara had to have heard things wrong.

I can't focus. I can't breathe. I can't sleep. All I can do is think about what Amara has told me about Mikhail asking me to marry him. It wouldn't be the worst thing in the world, to be married to a sexy billionaire, and we have an awesome sex life, but is Mikhail really the sort of man that I would make vows and a covenant before God with? I can't picture it. But I can picture the money, the yachts, the jewels . . .

I wait and wait and wait. Mikhail says nothing; he doesn't drop any hints either. Everything is status quo. I'm convinced that Amara heard it all wrong until the night before we are to leave Mykonos and head back to the States. A lavish dinner party is planned and the Apostles are all to join us on board, but Mikhail tells me that I don't have to DJ. He asks me to put on something sexy, sophisticated, and white. He tells me that he has a very important announcement to make. This must be it.

I take special care in getting ready for the evening because I want to look my absolute best when Mikhail proposes. Me, a billionaire's wife! Who could imagine? I have the onboard stylist put my hair in an updo and apply my makeup in a soft neutral palette except for my eyes, which are smoky and exotic. I put on a Chloé chiffon gown with an empire waist that is funky and classy at the same time. And I wait some more and practice my surprised look in the meantime.

People begin to board the ship. The Apostles are all accompanied by women young enough to be their daughters or middle-aged women who have gone overboard on plastic surgery. Someone really ought to tell these women that less is more, and that you can get too much of a good thing. When they hug me, their rock-hard boobs poke me in the chest. Who do they think they're fooling with these mammoth mammaries? No one, and I mean no one, over the age of twelve with a real D cup can go without a bra in certain outfits, at least they *shouldn't*, but these women are so perky without the support of a brassiere that their breasts look like they levitate. I see more than my share of trout-pout lips filled to the outer limits with collagen and duck-billed platypus mouths plumped up with Gore-Tex implants. I have no idea why a woman would put the same thing that's in a winter coat into her lips, but to each her own, right?

When dinner is served there are about fifty people on board. Dinner is amazing. There's foie gras, which I won't touch because I don't want any part of a force-fed goose's or duck's or whatever's liver, but the guests rave on and on about how flavorful and tender it is. There are also all kinds of other gourmet appetizers and such, but the kicker is the Cajun food that's served as the main course. Since my family is from New Orleans, I know a thing or two about Louisiana cooking, and although I know that the chef is from somewhere over in Europe, you couldn't have told me that he wasn't flown in from the French Quarter; the food tastes totally authentic. There's shrimp étoufeé, jambalaya, seafood gumbo, dirty rice, red beans and white rice, fried catfish and grits: you name it, we've got it. I'm in seventh heaven and so glad that I chose not to wear something clingy because I'd look like a stuffed sausage if I did.

After dessert is served, which is bananas foster, red velvet cake, rice pudding, and peach cobbler, the 'itis (for those of you who don't know, the 'itis is when you get sleepy after eating too much) is kicking in, and all I want to do is stretch out like a pig and go straight to bed. I want all our guests to go home. But the end of the dinner party is nowhere in sight. A jazz band sets up on the deck and begins cranking out standards and classics.

"Come take a walk with me," Mikhail says. Amara looks at me with excitement in her eyes when we excuse ourselves from the party. We stroll along the deck until we reach the business center and then we step inside. Mikhail takes my hand and kisses it gently.

"Bobbi, you are the most amazing woman I've ever met. You give me a feeling deep in my heart that no one has ever given me before. Together, I know that we can rule the world," he says.

Mikhail reaches into his coat pocket and pulls out something that he keeps hidden in his hand. *This is it,* I think. *He's going to hand me a ring. Will it be ten carats? More?* But he doesn't hand me a ring. He opens his hand, and in it is a set of keys dangling from a platinum and diamond monogrammed *B* key chain. The key chain is gorgeous, but I don't get it. Is he giving me the keys to his heart? If he is, this has got to be the corniest shit ever. So junior high! I don't have to use one of my practiced surprised looks, because I am genuinely surprised as hell.

"Bobbi Hayes, it is my sincere hope that you will do me the honor of accepting a very special gift. I want you to be my partner," he says.

"Your partner?" I ask.

"Yes, Bobbi. I want you to be a partner in my newest business venture: the Babylon club in Miami."

"You want me to be your business partner?" I ask him in a stage whisper. I don't even know for sure what business Mikhail is even in.

"That is right." Mikhail smiles at me. "Bobbi, those are the keys to Babylon, your new club."

"*My* new club?" I ask.

"Yes. I have the transfer of ownership papers here for you. The club will be yours. I want you to run it. I want you to make it a success," he states.

"You do realize that I'm a DJ, right? I promote parties on

occasion, but I'm not that kind of businesswoman," I say. "I can't run a club."

"Yes you can. You will be an equal partner in the club, but more important, you will be the face of Babylon. And you will be paid very well for your services. In return, you will be expected to headline certain events and make certain appearances. You'll have plenty of support; the club will actually be run by a corporation. There's a staff already in place. However, your input will be highly valued, and you will have a say in many important decisions regarding the club."

"Yeah, but a club? It seems like a lot of responsibility. And it sounds like it will take time away from what I do, which is spin."

"You don't have to do much of anything but be your brilliant, charming self," he says with a grin. "And I assure you that there will be plenty of time for you to DJ. You will have the biggest and best venue to wow the crowds in."

"Yeah, but what if I want to do stuff? What if I want to learn?" I ask, because what happens when this ride is over? What happens when Mikhail decides he's tired of me and finds a new woman to court? What am I left with? Sure I'll always be a DJ and no one can take that away from me, but will I still have my fans? Will people still regard me as the hottest female DJ around, or will they think I've gone soft and commercial? God forbid people thinking I've gone corporate!

"It all sounds great, Mikhail, really it does. But I've already had to fight so many battles with people thinking that I only am where I am because I come from a family with money. I've struggled even more because people think that the only reason I get gigs is because of my late fiancé, who was my mentor. It's not going to get any better if people think folks are constantly giving me things."

"Why do you care so much what people think? I do not care what others think of me."

"Sure you do. Everyone cares what other people think. Perception becomes reality."

"What is wrong with being perceived as rich? Rappers are always bragging about their wealth."

"Let me explain something to you about hip-hop culture. It's cool to be born poor and get rich through music. It gives people hope that they can make it out of their situations too. And it's acceptable to have a little somethin' somethin', you know, be middle class and come up through hard work and a hard hustle, but only if you've had to overcome some kind of unbeatable odds or unspeakable tragedy, like a crack-addicted mother or an abusive father. People can relate to that. For example, Kanye West had a very middle-class up-bringing, but what makes him different than say, Common? Kanye stared death in the face and told it to come back later. People root for you when they think that you aren't too different from them."

"Go on," Mikhail says, intrigued.

"If you get too large, if at any time your audience doesn't feel that it can relate to you, your game is shot. People accept me now despite my upbringing because I've proven myself, and I let it be known that I work my ass off. And it doesn't hurt that people know that my parents cut me off. I mean, my dad was quoted in a *Black Enterprise* article as saying that he cut me off because he wanted me to value hard work and because he believed that I was so gifted that I could make it in this world without his money and influence. But that was all media spin. It kept him from looking like an asshole who turned his back on his only child because she refused to step forward and take her place in the bougie elite. And it kept me from looking like a poor little rich girl who's been handed everything on a silver platter."

"I see. And I understand your reservations. But trust me," Mikhail says and I almost bust out laughing. *Trust me* are the most famous last words heard before a fall. "I am a very smart man. I didn't get this rich and this successful without taking some calculated risks. It is time for you to take such a risk. If you say yes, you will reach the highest levels of success attainable. And if you wish, we can keep any mention of our personal involvement hush-hush. This is your spotlight to shine in. I want no credit or attention at all."

Mikhail reaches into his desk and pulls out some documents.

"Look these over and tell me what you think," he says, shoving the papers at me.

I give the papers the once-over. I know a little about legal jargon and contracts because of my dad and my old job as a real estate agent. But I'm no lawyer; there could be a clause in there that sells my firstborn child to Rumplestiltskin and I'd have no clue. I read the papers again, this time scanning carefully for anything that stands out, but I don't see anything suspicious. As a matter of fact, the more I read things, the better they sound.

The MD Entertainment Corporation is the contractor that will oversee the operations of the club. The land and physical building are mine. I am obligated to appear as a DJ once a week, and as a party hostess once a month. However I can appear more if I choose. My salary is a whopping $10 million, half payable when I sign the contract, the other half payable on the first year anniversary of the club. From that point onward, I receive $10 million a year. There's a clause about early termination, but who'd want to terminate? Plus

I receive the exotic car of my choice, and I can upgrade or switch cars every year as well. I've seen enough. I just have one question.

"So what's the catch?" I ask Mikhail.

"The catch?" he asks. "There is no catch. You have everything there in black and white."

"There has to be a catch. This sounds fabulous, too fabulous. Millions of dollars, a luxury whip. If something seems this good, it's more than likely too good to be true. What's in it for you?"

"Lots of money, a serious tax shelter for my most lucrative corporation, and making you very, very happy. It's a win-win situation."

"Yeah, but what happens to us?" I ask. Mikhail likes to mix business and pleasure, that's obvious. And he loves to play games. "Things are good between us now, but I need to know that if we decide to stop seeing each other or if your feelings change, that you don't try to take this all away from me."

"Do you wish to stop seeing me?" he asks.

"No. Not at all. I'm happy," I say.

"I'd never dream of taking any of this away from you. It would serve me no purpose. I give it to you from the heart. I love you. No matter what happens between us, the club is yours."

"Mine, huh?" I ask.

"Yes," he says. I sit there thinking about the proposition.

"I would also like to ask you something else," Mikhail says.

"What?"

"Move in with me."

"Move in with you? What, here? Live on a boat?" I ask. I love the yacht, but there's no way I could live on it.

"No, Bobbi," Mikhail says with a laugh. "I have a wonderful home in Miami with more than enough room."

"Won't that make keeping our relationship low-key a little difficult?" I ask.

"Not necessarily. Who would really know?"

"South Beach is a small world after all," I tell him. "Can I take one offer without the other?" I ask. But I already know the answer. Mikhail has a definite modus operandi; he makes two offers at once, they're not mutually exclusive, and one is so good that you accept the whole package because you don't want to miss out on the other part of it. That's how he got me on the yacht in the first place.

"No. It's a package deal, of course."

"Wouldn't you prefer it if you didn't have to force my hand?" I ask. But I know the answer to that question as well. Mikhail is a type A personality if I ever met one; to call him a control freak would be a serious understatement.

Mikhail pushes a gold Montblanc pen at me.

"I just want to get what I want," he tells me. "Now, what do you say?"

Once again I am faced with the opportunity of a lifetime. Mikhail is dangling the keys to a whole new life in front of me. A life filled with yachts and private jets and multimillion-dollar nightclubs and jewelry, and did I mention tons of my very own cold hard cash? I look at the pen, the contract, and at Mikhail. And I say what anyone else in my shoes would say.

"Yes," I tell him, and I sign on the dotted line.

"I HAVE AN ANNOUNCEMENT TO MAKE," MIKHAIL SAYS WHEN we return to the party. Amara looks like she's about to burst.

"Dima, come," Mikhail says to Dimitri, who joins us.

Amara looks puzzled, like she wonders if she should join us or stay where she is.

"On behalf of MD Entertainment Corporation, I'd like to announce a new partnership. Ms. Bobbi is now the owner of the Babylon nightclub in South Beach, and MD Entertainment Corporation will be contracted to handle operations. She is exactly what we need to make Babylon the biggest and brightest of our venues. To Bobbi," he says.

"To Bobbi," our guests reply in unison.

"Guess you got it wrong for once," I say to Amara after the announcement.

"I guess so," she says, sounding confused.

"What did you hear, anyway?" I ask.

"He said that he had something to propose to you. He wanted you to be his partner and that he needed a woman like you in his life, that you would be good for him."

"Duh, Amara! He was talking about business. Now just imagine if I really wanted to marry him. I'd have been fucked up. You had me thinking that he was going to give me a fat rock!" I say, laughing.

"Mikhail has given you much, much more," she says. "He's given you the keys to your very own kingdom."

# CHAPTER NINE

*September 2006*

WHEN *KRIZIA* DOCKS IN MIAMI, AMARA AND I SAY OUR tear-filled good-byes. I'm going to miss her crazy ass while she's gone. She's going to spend some time with her mother in Brazil, or so she says, but one can never tell with Amara. We promise to stay in touch so I can keep her posted on all the details of Babylon and so I can report to her what's going on with her guy Dimitri, who will be staying on in Miami to oversee the club opening.

I take immediate occupancy at Mikhail's luxurious home. Well, maybe home is an understatement. I mean, would you call a fourteen-thousand-square-foot, fifteen-bedroom, twelve-and-a-half-bathroom residence a home? More like an estate, I'd say! Who wouldn't wish to live in such a spread with no financial responsibility? I still keep my condo though. I worked hard to get it, and I'm not going to just give it up. Besides, it isn't like I can't afford to keep it.

Mikhail's place is located on exclusive Indian Creek, a private island off the Broad Causeway. The mansions on Indian Creek Island are all ridiculously expensive, and we've got some pretty famous neighbors, like legendary crooner Julio Iglesias and former Dolphins coach Don Shula. There's even a private police force just to serve and protect residents, as well as a boat patrol just in case some fool thinks he's gonna pull a home invasion by sea. We've got at least six hundred feet of waterfront, and the boat dock is large enough to house *Krizia*, as well as a smaller craft that Mikhail purchased just for me called *Black Beauty*. There are even stables with Arabian horses and palominos, and a large portion of our twelve acres is designated just for riding. I'm not much of a horse lover, but I'm planning on learning the proper way to ride when I get a chance.

The lawns are manicured and as green as Mikhail's eyes. There's a swanky country club on the island, so naturally almost everywhere you look is a part of the golf course lawns, but the club is so elite that it isn't like crazed strangers are shooting balls in our front yard. There's so much land that they don't even come near us anyway. In the back of the estate there are flower gardens, herb gardens, a small plot of vegetables, and even some topiary that line a hedge maze, just like in an Agatha Christie novel, as well as an infinity pool that appears to dip into the Atlantic Ocean. In the front there are palm trees and a second swimming pool. I pity the pool techs and gardeners who have to mow all that damn grass and do all that cleaning, but maybe one of them will be a sexy young stud just like homeboy on *Desperate Housewives* and I can have a little fling. Hey, I may be in a relationship, but I'm not dead, and this leopard damn sure can't change her spots overnight.

The interior of the mansion is like nothing I've ever seen before, and I've seen some of the best mansions in Chicago, from Louis Farrakhan's "palace" to a Pulitzer Prize–winning author's town house on the North Shore. This place is so gorgeous, right out of an architectural magazine or something. Mikhail says if there's anything that I don't like I can feel free to change it, but everything looks perfect to me. We have the best of everything, from fine china and crystal to antique furniture to custom-made rugs that are hand looped. There's no skimping on quality around these parts, but would I have expected anything different from Mikhail?

On top of everything, I've got a really tight studio that takes up three whole rooms in the house. I don't know how Mikhail got it built so fast and why he committed to such a radical change for a live-in girlfriend, but when you have money like his, you can really make things happen. I've got my usual setup in one room: Numark CDXs, some Technic 1200s, a Pioneer mixing board, an Apple G5 laptop, plus a new toy I got, a Korg OASYS Open Architecture Synthesis Studio that I'm dying to fool around with. In the second room I've got a full-on recording studio that is comparable if not better than any other professional studio, and the third room is a soundproof recording booth. I can't wait to see what kind of mixes and beats I can create in my lab.

But I don't have much time to play at the moment. For my first official duty as the new owner of Babylon, Mikhail recommends that I hold a press conference. I select Skybar at the Shore Club as the location. My objectives are to announce the opening of Babylon and formally introduce myself to those in the media who aren't already familiar with me. I'm more excited about the press conference than I was about my debutante cotillion. I see the opening of Babylon as my real coming-out affair.

My family has declined to attend, which isn't surprising at all so I am not upset. Frankly, I think it's better this way because none of the attention is going to be taken away from me. It's my day in the spotlight. Mikhail is by my side, but he tells me to do all of the talking and that he's content to sit in the background and let me shine in the spotlight.

There are reps from all kinds of media at the press conference. The *Miami Herald, Ocean Drive, InStyle, OK, People, US*, and even the tabloids are there. Our publicist, a woman named Sascha Palmeri has mega contacts, and she hooked the whole thing up. It's better than I could have ever imagined! This is not your average run-of-the-mill, blah press conference. It's more like a junket for a major motion picture.

The journalists are all gathered into a holding room, where all kinds of appetizers and beverages are served. I treat them to all the tastes of Miami, from southern-style soul food to Latin American favorites. Footage of my performance at the Winter Music Conference is playing on a large projection screen in the middle of the room. Just when they are starting to grumble a bit and wonder where I am and when this show is going to get on the road, I make my big entrance.

A swarm of harem dancers arrives ahead of me and does a sensual and exotic belly dance. After their routine is over, more harem girls enter, tossing flower petals on the ground. And then a group of four hot, bare-chested men carry me while I recline in a sexy pose on a divan, dressed in an elaborate Arabian princess costume. At least it's the stereotypical version of what an Arabian princess looks like; I imagine real Arabian princesses leave a lot more to the imagination. My muscle boys set the divan down and I stroll behind a DJ setup in the middle of the room, the chiffon and beads of my costume swinging as I swish my hips.

There are flashbulbs popping and the cameras clicking away as I give the journalists a little taste of the magic I make whenever I get behind some turntables. I dazzle them with my skills for about five minutes; I just want to give them a sample. I can tell that everyone in the room is captivated. It isn't like people haven't seen a female DJ before, but while most DJs blend into the background and pump a subtle soundtrack, I'm totally brazen, absolutely outrageous, and I want folks to get a show. I want them to get an eyeful not just an earful, and that's what makes me so unique.

I step down from the DJ equipment and take a seat at a long table in the middle of the floor that is decorated with mini disco balls and shiny silver CDs. I open the floor up to questions.

"Ms. Hayes," a reporter shouts.

"Please," I say, "call me Ms. Bobbi."

"Ms. Bobbi, how long have you been a DJ?"

"For over five years now. But music has always been a major part of my life. I'm a classically trained pianist and I play guitar in addition to spinning records. I plan to branch out into recording in the very near future," I tell them.

"Ms. Bobbi, what can we expect of the new club?"

"Babylon is going to be wild, over the top, outrageous, and unique, just like me. You can expect an experience like you've never had. I'm taking all the elements of the best nightspots from around the globe—Ibiza, Mykonos, Saint Tropez, New York—and weaving them together at Babylon. There's going to be state-of-the-art sound, along with some of the best DJs in the world, a top-notch bar, excellent service, and a few little extras that I'm going to keep you guessing about." I wink and laugh. The journalists laugh too.

"Ms. Bobbi, when is the club set to open?"

"The club is going to open on Halloween. It's going to be a bash like no one has ever seen. Everyone who is anyone is going to be there, from models and celebrities to the locals who are in the loop and truly make the South Beach scene what it is, I can guarantee that."

"What about the competition with Las Vegas? Isn't Vegas the place to be on Halloween? Or at the Playboy Mansion?"

"Humility isn't my strong suit, so forgive me when I say

this, but there is no competition. Babylon is the only place to be this Halloween."

"Ms. Bobbi, how did you get your name?"

*Damn*, I think to myself. *I'm going to have to talk about my family.*

"Well, although I'm named after my father and grandfather, both named Robert, I wasn't too fond of the name Roberta. I prefer Bobbi. However, friends and family call both my father and grandfather Bobby, and that caused some confusion. My grandfather came up with the idea to call me Ms. Bobbi, and it stuck," I explain.

"Ms. Bobbi, I see that your father and grandfather aren't here today, nor are any other members of the Hayes brood. Rumor has it that your family is not pleased with your career choice. Tell us, how *does* your family feel about your new business venture?" one of the women journalists asks. She cocks her eyebrow at me like she thinks she's going to make me sweat. But I can handle her.

I smile a small, tight smile, and say, "Unfortunately, due to my father's and grandfather's hectic work schedules they can't be here today, and my mother is feeling a little under the weather, so naturally I want her to get some rest. But my family is wonderful. They are supportive of everything that I do and they're unbelievably happy for me," I lie, smooth as silk. You're damn right they're unbelievably happy for me; no one who knows us would believe it. But old habits die hard; I was raised to keep Hayes family business within the Hayes family, and to never speak against the family with outsiders.

On Sascha's cue, I wrap things up with the press. It's always a good idea to leave people wanting a little bit more, that way they maintain their interest. I can hear the journalists buzzing as they exit, and I know the conference has been a smashing success. I feel great.

Mikhail and I have dinner at The Forge, and when I get home, there are several red boxes engraved with gold on the dining room table. Cartier! I run over to the table and pick up a card that has my name on it. It reads: *These jewels pale in comparison to the way you shine. Love, Mikhail.* Corny, but sweet, I think. I tear into the pile of boxes and admire the fine selection of jewelry that Mikhail has chosen. There are rings, watches, bracelets, necklaces, pens, eyeglasses, you name it. If Mikhail weren't so classy I'd swear he got these from a heist of the Cartier store, there's so much stuff. Then I tear into Mikhail. We make love for hours, fucking in practically every room of the mansion.

"I don't know how I keep up with you, sweet angel," he tells me. "You're going to be the death of me."

"You've got to eat your Wheaties if you want to keep up with me," I tease him.

But later in the week, my body feels like it's been hit by a Mack truck. Every inch of me is aching, my head hurts, and my stomach feels like it's been turned inside out. I am sick as a dog and I chalk it up to nerves and stress; I have been going a hundred miles per hour since I got back, and I've got to be riding on fumes. I figure with a little rest I'll be okay. But it doesn't get any better as the days go by. It gets worse. Everything that I eat or drink comes right back up, even water, and it seems as if I've gained ten pounds overnight. I do some mental mathematics and realize that I haven't had a period in over two months. I was so caught up enjoying myself on the yacht, moving into the mansion, and doing press for Babylon that I hadn't even noticed it was missing.

Could I be pregnant? Of course I could. I'm a grown-up and I know how those things work, but I also know my body. I never used any birth control when I was with Kaos and I never got pregnant. Withdrawal had worked fine for me in the past. I think back to the night in the disco when Mikhail came inside of me. It stands out because that's the only time that he's done it; he prefers to ejaculate somewhere he can see it, like my tits, my face, my stomach, or my ass. If I'm pregnant, that's got to be the D-date. I know I shouldn't have let him come inside of me, but twenty-twenty hindsight isn't going to help me now.

Mikhail isn't stupid either. He calls me on the possibility of pregnancy after seeing me wretch and hurl for the better part of two days.

"Maybe you're pregnant?" Mikhail asks, and it sounds as if he is hopeful. I've been rushing back and forth to the bathroom all day. I don't answer; I just wait for the next wave of nausea to hit, and when it does, it's a tsunami.

"Bobbi, are you pregnant?" he asks while I'm on my knees in the bathroom, my face buried in the toilet bowl as I pray to the porcelain god.

"I'm not pregnant."

"Would you tell me if you were?" he asks.

"Were what?"

"Pregnant," he says.

"Of course," I lie. "You'd be the father. Why wouldn't I tell you?" I ask him. I can think of plenty reasons why I wouldn't, but he doesn't need to know that.

"Women are funny that way," he says.

"How would you know? Have you ever gotten anyone pregnant before?" I ask him.

"Yes," he admits nonchalantly.

"Uh, okay. Who?" I ask.

"It makes no difference," he says cryptically. I want to say, *Like hell it doesn't*. If I'm going to be thrust in the middle of some baby mama drama, I want to know about it. But I don't say anything. I'm too queasy to argue or probe him for info.

"Okay," I say, and resume puking until I'm dry heaving.

"Did you eat something bad?" he asks.

"Must have."

"And you're sure you're not pregnant?"

"I'm sick," I manage to say in between heaves. The nausea subsides and I go to the sink and rinse out my mouth.

"Yes, but how do you know for sure?"

"Oh, I know for sure. I have an IUD. For some reason I just don't get periods that often. But when I do, they're horrid." I don't know where I get the idea to say that. I'm afraid of IUDs because I just can't understand how a tiny little squiggly piece of plastic or metal or whatever it is can stop me from getting pregnant. I don't trust it.

"I didn't know that," he says.

"Oh yes. I wouldn't have let you come inside of me if I wasn't on something. I'm very responsible," I tell him. The lies just won't stop. Mikhail isn't buying it, and I know why. It's because when he asked to come inside of me, I distinctly said, "I don't want to get pregnant." But that's my story and I'm sticking to it.

"Don't you want babies?" he asks.

"Someday. But not nine months from today." Finally, I speak the truth again.

I go lie down and Mikhail slips the sheets over me, pats me on the back, and says in a low but stern voice, "I love you, Bobbi. But I don't believe you. Not for one second. I think you're pregnant. And if you are, don't abort my child. We will get married and raise it together. A child conceived in love can never be wrong; it can never be a mistake. If I find out that you've killed my baby, I will kill you," Mikhail says, leaving me alone in a state of shock.

Did this motherfucker really just tell me that he would *kill* me if I had an abortion? Is this the same man I made love to a million times just the other day? I don't know what the hell to say or do or think. He had to be dramatic, right? He wasn't serious, was he? Does he think I'd marry him after he's told me he'd kill me if I aborted? I mean really, what kind of shit is this? I try to block it all out and get some sleep; it makes no sense to get all worked up over what could still be a non-issue. Until a doctor tells me that I'm pregnant, as far as I'm concerned, I'm not.

But the pregnancy is officially confirmed by my ob-gyn.

"How far along am I?" I ask.

"Well, according to the date of your last menstrual period, you should be about eight weeks. But your blood tests make me think closer to six weeks. I want to do an ultrasound, just to see if things are progressing normally. When I do, I'll have a better idea."

"No," I tell her. I don't want to see the fetus. If I did, there's no way I could even consider abortion.

She asks me if I've given any thought to prenatal care.

"No," I tell her. "I haven't given much thought to this at all."

"Are you having thoughts of termination?"

"I'm not sure," I say.

"I really think it is in the best interest of you and your unborn child to have further tests if you want to carry this baby to term. You could run the risk of having a miscarriage if your hormone levels aren't where they should be," she warns me.

I don't say a thing. Would a miscarriage be God's way of giving me an out? I wouldn't have to choose between life and death for an unborn child that way.

"I know that being faced with an unplanned pregnancy can be difficult," the doctor says, as if she were psychic. "A miscarriage may seem like an easy way out, but it can be more traumatic than having to make a choice. If you experience any cramping or breakthrough bleeding, please call, okay?" she asks.

"I'll keep that in mind," I tell her. "Do you perform . . . terminations?" I ask her.

"No, I don't. But if needed I can make a referral," she says. "Just try not to wait too long if that's the route you want to go. Four weeks at the very most. Things get tricky after twelve weeks. And remember to call if you have cramps or bleeding."

I tell her I need some time to think it over and that I'll get back in touch with her. Four weeks . . . I've got four weeks to determine the fate of my unborn child and possibly the rest of my life. Can I really go through with having Mikhail's baby? Could we really live happily ever after? And if I don't and he finds out that I had an abortion, will he make good on his threat to kill me? As fucked up as it is, I hope for a miscarriage. I wouldn't have to decide. I wouldn't have to feel guilty. I could just chalk things up to being God's will.

I can't help but think about Kaos at a time like this. I was supposed to have his babies. If this had happened with him there would have been no questions as to what to do. In my fantasies, we would have been overjoyed, and we would have grown old together watching over our children and grand-children, and then died in our sleep together. Instead, I'm left alone to decide what is going to happen to the rest of my life. I wonder how God could be so cruel, how he could just leave me hanging like this. But my being pregnant isn't God's fault. It's mine.

I put off doing anything for the time being. I still have a little time left, so instead I concentrate my efforts on getting the ball rolling to make Babylon a world-class hot spot. Most of the hard stuff, like marketing plans and publicity and fi-nancial projections, is going to be handled by the staff that

Mikhail has hired, so I go to work on something fun, something to get my mind off my troubles even if it will only be temporary.

I begin by doing a total overhaul of the club's sound system. It's okay, but it needs some updating if it's going to compete with the up-and-coming spots on the beach. I make some calls to a few of my favorite audio equipment dealers and order everything that I think will make the club state of the art: new speakers, lights, lasers, smoke machines, foam and bubble machines, high definition video screens, I'm talking the works. And it feels amazing to shop carte blanche; Mikhail has made it clear to spare no expense to make my vision for Babylon a reality.

The club has been left the way it was under the old ownership and although it's functional, the played out décor and lack of a theme will never do. Not if I'm going to be the face of this place. It had been okay in the past and despite its bland interior, Babylon had been the spot in its heyday. It was fabulous as a result of the glamorous and famous patrons that frequented it. Celebrities from far and wide, representing every facet of the entertainment industry, made the old Babylon nightclub a priority stop when they were in town. There had been a ridiculously strict door policy that was legendary; Babylon had the reputation of being the most difficult club to gain entrance to on the entire beach, and we all know that when you make it impossible to get into a club, everyone wants to go there. Its location—right in the heart of the beach—further boosted its popularity, but visually there is nothing stellar about the venue. I have my work cut out for me.

Mikhail arranges for me to meet with some of the world's most renowned architects and interior designers. It feels like every waking minute of my life that isn't spent in the throes of morning sickness is spent approving blueprints, furniture, paint samples, and fabric swatches. It's hard to hide my puking from Mikhail, but somehow I manage. What's harder than hiding the pregnancy is making time to practice spinning, but once the new sound equipment arrives things get a bit easier. I practice in between meetings and crank the sound system up so loud that it drowns out the construction noises.

The old Babylon had been your average-looking South Beach megaclub, in that it used to be a theater and still resembled one. But I want the new Babylon to be an experience, not just a club, so the first thing I do is break up the space. The former club had only one room with two levels. The space is huge. But after partying at the luxe and opulent clubs of the Mediterranean, I want to take this club to another level.

I envision multiple rooms all tying in to a central theme, a Moroccan oasis. The architect and I decide to divide the club into seven different sections, three downstairs and four upstairs. The bi-level main room will remain, but downstairs we will add a hookah lounge resplendent with teak opium beds imported from Morocco. I also have the idea to add a smoke-free, oxygenated room complete with a waterfall and indoor koi ponds and aquariums for those who want to escape the smoke and smells of the hookah lounge and club. And then there's the dining room. I don't want to have a full-on restaurant, but a space where one can sip aperitifs, nibble on appetizers and tapas, and later relax with digestifs.

I want to reserve the upstairs for the exclusive clientele, with two VIP-only rooms, as well as a cordoned-off VIP section of the upper level of the main room. But the pièce de résistance is going to be a concept that I call "The Lair." It's a members-only skybox section. You will have to buy a membership key, much like the Playboy club did back in the day, and it will be unseen and virtually unknown to the normal club-goers. But those select few with a membership key will have an eagle's eye view of all the action. The Lair, situated at the very top of the club, next to the security offices, will have two-way glass so that patrons can see out but others can't see inside, and will only be accessible by being escorted by a member of security who uses a key-operated private elevator.

I want Babylon to come alive with brilliant, vibrant color. Most clubs look like crap when the lights come on, but I want to make sure that Babylon looks just as spectacular in the light of day as it does in the heat of the night. The ugly steel entry door will be replaced with a special-ordered, hand-painted zouak door that looks like the opening to a fortress in *Arabian Nights*. The entryway to the club will be completely redone in colorful, intricate mosaic tile. I'm even having the decorators design a huge tile *B* (for Babylon and of course Bobbi) above the mosaic tile fountain that greets guests in the foyer.

The old Babylon had maroon velvet drapes everywhere, even the carpet was maroon. And since maroon is just about my least favorite color aside from gray, it all has to go. The drapes will be replaced with brilliant, rich silks, sari fabric, and tapestries. The old carpet will also be ripped up and replaced with industrial-strength, stain and burn resistant Berber-style carpeting, which costs a fortune, but is well worth it because the end result will be awesome. Ornate antique-style chandeliers will hang from the ceilings, some hand-beaded and some crafted of fez brass with translucent Iraqi glass cutouts.

Mikhail and I spend little to no time together, but I'm cool with that, because I don't really want to face him right now. After becoming so wrapped up in getting the club together, I've realized what I have to do concerning the pregnancy. I have to terminate it. There is no way that I can be a mom and a club owner, because, as fucked up as it sounds, Babylon is my baby. It's selfish but it's the way I feel, and I have to take ownership of it no matter how ugly it is.

I call the doctor, get a referral to a specialty ob-gyn, and make an appointment. I'm a wreck the morning I'm scheduled to have the abortion. I front like I'm about to go for a run on the beach before an early morning personal training session so that Mikhail won't be suspicious. But me waking up early is suspicious enough. Mikhail questions me, but I tell him that I'm trying to turn over a new leaf and make some changes now that I'm a businesswoman. I tell him I want to be in peak physical and mental shape. What a load of horseshit. I make a big show of putting on sweats and doing some stretches. Then I wrap a towel around my neck, grab a water bottle, and hop into my Range. Once I'm off Indian Creek Island, I drive to one of the multi-level indoor lots on South Beach and park the truck. I walk to a coffee shop and grab a triple espresso and a couple of magazines.

I go to the doctor's office by cab. A bright pink Range Rover isn't exactly inconspicuous and I don't want to take any chances of someone seeing my car parked outside a "specialist" ob-gyn office. Even though the doctor is located in Kendall, a pretty decent drive from South Beach, I'm taking extra care to cover my tracks. I hear Mikhail's voice echoing in my head. *If I find out that you've killed my baby, I will kill you.* I shake it off. There's no way Mikhail will find out, no way he'll be able to prove anything. Medical records are confidential and guarded well. And I damn sure won't tell anyone.

There is no wait at the abortion doctor's office. I'm led into an office for pre-termination counseling. A nurse asks me a bunch of questions.

"How many sexual partners have you had in the past year?"

"Too damn many," I grumble under my breath.

"Pardon me?"

"Two," I say, clearing my throat. "I said two."

Nurse Ratched peers at me over her spectacles and purses her lips.

"Have you ever been diagnosed with an STD?"

"No," I say.

"Is anyone forcing you to have the procedure or threatening you in any way connected to this procedure?" she asks.

I open my mouth to answer but nothing comes out. *Get it together, girl!* I admonish myself. *If you lose it now, they won't do the abortion and then you'll be screwed.*

"No," I croak.

"Are you sure?" she asks.

"Sure I'm sure," I say, and force myself to smile. She takes off her glasses and leans forward.

"I'm just scared," I tell her. "Honest."

She reaches into a drawer, rummages around, and pulls out a card. She hands it to me and says, "Just in case you ever need it." She makes some notations on my chart as I look at the card and wince. It's to a domestic abuse hotline. Great! Who knows what she's writing down?

"I won't need it," I tell her handing the card back. "I'm the dominant. He's the submissive. It's all consensual."

The nurse looks flustered and puts her glasses back on. She doesn't look me in the eye once when she draws blood, takes my vitals, and gives me a robe to change into before bustling out of the room. The robe is pink and soft, not faded blue or puke green and scratchy, like most gowns in doctors' offices. *It feels like a baby blanket*, I think, and then start to cry. I brush away the tears angrily with the back of my hand. *It's for the best*, I convince myself. *Yeah, but best for who?*

I'm given a valium to calm my nerves, and am ushered to a room with soothing, soft yellow walls with smooth jazz pumping softly out of a stereo system. Finally I am taken to another room, I'm given an IV, and before I know it, every-thing goes dark.

He comes to me while I'm sleeping, Kaos does. I won't say that I dreamed of him, because I swear that I can feel him. It's more vivid than a dream.

"I'm sorry," I tell him.

"Baby Girl, I could never be mad at you. I love you. Always have, always will."

"You don't hate me?" I ask him.

"Never. I'm proud of you."

"Yeah, but look at me. I'm a mess."

"You're not a mess. You're beautiful. Everything will be fine. Don't worry; I've got your back."

Then he starts to disappear. I reach for him, but he fades before I can touch him. I feel someone roughly shaking me.

"Baby Girl?" I think I hear a voice say. I can't tell if the voice belongs to a male or a female. It sounds warped and distorted.

"Kaos?" I ask, stretching my arms out and reaching around, grasping the air.

The voice gets clearer. "Roberta," it says. The shaking gets rougher until I'm jolted from my bleary-eyed state. I sit up and look around.

"He was right here," I say.

"We need you to wake up, Roberta," Nurse Ratched says, calling me by my given name. I'm given some cookies and juice to get my blood sugar up, and she comes around a few times to check my bleeding. I have cramps, but they don't even begin to compare to the way I feel mentally, which is like shit. My mind is as muddled as if it had been put through a blender. I have no idea how women can do this multiple times, because one thought keeps ricocheting through my brain like a sniper's bullet. *You're a murderer.*

# CHAPTER TEN

AFTER A COLOSSAL $7 MILLION OF MIKHAIL'S MONEY AND plenty of my blood, sweat, and tears, the club's renovations are ready ahead of schedule and now the time has come for me to meet with the staff, discuss my vision, and get to the meat of running a world-class nightclub. Mikhail has called a meeting to introduce me to the other members of the team that will run Babylon. I welcome the distraction to take my mind away from the abortion.

The initial meeting is full of surprises. First of all, any questions as to who the blonde is in the picture I found in Mikhail's office are answered. She is the managing director of the MD Entertainment Corporation. Her name is Rebeca Escobar and she's from Medellín, Colombia. Rebeca, I'm told, is the numbers lady; she's supposedly a whiz at making sure that the profits outweigh the losses. She's attractive in a bland sort of way, looks to be in her mid-thirties, and has worked with Mikhail and Dimitri at several of their other clubs over the past ten years. I immediately don't like or trust Rebeca. She makes it obvious that she knows Mikhail and Dimitri well and is familiar with the way they do business, and she doesn't try to hide her attempts at making me feel like an outsider. Whenever I suggest something, Rebeca is quick to shoot my ideas down because "we don't do things this way."

The publicity director is Sascha Palmeri, the lady who organized the press conference, and she is overseeing all the marketing and public relations efforts. Sascha and I see eye to eye. She's flashy and doesn't believe in doing things in a small fashion. Plus she's got a good attitude, nice and easygoing. I like her and I'm looking forward to exchanging outrageous ideas with her to make sure that the club is hot.

The food and beverage director is a middle-aged homosexual man named Joey J. He's a laugh a minute and I think that having him around is going to be a blast. He's got impeccable taste and a ton of experience working in the hospitality industry. He's going to make sure that nothing but the highest quality food and drink will be served.

But I think the biggest staffing surprise of all is the security director, who is none other than Q, the snotty bouncer that was at Mansion the same night I met Mikhail. Seeing him throws me for a loop. He was present both the night I met Mikhail, as well as the night I saw Mikhail and Misty at Nikki Beach Club, but I had no idea that he and Mikhail knew each other. I never saw them talk to each other or even acknowledge each other's presence. I've never heard Mikhail speak of him, and he hasn't been a player on the South Beach scene. So how did he go from a bouncer to head of security at my club? I think of the folder I saw when snooping in Mikhail's office on the ship. The label said Q. Could they be one and the same? It makes sense. Q is in charge of security; I'm sure he's into surveillance and other detective shit. I wonder what else he knows about me.

Q, whose government name is Quentin Robinson, isn't any nicer than he was the night I first met him, keeping his responses to my questions to him very minimal and gruff. Oh yeah, there's something suspicious about this dude. He acts like he doesn't even want to look at me. I can tell that unless he changes his attitude we're going to have problems.

We gather around a large conference table and nosh on a delicious meal provided by Joey J. while Mikhail and Dimitri facilitate the meeting. We discuss the hiring process and other staffing issues like insurance and benefits; we go over our list of preferred vendors, and hash out revenue projections. Frankly it all bores me to death so I'm quite happy that Mikhail has brought the others on board to handle things. I thought I'd be more interested in how much money we're going to pull in, but I just can't force myself to get excited about a bland PowerPoint presentation filled with spreadsheets and graphs and charts. Shit, just show me the money.

After hours of ennui, the meeting finally ends. I shake everyone's hand and say something complimentary just to get everyone as motivated and pumped as I am. Joey J. and Sascha seem genuinely happy to be working with me, and that's a good thing, because Rebeca is not, and she has the nerve to not even try to hide it.

"I'm really looking forward to working with you, Rebeca," I lie while pumping her hand up and down. Her grip is weak, as if she feels I'm beneath her handshake.

"I'm sure you are," she says. "It isn't as if you know the slightest thing about running a club."

"Pardon me?" I ask her, shocked.

"Oh you heard me, Ms. Bobbi," she says, crisply. "I'm not used to working with amateurs. So just stay out of my way and let me do my job. You just do . . . whatever it is you do," she finishes. Now I know I need to put this ballsy broad in check immediately, but I'm so stunned that I don't know what to say. That's a first for a smart-ass like me. I damn near faint when I watch Rebeca walk away from me and over to Mikhail, who immediately drapes his arm around her shoulder. They whisper a few things back and forth and start to walk out of the meeting room, but I stop them.

"Baby, what's up?" I ask Mikhail casually. "Where are the two of you slipping off to?"

"Don't wait up," is all that Mikhail says.

Before I can object, Q walks up to me. I make an attempt to maintain myself and act unaffected as he greets me.

"Congratulations," he says to me as he shakes my hand. He doesn't sound happy for me, but damn he looks good.

"Thanks," I tell him. "Congratulations to you too. Welcome to the team." Q isn't just eye candy—he's the whole candy shop. Brother is fine as hell. I look him over from head to toe. He's wearing an all-white linen casual pantsuit with a white wifebeater underneath that makes his smooth, bronze complexion glow. He's also wearing sandals, which I usually hate to see on men because, face it, who wants to look at a dude's grungy toes? But Q is obviously into grooming and such because his toes are clearly pedicured (but left natural, which is far more attractive than clear polish) and his fingernails are clipped short and buffed to a high shine. His hairline is razor sharp, like he just got his hair freshly faded, and his moustache and beard are perfectly clipped to accentuate his square jawline. But I still don't like him. And I don't trust him.

"Thanks," he says. "But I ought to be welcoming you to the team. I've worked with Mikhail before."

"You have?" I ask, hoping that he'll elaborate.

"I have," is all he says.

"I thought you were the bouncer at Mansion and Nikki Beach," I probe.

"Nah, I was just doing a favor for a friend," he says. "I have plenty of experience in private and upscale security. You know, *years* of running a successful business. Things haven't just been handed to me on a silver platter." He doesn't even bother to hide the fact that he's taking a dig.

"I see," I tell him. Not only has this dude been prying into my private life, but he obviously has a personal problem with me. "Is there something you want to say, Q?" I ask him.

"Actually there is. I'm not going to beat around the bush and drop hints," he says. "I'm not used to biting my tongue. So I'm not going to start now. I think that you should stick to what you do best, and that's looking pretty," he says, but I cut him off.

"You think I'm pretty?" I ask, flirting and trying to soften him up. If Q has been spying on me, I want to know why, and in order to do that I need for us to at least be cordial. Q ignores my comment.

"Stick to looking pretty and DJ'ing. Leave the real work up to the rest of us." He says *DJ'ing* like it's a menial job. I want to kick him in the teeth. But I'm bigger than that. Fuck him.

"You know, I don't appreciate your insubordination. If you want to remain a part of this organization, I'd suggest you change your attitude, and quickly," I say, tossing my hair in indignation.

"Whatever you say, Boss Lady," I hear him say sarcastically over the clicking of my stilettos on the floor as I walk away.

AS SOON AS I GET IN MY CAR I WHIP MY CELL PHONE OUT OF my purse and call Amara. I want information and she's just the person to give it to me.

"Bobbi, baby! How is everything?" she asks when she answers the phone.

"Things are going okay. I'm really excited about the opening. The club looks fabulous and I can't wait for you to see it," I tell her.

"Well, I'll be there for the opening, baby. I wouldn't miss it for the world."

"Good," I tell her. "But listen, honey, I need to ask you something," I say, getting to the point.

"Sure, baby," she says.

"Now this is just between us."

"Naturally, baby."

"I just had a meeting with the staff of the MD Entertainment Corporation. And let's just say that everyone isn't exactly on board. I'm catching flack from a couple of people and I need to know the scoop. I am so heated I can't even begin to tell you."

"Let me guess," she says. "Is one of them Rebeca Escobar?" Amara asks.

"Ugh, yeah," I say with disgust. "How did you know?"

"She's a barracuda. I should have known that the two of you crossing paths would be inevitable. Baby, Mikhail and Rebeca used to date," Amara says. That explains why they looked so close on the picture that I saw.

"Was it serious?" I ask.

"I'm not sure how serious Mikhail was, but Rebeca carried quite a torch. Whatever their personal relationship was, as far as I can tell it's over, and now Rebeca works for them. It's strictly business," Amara tells me. Amara obviously doesn't know how much Mikhail likes to mix business with pleasure. "Apparently she's very important to them. Even the Apostles seem to revere her," she says.

"Why? Isn't she like an accountant?" I ask.

"Exactly, baby. She makes everything they do look legal."

"*Look* legal? Wait a minute, Amara. Why would they need her at Babylon? Everything there *is* legal," I tell her.

"Sure, baby. I know you aren't doing anything wrong," she says.

"*No one* is doing anything wrong," I say. "The club is on the up-and-up," I tell her.

"Don't be naïve, Bobbi. I know of what I speak. If Rebeca is there, then something is going on. You can count on it."

"Are you sure, Amara?" I ask.

"Yes, baby, I'm sure."

"Amara, exactly what does Mikhail do? I've asked before and you weren't sure. But you seem to know a lot more than you've been letting on. My name is attached to this. My life is caught up in this more than you know. I need you to be up front with me."

"Okay, baby," she says reluctantly. She pauses for a moment, then speaks. "Here's what I've been able to figure out. The Apostles are like captains," she says. "They run the businesses in different parts of the world. They report to Mikhail. My Dimitri is the one who makes sure that the captains all stay in line. But without Rebeca or someone like her—and I believe that there are others like her—none of it would work. Her brother is some kind of diplomat or ambassador or something. He's their connection to all the crooked politicians. Rebeca is like a liaison, and she covers the money trail."

"Shit, Amara, this stuff you're telling me is dangerous. There are laws against those sorts of things: RICO laws and conspiracy laws and racketeering laws. Oh God, I'll be a co-defendant!"

"Look, baby, I understand why you're nervous. If I were in your shoes I would be too. But I know these guys. Calm down. Nothing is going to happen. Mikhail will never get caught. He's too smart, too connected, and too careful. Why don't you just get the money, and let things run their natural course?"

"Which is what? Get sucked in deeper?" I ask.

"Come on, Bobbi. You know how long clubs last on South Beach. A few years? By then, you'll be a very, very rich lady. Mikhail will move onto something else. You'll be free. It's happening with Dimitri and I. He is growing bored and so am I. We love each other, but he is not a suitable husband for me. We are not forever. You and Mikhail won't be either."

"Yes, but you didn't make Dimitri money, you cost him money. He may be more willing to set you free," I tell her.

"Maybe you have a point there," she says.

"I am so screwed, Amara," I say.

"No you aren't. You're rich. The rich always find a way out. You've got to stop worrying. But, baby, you said a couple of people were giving you trouble. Who else is there?" she asks. "That may tell me something."

"Well, his name is Q. Have you ever met him? He's a good-looking black guy. The first time I saw him was the night I met Mikhail. As a matter of fact, the only other time I've seen him before today was the night I saw Mikhail at Nikki Beach Club, the night before I met you. He seemed vaguely familiar the first time I saw him, but I thought it was because he reminded me of my ex. Now I'm not so sure."

"No, baby. I've never met anyone named Q. Never heard of him either. But that doesn't mean a thing. There are a lot of things about Mikhail and Dimitri that I don't know," Amara says, but she knows a hell of a lot more than me.

"Well, when we were on the ship, I did a little snooping in Mikhail's office. I found a picture of Mikhail and Rebeca and a folder with the letter Q on it. Inside the folder was a file with a bunch of information on me. I'm talking yearbook pictures, credit report, damn near everything."

"Why didn't you tell me that you found that?" she asks. "It's odd, isn't it?"

"Well, at the time I thought it was just a really, really thorough background check. I mean, I'm working for him. And when he asked me to go into business with him, it kind of made sense. I mean, you want to know who you're getting in bed with so to speak, right?"

"I guess so," Amara says. "So what's different now?"

"I don't know. It just seems too coincidental. And I'm not sure if I want someone from Mikhail's camp so involved with security, you know? How can I trust him when I know he doesn't have my best interests or the customer's best interests at heart, but Mikhail's? I've got Rebeca on one end being the bitch of life, and Q on the other side prying into my private life. I will not have them ruining this for me. What am I going to do?"

"You're going to keep your eyes open and watch your back," she tells me. "And you're going to be a legend. Not just on South Beach, but around the world. Go with the flow, don't make waves, but be smart. Learn what you're up against, and protect yourself at all costs," she says.

"Damn, Amara. That's gangster," I say. "Shit, are you a mafia chick?" I ask her, only half joking. "Is your family the Brazilian liaison?"

"No," she says, laughing. "I assure you that I'm no gangster. I'm a friend, Bobbi."

"I want to believe that, Amara. I really do. But I can't help but ask myself why you're telling me this. Why now? Why not before? Why did I have to come to you? If you were really a friend, wouldn't you have told me earlier? No offense, but nothing is as it seems anymore. I don't know who I can trust."

"You have some valid questions, Bobbi, that I can't deny. The only answer I have for you is that you can't trust anyone. Just trust the advice I have given you. I'm sorry, but that's just the way it is."

The conversation with Amara rattles me at first because I know in my heart that she's told me the truth. It was too much to think that Mikhail would just bless me with a club for the reasons he gave. There's too much money involved for everyone to be on the up-and-up, too much at stake for me to be naïve enough to trust everyone. But regardless of what's now been confirmed, I still want Babylon to be a success. So the dream is a little tainted. It's still a dream come true. I'm walking a fine line and taking some big chances, but to win big you've got to bet big.

I come to the realization that I need to play the game to win. I've got to think and move strategically. Like Denzel said in *Training Day*, "This shit's chess, it ain't checkers!" The way I see it, I'm the queen, the most powerful piece on the board. And every other piece should move to protect me because I am Babylon, whether they like it or not.

I hold my head high when I go to work, and exude confidence and professionalism. Regardless of the circumstances, or maybe even because of them, my club is going to be the biggest thing to hit Miami since Hurricane Andrew. Q remains cold and indifferent toward me. I'm friendly, but it's a wasted effort; talking to him is like talking to a brick wall. He'd rather grunt or nod than speak to me, but I don't stoop to his level. If I need to know something I ask him, and I don't stop asking questions until he's given me a satisfactory answer.

I also make a conscious effort to get along with Rebeca, no matter how difficult she is. You get more flies with sugar than you do with vinegar. Rebeca makes this especially hard though. She acts like I rode the short bus to special school, and I don't know how much more of her attitude I can take.

"That doesn't go there," she barks, when I replace a file in the file cabinet.

"Did you put this bill in this tray? It goes in the other one," she admonishes me when she finds the phone bill in the out bin instead of the in.

"What the fuck is wrong with you?" I finally snap on her.

"What the fuck is wrong with *you*?" she asks.

"Rebeca, this is my club. I *am* Babylon. Babylon is mine. I've tried to be patient with you and I've tried to be friendly. But you want this to be difficult. Well, let me tell you, I'm not going anywhere." I roll my neck like I'm back on the playground on the South Side, facing off with a school bully.

"You're so arrogant, but so naïve. You really overestimate your importance. You may be Babylon for now, but trust me, you won't be it forever."

I confront Mikhail about both Rebeca's and Q's behavior.

"Mikhail, why is Q so mean to me?" I ask.

"How is he mean to you?" he asks, his brow furrowing in concern.

"He acts like he has nothing to say to me. He makes me feel like I'm in the way or something. He's rude."

"Is that all?" he says with a chuckle.

"Isn't that enough?" I ask.

"That is nothing. He's the head of security, sweet angel. He's not supposed to be nice. He's supposed to make sure that everyone, including you, remains safe," Mikhail explains. *Is that why you had him spy on me?* I wonder. "If he's chatting and joking and laughing with people, how can he do that?"

"Maybe you have a point, but I don't like it," I complain. Mikhail runs his hands through his hair, exasperated.

"Is there anything or anyone else bothering you?" he asks me. He says *bothering* as if this is all in my head.

"As a matter of fact there is. What does Rebeca have against me?" I ask him. I wonder if Mikhail will tell me that they used to date.

"I don't understand what you mean," he says.

"She's a bitch," I say, cutting to the chase.

Mikhail laughs but I don't find anything funny.

"I'm serious. She's rude, patronizing, and stank."

"That's just her way," he says, defending her.

I don't like it. "Well, her way sucks," I tell him. "She's straight up insubordinate and I'm not going to take it. We already had words. And you're not blind; you see it. Now, Mikhail, I'm not telling you how to run your business, but this isn't just your business; it's ours. I am the face of Babylon, and I don't need her giving me shit for doing what I'm supposed to do."

"I'll have a chat with her, sweet angel," he says.

But whatever he says to her doesn't do squat. Things come to a head again when I ask Rebeca to see the liquor license. I have a meeting with a wine vendor, and I need it for the paperwork.

"I'll have to talk to Mikhail," she says.

"Why? This is my club," I say.

Rebeca ignores me.

"Do you hear me?"

"Yes."

"Well, then let me see it. I just need to write down the license number."

"I'm afraid I have orders," she begins.

"Orders? From whom? This is *my* club," I repeat.

"Yes, but all operations are handled exclusively by the MD Entertainment Corporation. I'm afraid that when Mikhail isn't around, all the important decisions—you know, the one's that will keep this club afloat—are made by me," she says.

"What?" I ask incredulously.

"Didn't you read your contract?" she smirks, and walks away.

I chirp Mikhail immediately on his cell phone.

"What is it, Bobbi?" he asks curtly. "I'm busy."

"It's your girl Rebeca. She's tripping again, and I think she may be in need of professional help because she's obviously not thinking clearly."

"Can you make this quick?" he asks.

I sigh, exasperated. "I need to see the liquor license for a meeting, and she says she needs to talk to you first," I say.

"I'll talk to her," he says. Yeah right! I've heard that before.

"Yeah, but I need it now. As it is I'm already late," I say.

"Reschedule the meeting," he replies.

"What?" I ask. Surely there's got to be some interference on the line.

"Reschedule it. Rebeca is just following protocol."

"Protocol? I'm the owner," I say.

"Later, Bobbi," he says. "Can't talk now."

Mikhail doesn't answer any more of my chirps that afternoon; I have no choice but to do as he says and reschedule the meeting. Mikhail also doesn't return any of my phone calls or reply to the text messages I send when "later" comes and goes. Afternoon blends into evening and evening into morning. Mikhail never makes it home. I'm sick with worry. The first thing I think is that he's been arrested, or even worse, kidnapped. Right now he could be getting tortured. Right now an assassination squad could be on its way to my house to retaliate for some of Mikhail's business doings. I don't even want to think that he's been in an accident. God would never be that cruel to me. He'd never allow me to lose two men that way.

I nearly jump out of my skin when Mikhail finally comes home. I'm dozing on the couch near the front door when his keys jingle in the lock.

"Why didn't you call?" I ask him as soon as he walks in, trying not to sound whiny or confrontational. I wrap my arms around him, happy to see him in one piece. Mikhail's body doesn't respond and he pulls away from me.

"I wasn't aware that I had to check in," he says nonchalantly.

"It's not about checking in," I tell him. "I was worried about you. I called and left messages and you still didn't call. It's inconsiderate. You're a grown man, do what you want. I just think it's respectful to call me and let me know you aren't coming home so I don't sit up worrying all night."

"I'll keep that in mind," he says.

"Yeah, well, you should," I say, growing angry. Mikhail hasn't offered any explanation as to his whereabouts. "You would have a fucking cow if I pulled some shit like that."

"You're smart enough to not ever try my patience like that," Mikhail says, his voice bearing the faint signs of irritation. He's got some nerve being mad at me when he's the one who stayed out all night! He's trying to flip the script. But I know all about those tricks, and I'm not falling for any of them.

"Mikhail, were you out with another woman?" I ask.

"Bobbi, don't be immature and insecure. It isn't flattering," Mikhail says. "Now if this interrogation is over, I'm going for a swim." Mikhail walks coolly out of the room.

"You didn't answer the question," I yell after him.

I pout in frustration. Why is it that men always change up once they've won you over? They're always flowers and candy and candlelight when they want you. Once they've got you, that shit comes to a grinding halt. *Fuck it*, I think silently. *Fuck it and fuck him.* If that's the game he wants to play, then fine. As long as I'm getting what I want out of the deal—money, fame, and a world-class nightclub, then that's all that matters.

THINGS WITH MIKHAIL CONTINUE IN THE SAME DIRECTION. HE begins to spend less and less time at home with me, and more time out at overnight "business meetings." I'm not stupid; Mikhail is spending time with another woman. If the meetings were all "business," how come I didn't need to be at any of them? After all, I am his business partner. I have the suspicion that he's keeping time with Rebeca. The more I'm around her, the more smug she is; I'm catching a definite "I'm fucking your man" vibe from her. And I'm not sure if Misty is out of the picture. My gut tells me that a woman like her won't go away quietly, and I'm just waiting for her to rear her ugly head again. It wouldn't surprise me at all.

I can't front like I'm not upset. I was so certain that I had Mikhail eating out of the palm of my hand. Now I feel like I'm losing a hold on him, and a little part of me is afraid that the club and all my dreams for it may slip away as well. I go to work every day, tending to the little details that need to be taken care of before the opening. I know that I don't have to do these things, that they're just busywork, but I can't just sit around the mansion twiddling my thumbs and waiting for Mikhail to pay attention to me, nor can I sit idly by and let life happen to me. I intend to hang on to Babylon with all my might. I've come too far to let Rebeca or Misty or any other woman run me off.

I find solace from the uncertainties in my life through my music, pounding out my frustrations on the ones and twos. I love spinning in the club and spend most of my free time practicing and experimenting, getting myself prepared for the opening. The acoustics are the bomb, and it just gives me a thrill unlike any I've ever experienced.

A couple weeks before the opening, I'm in the booth mixing Wu-Tang with Linkin Park, Eminem with Three Doors Down, the Sex Pistols with Nas, and Bad Religion with Public Enemy. The results are a loud, angry, cutting edge, rap/rock/punk fusion that relieves my tension and frustration.

"Yo, Boss Lady!"

I look up from the turntables to see Q standing below the DJ booth, yelling into his hands that are cupped in front of his mouth. I yank my headphones off and cut the volume down.

"How long have you been standing there?" I ask.

"A few minutes," he says. "You were really into your music. You didn't hear me at all."

I hold up the headphones and shake them. "Yeah, well, it's loud under here."

"Yeah, well, Mikhail left a message for you," he says. "He said to not wait up for him tonight."

No big surprise there.

"Hey Q?" I ask him. "Do you know where Rebeca is?"

Q looks a little uncomfortable, like he doesn't want to answer the question.

"Yeah," he says.

"Well, where is she?" I ask him.

"With Mikhail," he tells me. My face drops. How embarrassing. I'm almost certain everyone knows Mikhail and

Rebeca are fucking; the signs are clear. But couldn't they at least show some decorum? Couldn't they at least try to be slick about it? Doesn't Mikhail realize how disrespectful he's being, how stupid he's making me look?

"Boss Lady?" I hear Q shout. I snap out of my daze.

"Yes?"

"That mix was tight," he says. "I never heard anything like it before." I look at Q suspiciously; he's looking at me like I'm a lost puppy dog. Good God! Don't tell me he's feeling sorry for me because I'm getting played. How humiliating!

"What? Are you giving me my props?" I ask sarcastically, trying to play things off.

"I never said you couldn't spin," Q replies, equally sarcastic. He turns to walk away.

"Q," I yell at him.

"Yeah, Boss Lady?" he asks.

"Come here for a second, please?" I ask. He looks like he wants to say no, but he comes up the stairs and enters the booth. I'm greeted by his scent and my body instantly responds. It's Be Delicious by Donna Karan, one of my favorites.

"Can we talk?" I ask him.

"About?"

"About our work relationship."

"What is there to talk about? I have a job and I do it."

"Yeah, but what's your beef with me? I'm not trying to stop you from doing your job. I never have. But you've never given me a chance. You always act so foul towards me."

"There's no chance to give. I work security. I don't get paid to be friendly," Q tells me, echoing Mikhail's earlier sentiments.

"You don't get paid to be rude either," I counter.

"Are we done?" he asks.

I don't say anything. Q turns to walk away.

"Why have you been spying on me?" I blurt out. Q freezes.

"Excuse me?"

"I know that you've been spying on me," I say. "I saw the folder."

"I don't know what you're talking about," he says coolly. But his eyes and body language betray him. I've caught him off guard.

"The background check. All my personal info. I saw it. The folder of files had your name on it. I want to know why. I know it wasn't your typical pre-employment screening."

Q gauges his words carefully.

"I'm just doing what I'm told," he says. "I can't divulge any more."

"It's like that, huh?" I ask, pissed off. "Fine, *brother*," I say, pulling the race card. It's a cheap shot, but I'm taking it. "Got no love for a sister, huh? It's fucked up that I get this opportunity of a lifetime, and the only brother onboard gives me shit and spies on me. This is just what I thought. You work for Mikhail; you're one of his flunkies. A fucking do-boy!"

"I'm not a fucking do-boy!" Q spits at me. He takes some deep breaths and speaks again. "Look, Ms. Bobbi," he says.

"Just Bobbi! Damn, do you have to be that formal?" I yell.

"Look, Bobbi. It isn't like that," he says.

"The hell it isn't," I say. I feel my eyes start to water. I'm partly mad, partly frustrated. It seems as if the entire world is against me. I feel a wave of emotion building up within, and I can't contain it. I do the unthinkable. I start to cry.

"Shit, Q. You can see with your own eyes that Mikhail and Rebeca are fucking. Do you have to be so smug when you bring me fucked up messages? I know that you work for

Mikhail, but do you have to do your share to make me miserable? Do you have to bring me the fucked up message and attitude too?" I'm embarrassed to be crying in front of him, but I'm so frustrated that I don't know what to do. Q's expression softens a little.

"Stop crying," he says. "What are you crying for? Mikhail is with Rebeca. So what? What difference does it make? You're getting the money. That's all you're in it for, right?" I don't answer, I keep crying. Q looks around nervously.

"Shit! The last thing I need is for someone to come in here and see us here together with you crying like that. Let's get out of here until you calm down," he says.

We walk outside the club and get inside his truck, a white Explorer that is parked up front. A blast of cool air hits me and I inhale deeply as he starts the engine and the sounds of Bob Marley pump through his speakers.

"Want to get something to eat?" he asks. I nod yes.

We head for the causeway and Q drives toward the city.

"You like seafood?" he asks.

I nod yes. I stop crying and stare out the window as we leave the turquoise waters and art deco buildings behind and the scenery changes to a darker, grimier backdrop. We roll through Liberty City and head to a spot called Jumbo's.

"You ever been here before?" he asks me.

"Yeah," I say.

"What? A princess like you?" he teases. He takes the liberty of ordering fried shrimp and conch for both of us.

"I'm no princess, Q. I see you only scratched the surface when you did your spying on me," I tell him, dryly.

"Bobbi, I don't know what to tell you about that. It was business, not personal," Q says as we sit down. I take a sip of my sweet tea.

"You've been making it personal," I say. "What do you

have against me? From the looks of that folder, you've been watching me a long time. You've got to be able to tell that I'm not that bad a person," I say.

"I think you have the wrong idea about what you saw," Q tells me.

"Then set me straight," I say.

"You're making more out of this than what it is. Yes, I pulled some public records of yours. I work for Mikhail. He asked me to do it and I did it, and I really didn't think anything of it. He does that kind of thing with everyone he does business with. Then Mikhail told me to come to a couple of clubs and keep an eye on you."

"For what?" I ask.

"I don't know. He just said to observe you. I didn't even know what I was looking for. But he pays me well, so I did what he asked. I saw you come to Mansion alone, work, and leave with Mikhail. I saw you come to Nikki Beach Club alone, and leave alone." I wonder if Q caught my interlude with Bentley.

"Is that all you saw?" I asked.

"That's all I reported," he tells me.

"I don't believe you," I say. "I saw clippings from magazines and my yearbook photo in that folder. There was even a picture of me and my dead fiancé, Kaos, in there. It looked like it was taken by a spy camera or something, you know what I mean? It was from far away. You mean to tell me you didn't do that?"

"No, I didn't do that. Mikhail has lots of people working for him. It could have been anyone," Q explains. I'm still not buying it.

"Kaos has been gone a few years," Q says. "When he was alive I was just getting involved with Mikhail." The statement arouses my suspicions. I cock my eyebrow at him.

"Bobbi, I'm telling you the truth. I won't deny that I knew him. I did. We worked out together; we had the same personal trainer. We were cool. I wouldn't have done him like that."

"You knew my Kaos?" I ask him.

"Yes, Bobbi, I knew him, but just in passing, you know? Nothing deep. But he used to talk about you all the time. I guess that's why I didn't care for you much when I met you. In my mind you'll always be Kaos's girl. And I don't think he would be happy with you dating a guy like Mikhail."

That statement feels like a kick in the gut. The tears start rolling again.

"I don't think he'd be too happy about someone he was cool with giving me such a hard time either," I say.

"I'm sorry if that upset you. And you're right, Bobbi. I should be looking out for you instead of hassling you. But I felt like my loyalties were divided," he says. "I work for Mikhail and I've got responsibilities."

"Your loyalties don't have to be divided," I say.

"They're not anymore. I'm sure I can do my job and go a little easier on you. I'm sorry, Bobbi. Let's start over, okay?"

I look in his eyes to gauge his sincerity. I know that I can't trust anyone, but I'm happy that Q has at least stopped being so antagonistic.

"Sure, let's start over," I finally say. Q extends his hand and I shake it.

"Don't take this the wrong way, Bobbi. I really hope we can be cool now, but I just don't see what you see in Mikhail. How could you get caught up with him?"

"I'm sure it's the same way you got caught up," I tell him. "I see the same thing that everyone else sees. Dollar signs," I say.

"Is that all?" Q asks.

"Not really. I mean, I liked him. In the beginning he was

cool. I liked his style. He was a mentor. Mikhail offered to take my career to the next level. It was too good of an opportunity to turn down. I wanted to be like him. I wanted to feel the money and the power that he offered. That was until I got to know more about him and got to know him better. Lately, he's been treating me more like his employee than his girl, and I realize that he sees everyone as a subordinate. I'm also finding out that Mikhail is a little bit unstable. I can't quite put my finger on what it is, but there's a darkness to him that goes beyond any shady business dealings he's involved in."

"You don't know the half of it," Q says.

"Are you going to tell me?" I ask.

"If you really need to know something, I'll let you know," he says. That, I figure, is better than what I've been getting.

"Just tell me one more thing?" Q asks me.

"Sure," I say.

"Is this worth all the trouble?" he asks.

"I don't know," I say.

FROM THEN ON, THINGS ARE COOL BETWEEN Q AND ME. A couple of times we even grab a bite together and just chop it up about whatever's going on in Miami that day. I even gave him a DJ lesson once, and he isn't half bad. He's a quick study with anything technical, he says, and it shows, because he gets the hang of my Scratch Live software in no time. I get to know Q more, but in doing so, I learn more about Mikhail. Things I don't necessarily want to know.

"How did you meet Mikhail?" I ask Q one night. We're the only people left in the club and we're gathering our things, getting ready to walk out.

"You don't want to know all that," he says.

"Yes I do," I tell him.

"Well, I played football at UM. I used to meet a lot of hustlers and gamblers who liked to bet on the games and stuff. When I got injured senior year, my life changed. I wasn't going to the draft. I had to get a regular job. My major was criminal justice and there's nothing I could do with that except become a cop or a lawyer. I'm not smart enough for law school and cops don't make shit."

"So then what did you do?"

"I started hustling. I already knew all the players in the game, and I had knowledge of the law. I know how cops think. It made me a better criminal," he admits.

"And you're some kind of drug dealer?" I ask him.

"Not at all," he says. "Not anymore. Now I negotiate and broker deals. I make introductions. I scope things out and measure risks for both sides involved. I don't touch any drugs."

"But you do something illegal?" I ask.

"I do security, Bobbi. I deal with problems and problematic people. My size is intimidating. My demeanor scares people. Security comes natural to me. I make sure that Mikhail is taken care of."

"I thought that was Dimitri's job," I say.

"It is."

I ask the inevitable question. "What is Mikhail involved in that he needs so much protection?"

"You mean you don't know?" he asks in disbelief.

"No, I don't."

"Come on, Bobbi. You don't know what's going on around here?"

"Well, I know there's something, but I always figured the less I knew the better."

"So then what's changed?"

"I don't know. Mikhail, I guess. I used to think I could trust him, that he wouldn't let anything bad happen to me. Now I'm not so sure. I'm clearly not the only woman in his life, and I feel like I ought to watch my own back a little more."

"You're serious, aren't you?" he says.

"Yes. Are you going to tell me anything?"

Q looks reluctant. "I don't know. Maybe not knowing is better for you," he says.

"You know, I'm tired of other people all getting a say in what goes down in my business while I don't know shit. This is no better than it was when I was growing up. I'm not a little girl, I'm a woman. I deserve to know what's going on!" I say.

"Bobbi, you've got to trust me on this," he says.

"I don't trust anyone," I tell him.

"You've got to trust somebody sometime," he says, leaving me frustrated.

MIKHAIL DOESN'T SEEM TO APPROVE OF Q'S AND MY BUDDING friendship.

"I think that maybe you're getting a little too friendly with Q," he says.

"What do you mean?" I ask.

"I just think that the two of you should spend less time together. It isn't professional," he tells me. *Like you and Rebeca?* I think.

"It's totally professional. I don't hang out with him any more than I hang out with Sascha or Jimmy J. I'm just kicking it with my coworkers."

"It's different, Bobbi," he says, "and you know what I mean."

"Mikhail, I've noticed something about you," I tell him.

"Oh really?" he says with a smirk. "And what is that?"

"You have a problem with me associating with black men. You tripped over Bentley and now you're tripping over Q," I say. "You have no problem with me being surrounded by your male friends, but if I make any of my own, there's drama."

Mikhail turns beet red.

"Are you saying that I am threatened by black men?" he asks.

"Take it how you want to," I tell him. "We both know what the deal is."

Mikhail is so angry that he doesn't say anything else. And he doesn't bring up my association with Q again. But he watches us. I can sense it. He can watch away, though. Nothing's going on. Q and I are just friends.

# CHAPTER ELEVEN

THE DAY OF THE CLUB'S OPENING, MY BODY IS LIKE A LIVE wire. Excitement flows through my veins like a current as I prepare for the big night ahead. Amara arrives on Dimitri's G4, and I pick her up from the Tamiami Airport. We head straight to the Agua Spa at the Delano to be primped and pampered. We indulge in massages, bath treatments, body polishes, manicures, pedicures, and the like, and then have a light lunch from the Blue Door Restaurant. We don't have a chance to talk much; I need extra time to get ready because I am arriving in typical Ms. Bobbi fashion, outlandish as I wanna be. I'm just glad that my girl is able to support me on what is undoubtedly the first night of the rest of my life.

An artist meets us at the mansion and he paints my naked body (save for a very tiny g-string) with airbrushed tiger stripes, accented with citrine- and amber-colored crystals. My hair is wild and loose, with streaks of black, gold, and orange sprayed in, and gold glitter sprinkled throughout. I rock a pair of black soft leather ankle boots and black leather gloves, and wear a real diamond collar with a chain.

Amara dresses up like Lil' Kim, which I find hilarious

because there is nothing little about Amara. She wears a purple lace jumpsuit that only covers one boob, a purple flower-shaped pastie over the other boob, and a rhinestone belt with letters that spell out Lil' Kim. She tops it all off with a purple wig and lots of bling.

Mikhail and Dimitri are party poops and don't dress up, but Amara and I don't let them ruin our fun. We pull up to the club, Dimitri and Amara in an Aston Martin and Mikhail and me in my Ferrari, and immediately the attention of the multitude of people waiting in line shifts to us. The engines of the sports cars roar as we park our cars directly in front of the club. The valets open our car doors and members of the security staff stand by as we cross what would normally be the red carpet. Just for tonight, I've got sand spilling out onto the sidewalk from the entryway so that it looks like we're crossing the desert.

There are photographers lined up near the entrance, snapping pictures of the club's exterior, the crowd, and now Amara and me as we make our way toward the door. Amara and I cause quite a stir and we pose suggestively with her holding my chain. I ham it up and act like I've gone wild; I bare my teeth and pretend to maul Amara's dangling breast.

We enter the club and are hit by a wave of sound. DJ Tracey Young is spinning house in the main room, and her mix is being pumped throughout the entire club. Mikhail and Dimitri bail on us early and disappear into the thick crowd, but for the moment my focus isn't on them, it's on myself. People are coming at me from all angles, bussing me with air kisses, admiring my costume, and schmoozing with me as if I can make all their dreams come true. And I have to admit that it feels good. I enjoy the surge of power that I feel when people kiss my ass and try to impress me. When I was growing up, I hated that feeling, but I realize that it was because those people weren't feeling me, they were in awe of my family. But now it seems that everyone is beginning to realize what I've known all along—I'm a star in my own right.

Scantily clad go-go dancers bump and grind atop podiums and speakers, and swing on perches inside giant birdcages that dangle from the ceiling. Troupes of bellydancers wind their way through the crowds, throwing rose petals and clinking tiny finger cymbals as they undulate in an erotic fashion. Buffed and muscular shirtless men jump on top of the bars at random and breathe violent bursts of fire. My version of Babylon is just what I imagine the ancient kingdom of Babylon to have been like: rich, decadent, and wild.

There are loads of celebrities in the house. A few of the Miami Heat players are there; Shaq and his wife, Shani, are dressed as Frankenstein and his bride, D-Wade is dressed as Scarface, and Zo and his wife, Tracey, are there as Bobby and Whitney. I see a few renegade Playmates that have foregone Hef's party and I smile inside. Every hotboy and hotgirl on the South Beach scene is also in the house, the guys subliminally competing to see who has the sexiest and skimpiest-dressed girl. I love that Halloween allows normally prissy chicks to unleash their inner ho. The guys love it too!

Q's eyes nearly bug out of his head when he sees me.

"Damn, Boss Lady. You killin' it tonight," he says, his smile a mile wide.

"Thanks," I say. "You too," I tell him.

"I'm not wearing a costume, Boss Lady," Q says.

"I know," I say with a wicked grin.

"Who was that?" Amara asks, once Q leaves.

"Oh that's just Q, the head of security."

"The one you were having trouble with?"

"Nah, we're cool now," I say.

"I see you're cool now, baby. You've gone from being enemies to making goo-goo eyes at each other," she says.

"Are you kidding? We were not making any kind of eyes at each other. That's my dog."

"Oh, you were making eyes. You were definitely flirting with each other, and I don't blame you. Ooh, baby, he's delicious," she says, smacking her lips.

"He's all right," I say, playing it cool. But she's right. He *is* delicious.

"Amara, he was cool with my ex that died a few years ago. It's really not like that," I say.

"You're a fucking party pooper, you know that? Bringing up the dead," Amara says with a pout. "This is a happy occasion."

"No, Amara, it's all good. I'm still happy. Kaos was my heart. I miss him like crazy, but he's always with me. He's the one who taught me how to DJ. There's no reason to pretend he didn't exist."

Amara smiles at me. "Well then, to . . . What was his name again, baby?"

"Kaos," I tell her.

"To Kaos," she says, grabbing a champagne glass.

"To Kaos," I say, raising my glass. We take a sip.

"Ooh, and to great asses," she says as we watch Q walk across the VIP section.

"Amen to that," I say.

At the stroke of midnight, Guns N' Roses's "Welcome to the Jungle" plays, right on cue. I step inside a giant cage that is wheeled into the party. I prowl my confines like a sleek jungle cat, clawing at the air and through the bars, growling as I crawl along the velvet-lined floor. The men that wheel the cage into the room brandish long whips that they crack in the air in an effort to subdue and contain me, but with one well-rehearsed motion, I cause the walls of the cage to fall around me, and my "trainers" bow down in submission and fear. The room is pulsating; my guests stare in amazement.

Lights and lasers flash around the room and sirens blare. "Welcome to the Jungle" fades into a recorded intro that one of my favorite DJs from the crib, Boolu Master, has done for me. I slink my way over to the DJ booth, and make my way up the stairs and to the turntables. I yell into the microphone, "Yo, yo, yo. For those of you who don't know who the fuck I am, I'm Ms. Bobbi. Welcome to my brand-new nightclub, Babylon. So now that we all know each other, let's set this motherfucker off right!"

The crowd responds enthusiastically as I play banger after banger. Everyone is dancing and having a good time. The opening is a smashing success, and I couldn't be happier. When I finish my set, my replacement, a New Yorker named Mixtress Betty, takes over. I search the crowds for Amara and the men, who are nowhere to be found. It's pointless though; the club is so huge and the crowd is so thick that finding them would be like finding a needle in a haystack. I decide to go to my office to have a celebratory drink in relative silence.

I have a bartender fix me a large glass of Jack on the rocks, and punch the keycode into the security door that leads to the offices. As I walk through the maze of storage closets and offices, I pass Rebeca's door, and I hear the sound of muffled voices. It sounds an awful lot like someone is getting their fuck on. *She can't be in there with Mikhail,* I think. He wouldn't be that disrespectful. Curious, I test the door handle to see if it's unlocked. It is, and I grin in the anticipation of catching Rebeca screwing around with someone else while on the job. I can't wait to see the look on Mikhail's face when he finds out his chick on the side is fucking someone else on his dime. Slowly, I turn the knob and pop my head inside.

Rebeca is sprawled out on her desk with her legs wide open and her skirt bunched up around her waist. Her eyes are tightly squeezed shut as she throws back her head in sheer ecstasy. All I can see is a thick mess of dark hair grasped between her fingers; her lover's face is buried deeply in her pussy. But that's all I need to see. I'd recognize that hair anywhere. I've even seen it plenty of times from the exact same vantage point Rebeca is in right now. It's Mikhail's.

I shut the door and go flying into my office. I toss my drink back in one gulp and feel the effect of the whiskey burning in my chest. I stamp my foot in frustration. I pace back and forth. This is not good. Mikhail and Rebeca's extracurricular activities seem to be more serious than I thought. I sit in my chair and swivel it from side to side until I start to feel dizzy. I can't tell if I'm dizzy from the Jack or from the swiveling or a combination of both, but I don't want to hurl, so I stop swiveling and start rapping out a beat on the desktop with two pencils. I'm so full of conflicting emotions that I'm all fidgety. And I'm so distracted by my drumming that at first I don't realize that someone is knocking on my door, but it gets louder and more persistent until finally I get up and stagger toward the door. I fling it open and Q is standing there.

"Hey, there's some woman named Julia outside. She's from *Ozone* magazine and says she wants to talk to you," he tells me.

"Oh, okay," I hiccup.

"Boss Lady, are you okay?" he asks.

"I'm great," I say. "Don't I look great?"

"Yes, you do," Q says, and then he starts laughing. "Are you drunk?"

"You betta know it," I tell him. "Drunk as a skunk."

"Oh my God," he says and keeps laughing. "Girl, you better straighten up if you're going to be talking to anyone from the media. Do you have a coffeepot in here?" he asks.

"Not just a coffeepot, but an espresso maker," I say.

"I'm gonna fix you some, okay?" he says.

"Why do people in Miami call espresso Cuban coffee? I've always wanted to know that. I mean, espresso is Italian. Is it because a Cuban person is making it that they call it Cuban coffee?" I ask with a giggle. I check out Q's ass while he makes the coffee.

"Damn! You got a nice ass," I slur.

"Uh, thanks, Boss Lady," he says. I can tell he's a little embarrassed, which makes me giggle. I'm still giggling when Q hands me a cup of steaming hot espresso minutes later. "Drink it all," he orders.

"I'm not *that* drunk," I tell him. "I don't need no coffee."

"Well, just in case," he says, making me drink.

I gulp down the coffee, inch closer to Q, and ask him, "Do you think that if we met under different circumstances, if you never knew me as Kaos's girl or Mikhail's girl, do you think you would have been attracted to me?"

Q looks really uncomfortable, which just spurs me on. "Sure," he says. But even though he's uncomfortable, he doesn't budge an inch. And why should he? I'm naked save for some strategically placed body paint and crystals, and I'm pressed up against his body. He may have integrity, but he isn't dead.

I lean forward and part my lips. Q pulls away. I grab him by the sleeves and pull him toward me again. Q pulls away again but it takes him longer to do it.

"Don't you want me?" I whisper.

"Boss Lady . . ." Q begins.

"Hmm," I say as I keep leaning closer and closer to him and wrap my arms around his neck.

"This is not the time or place," he says.

"When?" I ask. "Where?"

"I don't know the answer to that. When the time is right, if the time is right, we'll both know," he says. "But for now you need to go talk to this lady, Julia, okay? Get out there and handle your business, Ms. Bobbi."

I feel like a fool for throwing myself at Q. He's right; this is not the time or the place. I straighten Q's tie for him and kiss him on the cheek.

"One day," I tell him with a smile. "Maybe."

He smiles back at me and kisses me on the forehead. "I hope so."

We step out of my office together and smack into Mikhail and Rebeca, who are hand in hand and heading back out to the party. This is a truly awkward moment; we're all waiting for someone to speak first. Rebeca doesn't look guilty. She looks smug, but I'm sure I look like I just got caught with my hand in the cookie jar. Q, however, is as cool as the breeze.

"Good evening, Mikhail. Evening, Rebeca," he says.

"Good evening," Mikhail says, eyeing us suspiciously. I give the look right back to him.

"Ms. Bobbi, that magazine publisher is waiting," Q says to me. "If you just follow me, I'll take you to her."

"Magazine publisher?" Rebeca asks. I want to scream at her that this is none of her business, but I don't.

"*Ozone* magazine," Q says to Mikhail. "They want to talk about a feature. I'm going to make sure Bobbi gets through this crowd undisturbed."

"Good idea," he says, but he still doesn't drop Rebeca's hand. I'm so tempted to say something, but before I can, Q ushers me out of the hallway and back into the club.

THE NIGHT ENDS AT 5:00 AM. MIKHAIL, DIMITRI, AMARA, AND I head home while Q, Rebeca, and the rest of the staff tend to closing things up. I want so badly to confront Mikhail, but I don't know where to begin.

"Well how do you feel?" Mikhail asks as sweetly as if nothing had happened between him and Rebeca earlier.

"Great. Just a little tired is all."

"Well, you're officially South Beach royalty," he tells me. "And this is just the beginning for you."

"You think?" I ask.

"I most certainly do. I never invest in anything that fails," he says.

"So is that what I am to you?" I ask him. "An investment?" I wonder what the return is that he's hoping for.

"Of course not! You are that and other things," he says with a wink. "You're my sweet angel." *Bullshit*, I say to myself. *You spent the night searching for buried treasure between Rebeca's legs.*

*Everything is business for Mikhail. Everything.* That's what Amara told me aboard *Krizia*. I wonder just what business Mikhail has with Rebeca that he has to eat her pussy to accomplish.

"And what is Rebeca to you?" I ask brazenly. Mikhail doesn't seem to get the hint.

"Why do you ask that? You know what she does," he says, innocently.

"Do I?" I ask, testing him. "What I know is that she's a nasty little bitch," I sneer.

"Rebeca isn't a warm fuzzy person. She takes some getting used to. But she's very good at what she does; she's very efficient," Mikhail replies. "I don't know where I'd be without her," he goes on. "She's an integral part of so many of my businesses."

"I'll bet she is," I say sarcastically, but it's lost on Mikhail.

When we arrive at the house the sun is coming up. Mikhail doesn't get out of the car. He just pulls up to the front door and tells me that he's meeting Rebeca for breakfast.

"This early?" I ask. "The sun isn't even up. And haven't you spent enough time with her? Damn, Mikhail, I'd think you were fucking her from the way you two seem joined at the hip," I say. Surely Mikhail will notice that I'm on to him now and confess. But what will his knowing accomplish? I'm not sure what it is I expect to gain from busting him. A tear-filled, heartfelt apology perhaps? Promises to get rid of her maybe? But it doesn't matter what I expect. Mikhail just laughs at me.

"Get some rest," he says. "You're sleepy and you're getting cranky. I'll be back shortly, and I'll make up for lost time." He flashes me a smile and rolls down the long driveway and off the estate, as I stand there and watch his taillights disappear into the dawn. I have no intentions of letting him make anything up to me. I just want to know what Mikhail is getting out of all of this, and why he even needed me in the first place, because Rebeca seems to be all the woman Mikhail needs.

SASCHA THE PUBLICIST IS EARNING EVERY DIME WE'RE PAYING her. She scored me a photo shoot at the club for *Ocean Drive* magazine! They're doing a profile and photo spread on the renovation of Babylon and little old me. Never in my wildest dreams did I think I would be modeling anywhere for any reason whatsoever. It's not that I don't have the looks because, if I say so myself, I'm a cutie. But does the world really need another child of someone famous strutting the run-way? I'll leave that to Paris and Nicky Hilton, Ivanka Trump, and Brittny Gastineau. I don't knock their hustle at all, but I've got more going for me than good looks and famous DNA, and I intend for the world to know it. Plus, I'm kind of thick and I like to eat. I'm not starving myself to look all "ana" for any reason.

I watch *America's Next Top Model* and see those girls going through so much just to get other people to say they're pretty and I've just never wanted to be a part of it. They all seem so insecure. If that had been me, annoying ass Tyra Banks and that old bitch Janice Dickinson would have gotten the smack down the first time they said something out of pocket, be-cause they might be nice looking, but they are far from per-fect. I've seen girls in the hood in Miami that run circles around those broads. Still it's going to be fun to pretend to be a supermodel just for a day. Just as long as no one says any-thing stupid, like my face isn't exactly symmetrical or that my forehead is too short or that I should lose twenty pounds.

I'm so geeked to be doing my first magazine feature. I hope it's the first of many. The process is actually really fun and exciting; I arrive at the club at one in the afternoon and I'm immediately whisked into hair and makeup, which are actu-ally a beautician and a makeup artist that have set up camp in the ladies' restroom. They inform me that the shoot and interview are going to last about eight hours in total, includ-ing a lunch break, and that we're going to go through a variety of different looks.

I go through several different extremes. The stylists curl my hair and then they straighten it. They pin in hair exten-sions to make my hair super huge, and they also have me rock a short, cropped wig that frames my head like a sleek cap. My makeup goes from subdued to surreal and back again. And my wardrobe ranges from what could only be described as business/sexy to nearly nude, and everything in between. The cool thing is that they snap Polaroids and take pictures for me with my digital camera to capture all the looks for posterity. The wardrobe stylist even lets me keep a couple of the outfits that I fall in love with from the shoot. But I have to promise to wear them again because they're from the fashion line that she's trying to launch. The pieces and their designer are so nice that I promise her I'll break my (new) rule of never being seen in something more than once just for her.

The magazine offered to arrange catering for the whole deal, but I decide to have one of my favorite little soul food spots located in Overtown called People's Bar-B-Que to provide the craft service. I don't want any brown rice and vegetables; I want good old-fashioned meat and potatoes. The staff on the photo shoot all seem to be surprised when a table is filled with serving platters and dishes of collard greens, cornbread, baked macaroni and cheese, fried chicken and catfish, baked chicken and whiting, salad, coleslaw, and candied yams.

The writer interviews me while I'm posing for pictures from behind the turntables; she says she wants my authentic personality so she wants to talk to me where I'm most at ease. I practice scratching while she asks me questions, and very candid ones at that. She asks for my opinion on interracial relationships, on the state of hip-hop, about my family, and what it feels like to be called "the black Paris Hilton," something I had no idea that anyone referred to me as.

I answer frankly and honestly and hope to God she doesn't misquote me or distort my words. I don't want to end up looking like an asshole. The writer tells me that I did a great job (don't they always say that?) and that she's going to pull a few strings to make sure that the article will appear in the December 2006 issue of the magazine. She also assures me that pictures from the club will be featured in the Shot on Site section of *Ocean Drive* whenever I want.

Sascha is pleased to hear the news when I tell her, and she lets me know that requests for additional interviews are pouring in from every publication, from *Essence* and *Black Enterprise* to *Scratch*, *XXL*, and *Vibe*. She tells me that I'm a natural at handling the press since I've pretty much grown up doing it, but that it wouldn't hurt to go through some additional media training as a sort of refresher course. I agree and she makes arrangements and then she tells me the coup de grace, that I've got some offers for a few endorsement deals on the table. I've been offered a chance to be a spokesperson for Numark, an invitation to walk the catwalk in a Heatherette fashion show and do some print ads for them, and my name is on the guest list for just about every hot event in town.

I'm the darling of the social scene and it's a strange transition for me to go from worker to guest. Even when I was on the cruise with Mikhail, I felt as if it were more business than pleasure. I didn't feel like I was a part of that whole private jet set; I just thought I entertained them. When I'm DJ'ing, I'm an outsider, I'm on the fringes. I choose to be as involved or as uninvolved as I want. I can be seen and heard but not have to be all caught up in the bullshit and phoniness of the club scene if I don't want to. But now I don't have a choice. I'm going to have to be social and play well with others, and being the rebel that I am, I don't know how all of it is going to work out.

But apparently, my fears are for naught. I am the toast of the Atlantic coast, attending cocktail parties on SoBe and formal events in Palm Beach with Mikhail by my side. He still doesn't know that I know about his and Rebeca's affair. He plays the role of the doting boyfriend to a T when we're out in public. And I learn a thing or two from Mikhail's duality. I can turn on the charm I didn't know I had and schmooze with the best of them.

Everything is fine and I'm sailing along the scene smoothly until Mikhail and I attend a party at Casa Casuarina, the former Gianni Versace mansion. I'm the DJ at the party, which is held in celebration of a new clothing line called Dika, named after its creator, a model turned fashion designer. Dika is everything you think of when you hear the word supermodel. She's amazingly tall, around six feet two, and is all legs. She's got that ambiguous look that is so popular now; when you look at her you have no idea what her heritage is; she could be Latin, Asian, or African American. Her skin is creamy and smooth, her eyes are dark and exotic, and her hair is an unruly curly mop that sprouts out from her head in copper-colored ringlets. She has a very faint sprinkling of freckles across her nose and cheeks, and she's wearing a bright orange gown from her collection of sleek and sexy clothes that have more than a hint of South Beach style.

A party that honors a classy stunner like Dika is the last place I expect to see Misty Blue, but she's there, dressed inappropriately in a baby blue dress that would be more at home on the stage of a strip club than at an exclusive party at the luxe Mediterranean-style villa. It's floor length, with a slit up to Canada, and is made of stretchy Lycra that is dusted with glitter. Not sequins, not rhinestones, not crystals, but glitter. Her boobs are spilling out of the top, and her nipples are erect and beaconing men to come hither. She's even rocking the proverbial stripper/hooker clear platform shoes.

Misty checks me out behind the turntables then strides right over to Mikhail, who is standing with Dimitri and a bunch of men sipping on the signature cocktail, a huge mo-

jito served in a coconut shell "glass." She thinks that I won't
do anything or say anything to stop her while I'm working,
and she's right. I keep doing my thing, because I am not
about to let that tramp distract me from my duties, but I do
take notice that she and Mikhail disappear into the night.

I'm burning up inside; not because I'm jealous, but because I am sick of tolerating the blatant disrespect from
chicks like Misty and Rebeca. I've had it up to here with
pretending that everything is cool. These hos could at least
be discreet; they've got me fucked up if they think that I'm
going to continue to let them keep throwing themselves at
Mikhail in my presence and the presence of everyone on the
scene. This isn't about feelings, it's about the principle of the
matter. These broads obviously don't take me seriously. If I
keep letting them get away with shit like this, my reputation
could be irreparably damaged. Folks will start treating me like
I'm a joke and I've worked too hard and sacrificed too much
to get to this point.

I take out my frustrations on the turntables and crossfader,
cutting records up like a pair of dressmaker's shears. The
dance floor is packed, and people are shaking and bouncing
and grinding away. It's one of my best performances ever;
maybe I should spin angry more often. Even the elegant and
sophisticated Dika climbs on top of a giant speaker and starts
to get her groove on until she sweats. I finally see Misty and
Mikhail reappear. Mikhail is walking steps ahead of Misty,
pretending he can't hear her, but she's obviously upset. She's
shouting something at his back until Mikhail motions to
Dimitri, and he swiftly grabs Misty by the shoulders and
makes a hasty exit, practically dragging her.

"What was that bitch doing here?" I ask Mikhail as soon
as my set is done and supermodel/DJ Sky Nellor takes her
turn at bat.

"Bobbi, she's gone now. Don't make a scene," he says, quickly.

"Not going to. I just want to know why the two of you disappeared and what went down," I say, and guide Mikhail away from the action of the party to duck behind one of the manicured hedges. "I want to know why you've got her cheap silver glitter all over you."

"Look, I told you that there is nothing going on between Misty and me. Nothing," he says firmly.

"What, just like there's nothing going on with you and Rebeca?" I ask.

"There's nothing going on between me and Rebeca. You are being paranoid," Mikhail states.

"Please! I know you're cheating on me with her," I say. Finally it is out on the table.

"You don't know what you're talking about," he says.

"You don't know what I know! I saw you and Rebeca together the night of the opening. I caught the two of you in her office. You were eating her pussy like your life depended on it. And I know about Misty's side hustles for you. I know that you pimp her out to help your business."

I am silenced by a slap across the face. This isn't one of his normal bedroom slaps either. This is an Iceberg Slim, p-i-m-p slap with the back of his hand.

"You motherfucker," I yell at him. "You're the one cheating on me, and you hit me? We're over. You'll be hearing from my lawyers about Babylon," I spit and start to walk away. Mikhail grabs a handful of my hair and yanks me back to him.

"If you're smart, you'll stay out of things that don't concern you and you won't bring any lawyers into this. Rebeca and I are what Rebeca and I are. It doesn't concern you. And just forget about what you think you know about

Misty. I'm not sleeping with her. That's been over for a long time," he says.

"Oh, so you *were* fucking her? You were fucking a common prostitute and then you come back and fuck me raw dog with your dirty dick? You've got me all fucked up," I say. Mikhail still has me by the hair, but I take the heel of my hand and slap him upside the head with it as hard as I can.

Mikhail balls up his fist and clocks me one good time in the eye. I fall to the ground, but I'm so furious that I can barely feel the blow. I tackle Mikhail by the legs, sacking him like a defensive tackle on the gridiron. We wrestle and writhe on the ground, Mikhail trying to restrain me. It's not an easy job. I'm a whirling dervish of fury, swinging my arms, trying to scratch him, bite him, and kick him. My knee makes contact with his groin *hard*. As he balls up in pain I run out of the party and down Ocean Drive in a now filthy and ripped sheer printed chiffon, off-the-shoulder Versace dress and bare feet. I don't even stop to pick up my shoes. For all I know, this motherfucker will try to kill me.

I don't stop running until I've reached a café a few blocks down the road and duck inside. Of course one of the servers tries to stop me from entering since I'm not wearing shoes, but another one, a guy that I slept with a couple years back, lets me in. He escorts me to the restroom, and comes back a few moments later with a pair of flip-flops. I don't know who they belong to or where he got them from, but at that moment I don't care; I'm no Britney Spears, so the thought of being barefoot in a public bathroom makes me sick to my stomach. I gratefully slip the shoes on my feet.

"I always knew that mouth of yours would get you into trouble one day," quips Tony, the server I used to bone. "Who'd you go off on this time, Ms. Bobbi?"

I start crying. I mean straight up bawling. I'm immediately

ashamed and I cover my face with my hands. Tony locks the door to the ladies' room.

"Are you okay?" he asks. "You aren't hurt, are you?"

"I'm fine. I just had a fight," I explain, my voice trailing off.

"Want a line?" he asks. I haven't touched coke in years, mainly because for me it's like potato chips. I can't stop with just one bump or one line.

"Got anything else?" I ask.

"Tina?" he says, referring to crystal meth. No way am I going to do crank. The last thing I need is to be on fast forward for the next eighteen hours.

"I need to relax," I tell him.

"Vicodin," he says. *What the fuck is this guy, a drugstore?*

"Cool. But as you can see I don't have a purse. It'll have to be a gift," I say.

"No problem," he says. "Just make sure I don't have to wait in line forever when I come to Babylon. I heard you're doing big things over there."

"Yeah," I say dryly.

"Is everything okay?" he asks again as I pop the Vicodin into my mouth and swallow it dry.

"Peachy fucking keen," I say as I wait for the muscle relaxant to begin to take effect.

# CHAPTER TWELVE

FROM THE CAFÉ, I HOP IN A CAB AND HEAD TO MY OLD condo. I'm so glad that I didn't sell it, and although I was looking for someone to rent it out, it's not occupied and some of my old furniture is still there. I don't have my purse or keys, but the doorman lets me in when he sees my disheveled state, and offers to send someone out if I need anything. When I finally take a look at myself in the mirror, I start crying. My mouth is swollen and my eye is black. I can't believe that my boyfriend actually beat me. Luckily my pity party doesn't last long, and I doze off from the effects of too much stress and the Vicodin.

I camp out at my old crib for a couple of days, but I know that I have to face the music at some point. Pissed at Mikhail or not, I have a business to run, and there are things that need to be done. I'm not sure what kind of vibe Mikhail is on. He might still be on some old Ike Turner bullshit, so the last place I want to go is the estate. But I have no money, no credit cards, no ID, and no clothes to change into. I've decided that I'll stay at my place until some alternate arrangements can be made, but I desperately need to get back to the home I share with Mikhail in order to get some necessities.

Luckily, I have a credit card on file with Take Out Taxi, so I can get food from my favorite restaurants delivered. I order a pizza and a calzone, and decide to pig out and then face my problems on a full, if not bloated, stomach.

I turn on the television and absentmindedly surf the channels while I wait for my food to arrive. I know I look like a hot mess, because when the deliveryman arrives he gives me a look that says *What the hell happened to you?* The ring around my eye hasn't gotten any lighter, and my top lip is still puffy.

"This was on your doorstep," he says, handing me a newspaper. It's a mistake—I don't subscribe—but I decide to take the copy of the *Herald* anyway.

"I just got plastic surgery," I say to him since he's staring at my bruised and swollen face. He nods knowingly and leaves. Then I settle on the couch, dig into my food, and start thumbing through the paper.

The first thing that grabs my attention is the headline of the local news section. ADULT FILM STAR FOUND DEAD IN APPARENT DRUG OVERDOSE. A large picture of Misty Blue is beneath it. I almost choke on my pizza. I can't believe it! Misty, dead? I read the article quickly. *Misty Blue, adult film star and Russian national, real name Ivanka Zernova, age twenty-six, was found dead of a heroin overdose in her Coconut Grove apartment.* I sit there and let it sink in. It's no secret that I was no fan of Misty's, and there were many times when I wanted to kill her myself. But I had no idea that she was some sort of junkie, and I couldn't help but wonder if her overdose was an intentional suicide. She was probably a very unhappy woman, and plenty of porn stars have offed themselves when life just got to be too much. Russian national, huh? I guess that's part of the reason why she and Mikhail were so buddy-buddy.

I pick up the phone to call Amara to see if she's heard the news.

"Hello?" Amara says when she picks up the phone. She sounds a little hoarse, like she's coming down with a cold.

"Amara, it's me, Bobbi. Are you okay?" I ask. "You sound sick."

"Bobbi, baby. I'm so glad to hear from you. I was just sleeping, but I have been worried sick about you."

"Worried sick about me? Why?" I ask Amara.

"Baby, Mikhail called and asked if I'd heard from you. He said you've been missing for days. He sounded really concerned." Oh yeah, I did have my cell phone shut off, considering Mikhail had been calling and texting me like crazy.

"I'm not missing, Amara. I'm at home," I tell her.

"But that's impossible, baby. Mikhail said you hadn't been home in days."

"I haven't been to *his* home in days. I've been at *my* house. I have my own condo, and Mikhail knows exactly where it is," I say. "I just had the doorman say that the unit had been rented if anyone asked for me."

"So what happened?" Amara asks.

"Mikhail didn't tell you what happened?" I ask.

"No, he didn't. Are you going to tell me?"

"Mikhail and I had a fight. A huge fight," I say.

"Over what?" she asks.

*Wow, where to start?* "More like over *whom*. Who's our favorite person to argue about? Misty Blue, of course," I say.

"That hag. She's vile. I don't know why you let her get to you. Mikhail has the woman that he wants," she says. "He's not interested in that whore."

"He *wasn't* interested in that whore. Misty is dead," I say dryly.

"Dead? Baby, what are you talking about?" she asks. She obviously hasn't heard the news.

"Misty was found dead in her apartment in the wee hours of the morning, according to the newspaper," I tell her.

"What?"

"You heard me. Misty is dead," I say. "It was in yesterday's *Herald*. It's so weird because I was ready to kill her just a few nights ago, and now she's dead."

"Careful what you say, Bobbi. You don't want anyone poking around in your affairs and considering you a suspect," Amara says.

"I doubt that would happen. I've got an alibi. I've been gorging myself like a pig nonstop. The delivery guys of every joint in town can vouch for my whereabouts," I say with a laugh. "Besides, Misty wasn't murdered, she overdosed. But even if I was going to kill someone, Misty wasn't at the top of my hit list, Mikhail is."

"What happened, baby?" Amara asks. "Tell me everything."

"I was DJ'ing at a party for Dika, the model. You know her, right? Anyway, of all people, Misty shows up and as usual she's all over Mikhail. But I can't confront her because I'm working. She and Mikhail disappear, and then reappear with Misty crying her big blue eyes out. Then Dimitri drags her out in a hurry. I confronted Mikhail and things got real ugly real quick."

"You say that Dimitri dragged Misty out of the party?" Amara asks me.

"Yeah. Misty was making a fool of herself in front of everyone and trying to put Mikhail on front street," I say. "Only I have no idea why."

"So Dimitri was the last person to see her alive?" Amara asks.

"I don't know. Knowing Misty, I doubt it. I'm sure she had a gentleman caller or two or twenty before she kicked the bucket," I say.

"Finish telling me what happened that night. Don't leave anything out," Amara says, dramatically.

"Uh, okay," I say. "Where was I? Oh yeah . . . I confronted him about sleeping with Rebeca . . ."

"Mikhail and Rebeca? You've got to be mistaken," Amara says.

"I saw it with my very own eyes, Amara. It was the night of the opening after my set."

"Why didn't you tell me, baby?" she asks.

"I don't know. I didn't feel like talking about it, I guess. It's embarrassing. Here I am, the toast of South Beach. Everyone seems to think that I have it all. But it's like I'm one of Mikhail's possessions. It's suffocating. Anyway, I told him that I knew about the two of them, and then Mikhail slapped me, and all hell broke loose. I was not raised to let some man whoop on me, so I fought back. We had a knock-down, drag-out brawl that resulted in me having a great big shiny black eye and camping out at my crib. I lost my brand-new Louboutin sandals too. I'm almost as mad about that as I am about him jacking up my face," I tell her.

"Mikhail hit you?"

"Yes. He hit me hard as fuck, ma. I said we had a knock-down, drag-out fight and I meant it literally. We are so over. I can't deal with the drama. What is it about Mikhail that is making broads go crazy?" I ask.

"I—I don't know," Amara stammers.

"What's wrong with you?" I ask.

"Nothing," she says quickly. But I'm not buying it.

"Amara, this is me, Bobbi. I know that something is wrong, girl," I say.

"How did you say that Misty died again?"

"She OD'd," I remind her, sighing. "She was a druggie or something. You know how that goes."

"There's no mention of anything suspicious," she says.

"No, Amara," I snap. "Why are you focusing so much on Misty? I've told you that Mikhail has gone all psycho on me and all you can think about is the dead porn star. What, do you think she was trying to kill herself?" I ask. "Is that why you're so stuck on Misty?"

"I—I don't know," Amara stammers.

"Can you say anything besides 'I don't know'? God, Amara. I'm trying to figure out what move to make next. What should I do?" I ask her.

"Bobbi, baby, there is only one thing for you to do. Get out," she says.

"What do you mean get out? I can't just leave my club and all my hard work. Besides, if I leave now I leave with nothing. There's a clause in my contract for early termination. I'd have to pay a fine of five million. Why should I suffer anymore? He already beat me up. My face is tore up."

"Consider yourself lucky. Mikhail very rarely shows restraint when he explodes. He can be very dangerous once you're on his bad side."

"His bad side? I didn't do anything wrong," I say.

"Oh there's something," she tells me. "Have you done anything that would anger him?"

"Besides confronting him about Rebeca and Misty and his cheating and whoremongering?"

"Yes, besides that. Throwing those things in his face would definitely anger him, but not to the point where he'd beat you. He'd consider an act like that beneath him. It's not his way."

"Well, it was his way the other night."

"Think, Bobbi. Did you overhear something? See him doing something? Oh God, Bobbi, please tell me you aren't cheating on him," Amara begs.

"Calm down. I haven't seen or heard anything out of the ordinary. I haven't done anything! Everything had been cool between us until Misty showed up and I confronted Mikhail," I say. I think about how red Mikhail got when I accused him of being threatened by black men.

"Do you think? Nah, that couldn't be it."

"What couldn't be it?"

"Well, he thinks I spend too much time with Q. I accused him of being threatened by black men and he got really, really red. I'm not sure if he was mad or embarrassed, though."

"Are you having an affair with Q?" she asks.

"No. Of course not. I'm not the one fucking the help, Mikhail is! I'll admit that Q is sexy, and well, once I stepped to him. But I was drunk. And no one saw us and nothing happened," I tell her. "That's the truth."

"Then that probably isn't it," Amara says. "If he thought you were fucking Q, both of you would be swimming with the fishes. He'd kill you both."

"If he *thought* we were fucking?" I ask. "Shit, he's a crazy motherfucker!"

"Well, if he thought you were cheating he'd get evidence first. *Then* he'd kill you. Mikhail never acts unless he's absolutely sure."

I think of the abortion but quickly dismiss it. Mikhail said he'd kill me if I had an abortion, and I'm still standing, so he couldn't possibly know. I covered my tracks well, and Mikhail hasn't brought up any suspicions of me being pregnant ever since. And he hasn't been around enough to know if I've gotten a period since then or not.

"I'm telling you, there's nothing. Look, I know you're

Dimitri's girl and Mikhail's friend, but you're also my friend. Why are you blaming the victim?" I yell at her.

"It isn't that, baby, I promise you," she says. "Listen carefully, Bobbi. I think that Dimitri killed Misty."

"What?"

"Oh, Bobbi, don't you see it? You're right there. You've experienced Mikhail's wrath firsthand. Don't you know what kind of person Mikhail is and what happens when you cross guys like him? Remember how I told you that Dimitri is the one who keeps all the captains in line? That includes getting rid of anyone who poses a threat to Mikhail."

"Okay, let me get this straight. You think that Dimitri killed Misty because she posed a threat to Mikhail? How?" I ask.

"Misty knew something she shouldn't have," Amara says.

"You say that like you know what it is," I reply.

Amara is silent.

"Amara, are you still there? Hello?"

"We shouldn't talk about this over the phone," she says. "It's not safe."

"But when?" I ask. "Are you coming to Miami for New Year's?" I ask, but Amara doesn't answer.

"I have to go now, Bobbi," Amara says.

"Wait a minute, Amara," I yell into the phone.

"Watch your back, okay, baby? Be careful," she says, and the line goes dead.

I'm totally freaked out. Amara is always calm, cool, and collected. She's been the voice of reason, but now it seems that even she can't rationalize remaining involved with Mikhail. She was definitely scared. And she left me hanging without a clue except for the fact that my life could be in danger. What the fuck am I going to do?

I nearly have a coronary when the phone rings. I take some deep breaths to calm down. It's just the doorman, I tell myself, picking it up. No one else would call besides my mother; I never ever give out my home number.

"Bobbi?" Mikhail's voice barks on the other end.

"Mikhail?" I ask, shocked. I look at the caller ID box too late. "How did you get this number?" I ask. "It's unlisted."

"That means nothing to me. I've had this number for quite some time. But I only now confirmed that you were there."

"How did you do that?" I ask him.

"You just spoke with Amara, didn't you?" he asks. I can hear his sinister laughter on the other end.

"How did you . . ."

"Never mind how I knew, I just do. Bobbi, you need to come home immediately," he says.

"There's no way I can do that. I have a black eye and a busted lip. How do I know that there isn't more where that came from?" For all I know Mikhail has tapped Amara's phone and knows everything we discussed. There's no way I'm going back.

"How do you know there's not worse if you don't come home?" he counters.

"I don't," I whisper. "But maybe it's a chance I'm willing to take."

"I don't think so," he says. "Come home and we'll talk," he says.

"What's there to talk about?" I ask cautiously. For all I know, *we'll talk* could be code for "say hello to my little friend."

"Don't make me force you to come home, Bobbi. Don't make this harder than it has to be. It's better if you just come of your own volition."

"Force me?" I ask, unable to hide the fear in my voice.

"Things will be better for you if you come home. If you come home, I promise you that I will not lay a hand on you," he says. His promises don't mean shit! "If you don't, I'll see to it that you lose everything. You know this. Your reputation will be shot. I will ruin you. Your life, if I decide that you shall have a life at all, will not be so good. No matter where you go. You can't hide from me. I have eyes everywhere. And I have no problem breaking you in every way."

"I see," I say. "You haven't left me with many choices."

"Naturally," he says.

I weigh my options. I can take my chances and run, but to where? I can't go to my parents' house. There's no way I can drag them into this mess. And I can't just live on the lam. If I stay here, I'm dead meat. I don't have a choice but to go back to Mikhail.

"I'll be there shortly," I say.

"Don't make me wait too long," he says, and hangs up the phone.

"YOU MUSTN'T EVER DISAPPEAR LIKE THAT AGAIN. IS THAT UN-derstood?" Mikhail admonishes me upon my return to the mansion.

"What did you expect me to do?" I ask him. "I wasn't raised to be a punching bag. I can't allow you to beat me like that, Mikhail," I tell him. It's my natural instinct to stand up for myself, but I'm scared as hell of how Mikhail will react.

"You bring things like that on yourself. Bobbi, you need to stay out of matters that don't concern you. I don't want to hear you speak of Misty's involvement in my business," he says.

"You know that won't happen. Misty is dead," I say. "I read it in the papers."

"Yes, Misty is dead. Because Misty, like you, did not know when to be quiet," Mikhail tells me.

"What are you saying?"

"I am saying that unless you want Misty's fate to befall you, you will continue doing what I need you to do. Misty wanted to go her own way, but I couldn't allow that. She held too many secrets and she threatened to reveal them."

"Well, I don't know anything," I tell him. "You don't have to worry about that. I don't want anything to happen to Babylon. It means everything to me. I'd never betray you."

"Good. Then you will have no problem continuing to do what I need you to do."

"What is it that you need me to do?" I ask quietly. I'm afraid of what Mikhail might ask of me and I hold my breath. But I'm willing to tell him whatever he wants to hear.

"It's simple. You must continue to be the face of Babylon. You're a good girl, even if you pretend to be a badass. You have no record of criminal activity. You come from a good family. You were born and bred to be in the spotlight. You give me a certain amount of credibility. Sure, I may know some thugs, some insidious characters. I may associate with them. But it's because of my beautiful black girlfriend and business partner. She's hip-hop, but surely she's no criminal. Her father is one of the most prominent attorneys in the nation. You are the perfect front," he says.

I'm in shock. "You mean that I've been a mark all along? You were using me?"

"Bobbi," he says, walking toward me. I start to back up. "Must we really be like that?" he asks. "I told you I wouldn't hit you."

I keep backing up until I back myself, literally, into a corner. Mikhail reaches out and touches my shoulders. I wince. "See, I'm not going to hurt you." He looks at me with what I swear is kindness in his eyes. "Bobbi, I was using you, yes. But I wasn't misusing you, and there is a difference. I really do love you. Can't you see that I'm doing all this for your own good? I'm your savior, Bobbi. I rescued you from a life of boredom, of mediocrity, and I placed you on a pedestal. I've made you a queen. Make no mistake, you are the queen of this empire. What I have with Rebeca and what I had with Misty pales in comparison to what I feel for you. You're my heart," he says. He takes my hand and places it over his heart. "My heart beats for you." He kisses my palm, then the back of my hand, and wraps me in his arms.

I'm dumbfounded, confused, and yet still very, very afraid. My lips are trembling, as is the rest of my body, but I'm determined not to let him see me cry. I'm not sure why, but I know that I can't appear totally defeated right now. My gut tells me that it's better to go along with Mikhail willingly, or to at least appear that way. I want him to think that I'm on his side while I figure out a way to get myself out of this mess. Mikhail, whether he did the deed or not, is a murderer. I don't need to know about anything else he's into. Murder is enough. I want out.

"Come, sweet angel," he says. "Let us make love."

I want to run, scream bloody murder or fire, do anything so that someone, anyone, can rescue me. But there's no one to come to my aid, so I don't run. Instead, I go through the motions. I pretend it isn't rape, that Mikhail isn't making me give him my body against my will. Because what good would a physical struggle be? But make no mistake, I will fight him. What Mikhail doesn't realize is that no matter how backed into a corner he thinks I am, he doesn't own me. He may be controlling my body right now, but not my mind, my heart, or my soul.

I RETURN TO WORK AFTER THE INCIDENT, SHINER AND ALL. After all, Mikhail and I agreed that we'd continue business as usual. Maybe in doing so I can find something, anything that I can use as leverage to escape Mikhail's clutches with my body, my rep, and at least some of my finances intact. I rock a pair of oversized Chanel frames to hide the bruises until they go away. I wear Audrey Hepburn–inspired clothes, circa *Breakfast at Tiffany's*, in an effort to not look like a total fool wearing huge dark shades indoors.

"What's up with the Grace Kelly look?" Q says when he sees me.

"It's not Grace Kelly, it's Audrey Hepburn. I just feel inspired by her glamour right now," I say, avoiding his gaze.

"And I thought it was to cover that black eye," he says. I pretend not to hear him.

"You're not fooling anyone," he says. "At least you're not fooling me and I don't know why you'd try. You've been missing in action and now you come back in costume. Come on. I know Mikhail clocked you at that party at the Versace mansion."

"You're obviously misinformed," I tell him. I don't look at him; I pretend to be engrossed in a pile of receipts.

"Yeah, whatever, Boss Lady. But if you think that people aren't talking and that no one knows, you're wrong."

"It's just gossip," I say. "You shouldn't believe everything you hear."

"Don't have to. I know the signs a mile away," he says.

"Well, in my case, you're misreading the signs."

"If you say so, but I think I know a thing or two about domestic violence."

"What, did you see an after-school special?" I ask sardonically.

"No, I wish I had. My mother was battered. She used to make excuses, cover her bruises. Kind of like you're doing now. She thought things would get better. They didn't. She said she was going to leave, but she didn't. She pretended that nothing was wrong. But it was. Her boyfriend beat her to death," Q says.

I immediately feel like a complete and total asshole. "Q, I'm really sorry about your mom. That's really fucked up, but I'll be fine. I appreciate the concern, but everything's cool."

"It isn't cool. I don't believe any woman deserves to be hit under any circumstances. Only cowards hit women."

"Cowards and complete psychos," I say.

"Ain't nobody so bad they can't get their ass whooped," Q says. "The bigger they come, the harder they fall."

"Q, look, I'll be honest with you. I want out of this but I can't think of any way. Mikhail will destroy me if I leave. It's that simple. I'm stuck."

"Maybe not," he says.

"How?" I ask.

"Don't worry about how. Just know that every dog has his day."

"You're not going to do anything crazy, are you?" I ask him. But I want him to do something crazy, like kill Mikhail. I want someone, anyone, to step in and fix this for me because I haven't been able to come up with anything on my own.

"Don't worry your pretty little head off, Boss Lady. He's going to do it to himself." I have no idea what Q means by this, but somehow it comforts me enough to get through the day, and I guess that's all that matters.

# CHAPTER THIRTEEN

*December 2006*

WHEN THE ISSUE OF *OCEAN DRIVE* MAGAZINE ARRIVES AT the club, I'm astonished to find that there's a picture of me on the cover. I knew that they were doing a profile, but I really had no idea that they would plaster me on the front. I thought magazine publishers got all freaked out about sales when there was a black woman on the cover alone. It rarely happens, and I damn sure didn't expect it to happen to me. I'm not a huge celebrity or anything, but apparently *Ocean Drive* thinks otherwise.

I peep at the headline, which reads: THE QUEEN OF MIAMI. Mmm hmm, that's right! I excitedly flip through the pages to see a layout of myself that rivals that of any superstar. I look amazing. Watch out Halle, there's a new hottie in town! The article says glowing things about me, raves about my skills, and makes Babylon sound like the greatest place on earth.

"Queen of Miami?" Rebeca asks with more than a trace of sarcasm in her voice when she sees the magazine. She picks it up, looks at me, and rolls her eyes, and then throws it back onto the bar. "That's laying it on a little thick."

"Green is not your color, Rebeca," I tell her with a toss of my hair.

"You might be the queen of Miami," she says, "but I am the queen of Mikhail's heart."

"Well, if you're happy with my leftovers, then fine by me. I love giving to charity," I tell her, spinning on my heels. She can say whatever dim-witted, jealous comeback she thinks of to the crack of my ass as I walk away.

It's a good thing that not all of my staff is such a pain in the ass.

"I've got great news," Sascha tells me a few days later as we're discussing plans for New Year's Eve. "The folks over at MTV want to use Babylon as one of their countdown sites for their New Year's Eve telecast. They're doing something different."

"You're kidding," I scream. "That's great! What do we need to do?"

"Nothing much. They'll send a camera crew and a VJ to handle all the technical stuff. You just have to throw a fabulous party. I know you don't have a problem with that," she says with a smile.

"This is going to be so cool," I say, shaking my head in disbelief. Of all the clubs in the world, of all the clubs on South Beach, MTV chose mine to broadcast from on the biggest night of the year.

"I just had a great idea, Sascha. Tell me you can do it," I say to her, excitedly.

"I can do it. Now tell me what it is," she says with a smile.

"See, Sascha, that's why I like you. You're a cocky broad, just like me."

"Damn straight."

"Well, how about channeling all the girl power we can muster beneath this roof?"

"What do you have in mind?"

"A concert. Not just any concert, but the show of the century. I need you to get in touch with the agents and managers of a few acts. Tell them that they're invited to perform," I say.

"That ought to be easy."

"Well, tell them it's an ensemble performance. They may not want to share the spotlight, but sell it, Sascha. Let their representation know that their clients are going to be a part of making hip-hop history."

"Ooh, sounds juicy. What do you have in mind?"

"You remember that VH1 special, *Divas Live*, don't you . . ."

⁂

ON CHRISTMAS EVE, MY CELL PHONE RINGS IN THE MIDDLE OF the night. I'm tempted not to answer, but my curiosity gets the best of me.

"Hello?" I whisper into the phone.

"Are you alone?" a voice whispers back.

"Yes, Amara, is that you? Where have you been? I've called you a million times. I was worried about you!"

"Where is Mikhail?"

"We sleep in separate rooms. But he's not home. What's going on?"

"Dimitri isn't around, is he?"

"Nuh-uh. I hardly ever see that guy at all. I couldn't tell you where Dimitri is," I say.

"Well, that's not a comforting thought. He's probably after me. Look, I'm going to disappear for a while," she says.

"What does disappear mean? And what is a while?" I ask. "And what do you mean he's probably after you?"

"I mean that he's going to try to kill me. He knows what I've been doing. I don't know how he figured it out. But now I've got to get away," she rambles a mile a minute.

"Amara, what have you been doing?" I ask her.

"I've been playing for both teams and it's catching up to me. I'm going to leave all this behind me. I'm going to become someone else, if possible. For good. I wanted to tell you good-bye."

"What?! Wait! What do you mean good-bye? Amara, what the hell is going on?"

"Baby, I can't explain it all. But you've got to get away from Mikhail before it's too late. Do what you need to do, whatever it is, just get out as soon as you can," Amara says in a hurry. "Bobbi, the authorities are on to him. They have been for a while. They're closing in. I'm so sorry but I couldn't tell you what I was doing before and now there's no time. You've got to believe that I never meant to hurt you. I just didn't have a choice. I am so sorry."

"Amara, I don't like the sound of this at all," I say.

"Baby, just leave," Amara cuts me off. "Bobbi, listen to me. If Mikhail has to go down, he's going to take you with him. That's the kind of person he is. And I guarantee you, he's about to go down. Forget what I told you about him being a Teflon Don. I have to go, baby. Be careful. And Merry Christmas. Kiss kiss, love you much," she says, and the line goes dead.

I rub my eyes and try to call Amara back. It goes straight to voice mail. I try a few more times, but it's no use. Amara isn't going to pick up. I replay our conversation in my head. I've been playing for both teams and it's catching up to me. I consider the unthinkable. Could Amara be a snitch? If she isn't, then what is she running from? I wonder who she's more afraid of, Dimitri or the authorities? And I wonder, what the hell am I supposed to do?

I don't want to be alone right now. I look at the clock. It's 4:30 AM. The club is closed for Christmas Eve and Christmas. Something's got to be held sacred in clubland. We unanimously decided that the staff should be able to spend time with their families, considering how hard they've been working and how much we're going to need them on New Year's Eve. But I don't have any family or friends to share the holiday with.

My parents are off sunning on some island. Mikhail is probably off boning Rebeca somewhere and under the current circumstances I wouldn't want to spend Christmas with him anyway. Amara has gone underground. I have no one to turn to. I debate whether or not to make a phone call. I don't want to seem desperate or crazy. But I'm feeling a little bit of both, so what do I have to lose?

"Merry Christmas," I say, way too cheerfully for four thirty in the morning, when Q answers his phone.

"Bobbi?" he asks.

"Uh, yeah. Were you asleep?" I ask.

"Uh, yeah," he says, like I should have known the answer.

"I'm sorry. You're probably with someone," I say pathetically.

"Boss Lady, I'm not with anyone."

"You're not?" I ask.

"No. I can't spend the holiday with the person I really want to spend it with," he says.

"Is that right?" I ask.

"Yeah," he says.

"Would you settle for spending it with me instead?" I ask.

He laughs. "What are you saying?"

"What are *you* saying?" I ask him. This makes him laugh more.

"Want some company?" I ask.

"Yes," he says.

I hang up the phone, throw on a Juicy Couture velour sweatsuit and my K-Swiss, and put on a baseball cap. I hop in my Rover and head to Miami Shores, where Q lives. His home is cute and small; it's a white stucco ranch-style home with a basketball hoop in the driveway and freshly mowed green grass. There's nothing fancy about it, but it looks absolutely adorable, the perfect bachelor pad.

"Nice crib," I tell him as he greets me at the foyer. He looks too good for words in a pair of light blue basketball shorts and nothing else.

"Thanks," he says.

We go into his den and sit on the couch. We don't say anything at first, we just stare at the TV. Finally, Q wraps his arms around me and holds me tight.

"Merry Christmas, Bobbi," he says.

"Merry Christmas, Q," I tell him, snuggling into the crook of his arm.

Q looks at me and smiles, stroking my face softly.

"I'm glad you're here. I don't know why you're here, but I'm glad," he says.

"I didn't want to be alone," I tell him. I want to tell him everything that's going on with Amara, but I don't want to ruin the moment. Those problems will still be here later, so for now, I'm going to enjoy this time alone with Q.

"Where's Mikhail?" he asks.

"Probably with Rebeca," I say. "I don't want to talk about him, though."

"Me either," he says.

Q pulls me close and kisses me. Our tongues dance sensuously, our kisses growing hungrier and more demanding. I let my hands run over his chiseled chest and powerful biceps and my juices begin to flow like Niagara Falls. I kiss his lips, his neck, and his chest before trailing my way down his ripped abs, lowering his basketball shorts. I drop to my knees and pull out his dick. It's rock hard and feels hot beneath my touch. I can feel it throb as I suck him in slowly, running my tongue over the head of his member until he starts to squirm. Then I deep throat all ten inches of him and then do a little trick I saw in a porno movie; while he is still engulfed in my throat, I stick out my tongue and let it flick over the top of his nut sack.

"Oh my God, girl, how did you do that?" he asks, moaning in ecstasy.

I don't answer; I suck and suck while stroking his shaft. He grabs me softly by the hair and pulls me away, then scoops me up in his arms and carries me to the bed. Q removes my clothes, kissing my skin as it is exposed. He stands there in front of me after I am naked and looks at me lying there on the bed.

"You're so beautiful, Bobbi," he says and then kneels down and spreads my legs. Q licks me until the bedsheets are soaking wet and his face is glistening with my juices. Then he gets a condom, puts it on, and eases himself inside me. I close my eyes and sigh, but Q commands me to look at him. I do as I'm told and our eyes remain locked while we rock in perfect rhythm.

"I'm falling for you, Bobbi," he says.

"I feel the same way," I moan.

Q and I make love over and over, learning each other's bodies and discovering what brings each other pleasure. We kiss, we talk, we laugh. It's a better Christmas than I could have ever imagined. But when we're spent and can't make love anymore the dam bursts and my problems come flooding back.

"You okay?" Q asks me.

"Yeah, I'm cool."

"What are you thinking about?"

"Lots of stuff. My friend, Amara, for one. I spoke with her last night and it scared the shit out of me. She's in trouble, and I think I am too," I say. "If Mikhail ever finds out about this . . ." My voice trails off as I consider what would happen. Q sits up in bed.

"Bobbi, I think there are some things that you should know, before this gets any deeper," he says. "I have no idea how to tell you, and I don't know how you'll feel about me after I do."

"Just tell me," I say. "Give it to me straight."

"You are in trouble. I'm going to do my best to help get you out, but you've got to trust me. Can you do that?" he asks.

"Do I have a choice?"

"You always have a choice. It just doesn't always seem that way. You wanted to know what's been going on at the club. And I've wanted to protect you from this somehow, but I can't keep you in the dark anymore. You need to know what you're up against. Bobbi, Mikhail is laundering money through the club. It's drug money. He doesn't sell drugs, but he washes money for members of Colombian drug cartels. Rebeca introduces them, and she does most of the actual work."

"That's not hard to believe," I say. "This is Miami. Who isn't laundering drug money? I just get the feeling that there's more to Mikhail's empire than that."

"And your feeling is right. Mikhail's got his hands in some of everything. He's also been selling Russian submarines. Mikhail makes billions at this hustle; he doesn't need the Colombians losing shipments. They smuggle the coke into the country using the subs. They travel outside the Coast Guard's radar."

It all sounds like some plot from an action flick. This can't be my life. But as crazy as it sounds, it gets crazier.

"Okay," I say slowly. "Is there anything else?"

"Yeah, unfortunately there is. Mikhail is a player in the sex trade," he says.

"You mean like prostitution?" I ask.

"Yes, but on a deeper level. A part of Mikhail's business includes bringing women from Russia and the Ukraine to America to work as sex slaves."

I think of Misty Blue and wonder if that was how she became involved with Mikhail.

"Bobbi, almost everyone in a position of power at the club is into something dirty," Q continues.

"Like who?"

"Almost everyone," Q says. "Joey J., he's a legit guy. But Sascha's dad is in the Italian mafia in New York. They've got some kind of partnership going, which is how Sascha got the job. She knows what's going on, and it's her job to make Mikhail look like he's on the up-and-up," Q reveals.

"My girl Sascha?" I ask. I like her and she's such a good publicist. It's hard to imagine her doing dirt behind my back.

"Yes."

"Well, you've covered Rebeca and Sascha and Joey. But what about you? What's your part? You told me you assess risk, and you look out for Mikhail. What exactly does this mean?" I ask him.

"I hook the Colombian cartels up with distributors here in Miami."

"You introduce drug suppliers to dealers?" I ask him. "Those are the deals that you broker?"

"Yes," he says.

"Is that all?" I ask.

"That and I tip Mikhail off with what's going on with the authorities. I've got some connections with the police and the feds."

"Are the feds onto him?" I ask. "Amara mentioned that Mikhail's empire was going down and that he'd take any- and everyone down with him."

"The feds are definitely involved. It's all just a matter of time."

"What does this mean for me? For you? Are we going to go to jail?" I start crying softly. Q holds me in his arms, consoling me.

"Not if I can help it," he says.

I GO THROUGH THE DAYS BETWEEN CHRISTMAS AND NEW Year's Eve on autopilot. I have no idea where my life is going, but I keep things moving as if nothing has changed. The only alternative is a complete nervous breakdown, and by the grace of God, that doesn't happen. My body is going through all the usual motions, but underneath my cool demeanor I'm a wreck. Everyday I wake up and think, is this the day? Will today be the day that Mikhail reveals that he's onto me? Will I get arrested for conspiracy to all Mikhail's dirt?

I want to seek comfort in Q's arms, but that isn't possible. My body craves him, remembering how good we felt together; it was definitely more than a fuck. I ask Q how he's going to get us out of this mess unscathed, but he warns me not to discuss the matter at the club or over the phone, which leaves me with no other option but to pray that he's going to fix this mess. Somehow Q and I manage to act normal around each other, but it's hard. We both feel the spark between us but we know that doing anything out of the ordinary could cost us our lives.

I fantasize about transferring my money to a Swiss account, or better yet a Cayman Islands one. I could hop on a plane and just disappear. I wouldn't have my career but I'd be safe. I wonder if I should act on these dreams, but come to no solid conclusions. I just hope that I have time to do whatever it is I need to do before the walls come crashing down.

New Year's Eve begins like any other day. I wake up at around ten in the morning, work out for an hour, and then I have Mikhail's cook fix me a decadent breakfast of Belgian waffles with plenty of butter and maple syrup, a few strips of turkey bacon, some turkey sausage links, an egg-white omelet, and a bowl of tropical fruit salad. I wash it all down with a half pitcher of Bellinis. I may as well enjoy the benefits of living the high life while I can, because my days are numbered. I just don't know what will happen when my time is up.

To relieve my stress (but not my paranoia) I fire up a bowl of California Indo and take a few tokes before I hop in the shower. I take a few more hits when I get out. I put on some Rock and Republic jeans, an ornate wifebeater, and throw on some crisp white jumpers. I top it off with a vintage Kangol and head to the Agua Spa at the Delano for a relaxing massage, a skin smoothing body polish, and a mild and light facial. I can't help but think of Amara and wonder where she is and if she's managed to elude whoever was after her.

After my spa treatments, I head to Vidal Sassoon to get my hair and nails done. Then I eat a burger and onion rings at Johnny Rockets and down a thick chocolate shake before I roll to MAC to have my makeup done. I could have someone come to the mansion and do all those things there, but

I wanted to get out of the house and soak up the energy of my city. And I don't want to take any chances of running into Mikhail if I don't have to.

New Year's Eve is always an extra-hype night in Miami. There are several A-list celebrities in town to ring in 2007, and they'll all be at Babylon. I almost feel sorry for the other clubs on the beach. Almost, but not quite. Their little celebrations are going to pale in comparison to my fête. Not only is MTV broadcasting, but so is the television show *Deco Drive*. I'm going to do my best to enjoy all this success, even though it may end at any moment.

With a whole lot of prodding, begging, cashing in favors, and mad phone calls from Sascha and myself, we've managed to accomplish the impossible; all the top female hip-hop artists are coming to perform at Babylon. Regardless of her connection with Mikhail, Sascha is great at what she does. In an unprecedented event, we've got fresh-out-of-the-pen Lil' Kim teaming up with a healed Foxy Brown, as well as Miami's reigning hip-hop queens, Trina, Jacki-O, and Dez all doing a 2007 version of the hip-hop classic, "Not Tonight (Ladies Night)." Missy is singing the hook. Tonight is going to be off the chain.

Because of all the publicity and excitement around tonight, people recognize me on the streets now, and they wave or stop and say hello. Some just whisper and point at me, like I'm a movie star that they're too intimidated to approach. There are flyers in every boutique and shop, and ads have run in the papers as well as local entertainment magazines. The streets are talking and there's one word on their lips: Babylon.

At 5:00 PM I head to the club to prepare for the festivities. When I take out that diamond-encrusted key chain and turn my key in the lock, I wonder if it's the last time I'll do so. I practice a little bit and do a final sound check of all the audio equipment. Everything sounds great and I can't wait to throw down later on. At 6:00 PM the staff arrives for dinner and a meeting before the doors open. That was my idea, because Mikhail can afford it and our staff deserves it. Mikhail doesn't even care that his actions could put the livelihood of so many people in jeopardy. These people need their jobs, and if there's no club, there's no job. But of course he doesn't give a fuck about the little man.

As the dinner plates of chicken, beef tenderloin, fish, and plenty of veggies are cleared and coffee is served, Q, Rebeca, and I each make brief presentations about security policies as well as bar and door policies, and finalize the order of events for the night. The staff signs releases for MTV and ABC, giving them the right to use their images and likenesses on camera, and by nine o'clock, camera teams are on location setting up lights and testing feeds. Everything is in place and running like clockwork.

The employees are all changing into their uniforms. The cocktail servers are decked out in revealing little harem girl outfits, and the men wear masculine but sexy tunics and pants sets. The security staff is outfitted in black Hugo Boss suits that I've ordered for them; I want them to look uniform and classy, but not stand out too much. Everyone looks fantastic; I've never seen a more attractive and in shape bunch of people in one room. I swear everyone is good-looking enough to be a part-time model or actor.

La La is the MTV on-air correspondent, and she arrives looking amazing in a cobalt blue dress that flatters her coloring, hazel eyes, and buxom figure. We chat for a while about her upcoming nuptials to Carmelo Anthony, and go over marks and placement with the cameramen, and then I bid them adieu for the moment so that I can go to my office to

get changed into the first of my many outfits for the evening.
My stomach is all fluttery and I hope to God that my palms
aren't all clammy since I've been shaking everybody's hand.
I sniff under my arms, and after I see that I still smell fresh,
I pat my pits with tissues, slick on a couple of precautionary
swipes of clear deodorant, and slip into a shimmery metallic
gold Zac Posen cinched-waist number that really accentuates
my curves.

Meanwhile, people are filling in downstairs and I hear the
thumping sounds of the warm-up DJ, who's playing some
garage house. I go down the back stairs and out to my Range,
which is parked by the exit. I look at the sky and see the
spotlight beckoning for one and all to come check out my
club. I look at my watch and see that I'm right on time. La
La and the MTV crew, the camera crew for *Deco Drive*, and
a plethora of other photographers should be camped out
front, ready to snap pictures of the glitterati as they walk the
red carpet. I start up the truck and the sounds of Frankie
Beverly and Maze's "Before I Let Go" wash over me. I'm in
a groove as I pull around to the front of the club so I can be
interviewed and photographed on the red carpet, and then
I join the special VIP guests for cocktails.

I sail through everything looking beautiful and confident.
I am poised and charming as I mix and mingle with the celebrities from every level: national, local, and even ghetto. I
think to myself that, aside from the illegalities, Mother really
ought to be proud of my club. I'm glamorous, my guest list
has just the right mix, and everything looks fabulous. The
only difference between what I do at my club and what she
does with her fundraisers and society soirees is that people
are actually going to have fun instead of faking it.

At 10:30 PM I go to change into my second outfit, a sassy
Atelier Versace gown that makes that famous JLo dress look

like a burkah. I have no idea why something so skimpy costs well into five figures, but when I slip it on and the soft, silky fabric kisses and caresses my body I truly feel like the Queen of Miami. It's worth every penny. The neckline plunges all the way to my navel, and my boobs barely stay inside the skimpy top. A pendant of rhinestones connects both sides of the top of the dress and dangles provocatively in my cleavage. The bottom of the dress is split so high that I'm afraid I'm going to give someone an eyeful of smiling snatch at any second. It's a very dressy gown and no, this ain't the Oscars, but it *is* New Year's Eve and this is my party. I'm going to be up on stage and beamed into millions of homes introducing some of hip-hop's finest, so I want to make sure that I stand out.

I touch up my makeup and slip on a pair of custom-made shoes that are encrusted with genuine white and canary diamonds and accented with citrines that match the bright yellow of the dress. My skin is glistening thanks to an application of NARS Body Glow; I'm as radiant as the sun. I can hear the crowd ooh and ahh as I make my way to the stage, verification that the outfit is perfect.

"I want to welcome you, on behalf of myself and the amazing team that makes this club run, to Babylon!" I say excitedly into the mic.

"That's right," La La says. "You're here at the hottest nightclub on South Beach to witness a historical event. We've got the hottest DJ in America, the first lady of the club scene, the queen of Miami, Ms. Bobbi here." The crowd cheers and applauds and I have the nerve to damn near blush.

"And we've got MTV and the hottest MTV VJ here. La La Vasquez in the house!" I scream and the crowd takes the energy up a notch in anticipation.

"And we've got the female all-stars of hip-hop here to perform a new take on a classic hit, 'Not Tonight (Ladies Night)'!"

La La concludes. The curtains are pulled back, and a mini pyrotechnic show lights the club up with sparklers, flames, and lots of smoke. I pray to God that nothing catches on fire as Missy steps onto the stage looking trim and fit, singing and dancing her heart out and winning the crowd over with her megawatt smile.

I can barely hear the women rapping over the screams of the crowd. The performance is viewable on the giant projection screens situated around the main room, as well as in the other rooms and all the VIP sections. Kim has never looked better and I'm so glad she's home. Foxy sounds great and appears healthy and refreshed and I'm sincerely happy that God and surgery have healed her deafness. Trina looks toned and in shape even though she still has ass for days, and her hair and makeup are perfect, even if I don't care for her outfit. Jacki-O is very ladylike and raw at the same time, and with most of her monetary troubles behind her, her fans seem to be happy to see her back on top. Dez is absolutely phenomenal; not only does she have flow, but she looks breathtakingly beautiful. I can't believe that with all the beefs that have gone down among various members of this ensemble, everyone seems to be getting along.

When they finish and take their bows we all gather on the stage for the countdown to 2007. A round of Krug is served to us, and we wait to toast in the New Year. The screens now show a split shot of Babylon and Times Square as the crowd begins to chant, Ten . . . nine . . .

I can't believe that this is my life. I became an internationally known DJ, I opened a nightclub, and I've arranged for one of the most anticipated events in hip-hop to take place. My status as an industry legend can't be denied. To the naked eye I am a woman in control, and everything is running along as smooth as the ride in a brand-new Lexus.

Eight . . . seven . . . six . . .

As hard as I've worked, I'm still not free. Instead of having my parents controlling my life, it's Mikhail. As a result, I can't share this night with my friend Amara or the man I genuinely care for, Q. I've got the whole world in my hands and yet I can't have the one that I want on my arm.

Five . . . four . . .

Fuck it! I'm the queen of Miami. I can reign alone.

Three . . . two . . . one . . . *Happy New Year!*

Confetti drops, a laser light show ensues, and everyone around me is hugging and kissing their friends, loved ones, and lusted ones. Everyone but me. I smile and survey my kingdom, full of mixed emotions, perhaps a little empty inside, but still quite satisfied with my accomplishments. I look at the screens that are showing couples smooching in the New Year. It does make me feel good to see everyone look so happy. I feel good for everyone except for Mikhail and Rebeca, whose image gets shown on the jumbo screen, entangled in a passionate kiss. Knowing Rebeca, she probably arranged for it to happen; she's such a bitch. Doesn't she understand that I don't want Mikhail, that she can have him?

I don't have the desire or the time to think about Rebeca or Mikhail. I'm about to spin, so I run and change clothes once again. This time I'm rocking a dress made entirely of shiny silver CDs. I become one with the turntables as I deliver a set that leaves every seat and every wall empty. Everyone is out on the dance floor, on top of tables and banquettes, dancing and enjoying themselves. I force myself to get into it and have fun, because after all it is my night, and nothing but nothing is going to steal my joy.

After my performance I go straight to the bar, get behind it, and grab a bottle of Moet. I'd prefer Krug—my palette is spoiled now—but it's the first bottle of bubbly I can get my hands on. I go to my office, shut the door, and pour out a little bit of champagne.

"This is for you, Kaos, and for you, Amara, wherever you are. I hope you're okay." I guzzle some of the champagne and flop down into my leather chair. I am so frustrated with my situation, I don't know what to do. I never thought I'd be waging another battle for the sake of my career. I get up from the chair and pace the floor. The door opens and Mikhail and Rebeca barge into my office.

"What do you two want?" I ask bitterly. Rebeca is clutching Mikhail's arm and pushing her body so close into him that she looks like his Siamese twin.

"I have to tell you something," Mikhail says seriously.

I hope to God that he's telling me that he's going to walk out of my life and just let me have my club and that he and Rebeca plan to live happily ever after in a galaxy far, far away.

"Let me guess? The two of you are getting married?" I ask sarcastically.

"Bobbi, there's been an accident," he says firmly. Rebeca rubs his back soothingly and glares at me with her beady little eyes.

"What happened?" I ask, exasperated. This is probably some bullshit Mikhail and Rebeca have cooked up to throw another monkey wrench into my night. God, I am so sick of them. Enough already!

"Amara is dead," Mikhail says.

"This is not funny," I say.

"It is no joke. Amara is dead," he says.

"How?" I ask. I don't know what to think. Has something really happened to Amara or is this part of her plan to disappear?

"It was unfortunate," Mikhail says. "But it had to be done."

"What do you mean, it had to be *done*?" I ask. This doesn't sound good at all.

Rebeca and Mikhail look at each other and Mikhail nods at her. Rebeca locks my office door and stands in front of it.

"What the hell are you doing, Rebeca?" I ask her. She just smiles an evil smile. I head toward the door but Mikhail stops me.

"I'm afraid your friend Amara was cooperating with the police," Mikhail says, grabbing me by the neck.

"What is that supposed to mean?" I ask hoarsely, but I know what it means. Amara had been snitching. That's why she thought Dimitri might kill her and why she went AWOL on Christmas. It's what she was referring to as "what she'd been doing."

"I think you know very well what it means," Mikhail says. "We know that you and Amara spoke on Christmas Eve. We've checked her cell phone records."

"And? It was Christmas and she was my friend. She called to wish me a Merry Christmas."

"No, Bobbi, that wasn't it. That was the night she thought she could escape. After she talked with you she called an Interpol agent. There had been several calls to this agent, and I think you know why," Mikhail says.

"What's Interpol?" I ask Mikhail. I know damn well that they're the international police, but playing dumb is worth a shot.

"Don't play games with me, Bobbi. I guarantee that you will not win. Now, I asked you why you think she called an Interpol agent."

"I don't know. Why didn't you ask her?" I ask him.

"May I?" Rebeca asks Mikhail.

"Please do," Mikhail tells her.

Rebeca walks up to me and administers a kick to my mid-section. It hurts like hell and catches me totally off guard, but I don't fall or double over. I jump on Rebeca as swift as a panther. I do my best to whoop her ass, and I get a few good licks in, but I'm outnumbered and Mikhail isn't going to play fair. He stops the action by pulling out a gun and putting it against the back of my head. I feel the coldness of hard steel poking into my scalp and immediately stiffen. The shit has officially hit the fan.

"I think you know more than you're telling," Mikhail says. "But I have ways to make you talk." Mikhail whirls me around roughly and points the barrel of the gun at me. Rebeca dusts herself off and returns to her post blocking the door.

*Where is Q when I need him?* I wonder silently. He promised to have my back and now he's nowhere to be found. He made it seem as if all I had to do was sit back and he'd fix all this before things got worse. I should have come up with a backup plan and acted on it immediately, and now it's too late.

"Come now, sweet angel. We're going to go somewhere nice and private where we can chat," he tells me.

"I'm not going anywhere with you," I tell Mikhail. I've always heard that if you allow an abductor to move you from one location to another that your chances of survival decline exponentially. The way I see it, I have a fifty-fifty chance of escaping if I can avoid being moved somewhere else. If I can find Q, then I've got better odds of surviving. Mikhail isn't going to shoot me in the middle of my club in front of witnesses. And with the staff milling about, he probably isn't going to shoot me in my office. If I can only get to the main area, I can make a run for it. Mikhail is not about to take me to God knows where to do God knows what.

"This gun means that you will do whatever I ask you to do," he says.

"You're going to kill me either way," I say. "You may as well just do it now."

"My, aren't we courageous?" Rebeca asks sarcastically.

"Fuck you," I spit. "You won't get away with this. If anything happens to me, my father won't rest until you're brought to justice."

"If your father comes after me, your father is a dead man. Your grandfather and your mother as well," Mikhail threatens me.

"Then I guess we're at an impasse," I say to him. "Because I don't know anything. I can't help you. So just shoot me." I say a silent prayer that God will deliver me from this pit. I can remember my grandfather preaching a sermon from the book of Daniel, and I hope I will be shielded like Shadrach, Meshach, and Abednego, three slaves in Babylon who refused to bow down to a golden idol. They were thrown into a fiery furnace but emerged unharmed. I pray that God shows me mercy because I believe he can deliver me, just as he delivered Daniel from the lion's den without a scratch. And if deliverance isn't in my cards, I pray that my sins are forgiven and that I go to heaven. I just hope Q gets to me before a bullet does.

"Perhaps you will change your mind when you hear this," Mikhail says. "Make the call, Rebeca," he tells her. Rebeca whips out her cell phone and starts punching in some numbers.

She hands Mikhail the phone and he begins to converse in Russian. Then Mikhail shoves the phone against my ear.

"Boss Lady! Are you okay?" Q is on the other end of the phone. My eyes go wide and I feel all the blood draining from my body.

"Q? What's going on?" I ask him.

"Baby, I'm so sorry," he says.

"Where are you?" I ask and Mikhail snatches the phone away.

"You thought I didn't know about your little fling?" Mikhail asks me. I don't answer him. "I bet you thought that Q would be your knight in shining armor, didn't you? Did you think that he could protect you? Rescue you? Some knight. I just don't understand why you'd trust him instead of me. This hurts me. I've given you everything and this is how you repay me?" Mikhail says, looking hurt.

"I don't know what you're talking about," I lie. "Whatever you think is going on is just a misunderstanding. Baby, we can work this out," I say.

"Bobbi, I don't believe you. We'll see if you don't change your tune in a little bit. Once you see your little friend, I'm sure you'll cooperate."

Mikhail stops pointing the gun at me and uncocks it. He removes a magazine of bullets from the gun, puts the cartridge in his pocket, and twirls the gun until he's holding it by the barrel. He raises his hand and delivers a blow with the butt of the gun to my temple, and then everything goes black.

# CHAPTER FOURTEEN

WHEN I COME TO, I HEAR LAUGHTER AND THE CLINKING of glasses. I will my eyes to focus despite the throbbing of my head. When the room stops spinning, I see Rebeca and Mikhail kissing and doing shots of vodka. I'm not sure where I am, but my surroundings look vaguely familiar. Wherever it is, it appears to be a warehouse by the looks of all the crates and packing materials around the room. I am lying on a heap of rags and sheets, and I try to sit up but my wrists and ankles are duct-taped together and I can't gain my balance.

"Oh look, the queen of Miami finally woke up," Rebeca says sarcastically.

"What are you going to do to me?" I ask Mikhail.

"After I get the information that I need, I'm going to end your life," he says. "I don't want to do it, but you leave me no choice."

"You won't get away with this," I tell him.

"Oh yes I will," Mikhail replies. "But I won't get over it. I'll miss you."

"You can't just kill me. You'll be an automatic suspect. You're my business partner and my boyfriend. The police will come straight to you first."

"We own the police," Rebeca says.

"You don't own shit," I say to her.

"Let's not have this get uglier," Mikhail says. "Bobbi, Rebeca has figured out a way to keep things moving at Babylon without you. She's found another front. One who will remain loyal and who won't ask questions. One who won't betray me."

"Mikhail, I've never betrayed you," I say.

"How I wish that were true," he replies. "I want to believe you. But I can't take that chance. There have been too many breeches with people that I've trusted," he says.

"But I love you. I'm not like Misty," I say.

"Misty was in love with me too. She wanted me to leave you and be with her. That could never happen. She knew that our relationship was purely business. I never had those kinds of feelings for her. She threatened to reveal secrets to my enemies if I didn't leave you. She even threatened to go to the police. And I couldn't have that, so she had to die," Mikhail says.

"I didn't like that bitch anyway," I tell Mikhail. "And I'm telling you that I don't know anything I could tell. If you can't believe that I wouldn't betray you, can you at least believe that I wouldn't do anything to put Babylon in jeopardy? I can't do it without you. I need you. Why would I hurt you?"

"Yes, you say that, but I'm not sure if it is true."

"I swear, Mikhail."

"Even so," Mikhail says, "Amara was a snitch. Not only that, she was a traitor. She was given a simple task to fulfill: to befriend you. She was supposed to get you to feel comfortable and to trust me. She turned on me and told you things you didn't need to know. Then she tried to work with the authorities. How do I know you weren't working with her?"

"I thought Amara was my friend," I say. "I had no idea what she was doing. I wasn't involved."

My head is reeling from the information. Amara was playing me? Amara was playing everyone! I shake my head in disbelief. They're just trying to confuse me. Amara *was* my friend. She just got caught up. They forced her hand. If Amara wasn't my real friend, she wouldn't have tried to warn me. She would have totally sold me out. But that doesn't matter anymore. Mikhail thinks I'm a threat.

"I know that she's the one who told you about Misty's role in my business. She gave the police information, and in exchange she thought they could protect her. She signed affidavits," Mikhail says. He shoves some papers in my face. Rebeca is behind him, loving every minute of my torture. I can't decide who I hate more, her or Mikhail.

"I know she told you to leave me. I know she told you that she was going to disappear. That's why she called you. She thought she could enter a witness protection program. But we have eyes everywhere. How do you think we got those papers?" Mikhail says.

"Mikhail, I don't care what you're doing. I just want out. I won't say a thing to anyone, I swear. Keep the club. You'll never have to hear from me again. You know you can believe me. I've never lied to you."

"I wish I could believe you. But I have proof that you are a liar. You've shown that you can't be trusted."

"You can trust me," I say to Mikhail. "How have I shown otherwise?"

"I told you long ago you were a horrible liar. I can always tell when you're not telling the truth. Like when you told me that you weren't pregnant," he says.

"What?" I ask in shock.

"There's no need to lie and say that you weren't. I told you that I would kill you if you aborted my child and I meant it. I couldn't do it before now, but I wanted to. I had to wait until the time was right. And to be honest, I wanted to give you a second chance. You don't realize that I spared you."

"Mikhail, I wasn't pregnant," I lie.

"Bobbi, I know you had an abortion. I had you followed," Mikhail reveals. "You were acting suspiciously that morning. It was nothing to have someone tail you. You were crafty, I'll give you that, but not crafty enough. Someone was always watching you, Bobbi."

"I—I," I stammer.

"I couldn't have it any other way, sweet angel. It was for your protection. I would have never been able to forgive myself if something happened to you."

"Let me explain," I beg.

"Shh," Mikhail says, putting his fingers to my lips. "There's nothing to explain. It breaks my heart to have to do this, Bobbi, but I know that I can't trust you."

"I'm sorry," I say.

"If you had had my child, I would have spared you, even considering your other acts of betrayal. None of this would be happening to you. Now you have to trade my child's life with your own."

"I didn't mean to lie to you," I say.

"Yes, you did. You never cared about me. You only wanted to get ahead. I have always known that you were an opportunist. That was what people said about you. But I wouldn't hear of it. I was so blinded by my feelings for you. Like a fool, I thought that you would grow to love me. I knew that I could make you happier than that deadbeat boyfriend of yours," he says.

"I don't understand," I say through a flood of tears. "What boyfriend?"

"The gambler. Your boyfriend Kevin," Mikhail says.

"Kaos?" I gasp.

"Yes, that boyfriend. You think his fall off the motorcycle was an accident?"

"What are you saying?" I ask. I feel as if I'm about to vomit.

"Your boyfriend liked to play cards, but he got in over his head. He didn't know when to quit. He was good, so when he came to me for money, I obliged. I'd played with him several times, and he seemed like a good guy. I thought he'd be a man of his word. But he was a degenerate. He couldn't keep up the payments. And when I put the heat on him, he balked. He thought that because I was rich that I could afford to wait. He had no principles."

"No," I say. "That's a lie." I knew that Kaos had a poker game that he went to, but I had no idea that Kaos was in so deep. This couldn't be true.

"It's the truth, Bobbi. I had Dimitri follow him. I learned and studied his every move. And I looked for the thing he would miss the most in life so I could take it away from him. That was you. I was going to kill you to send him a message, but you were so beautiful that I spared you. I fell for you the moment I laid eyes on you. I knew that you would be of better use alive. So in order to settle his debt, he had to die. I will give him credit. He was a good rider. He put up a good chase. But ultimately there was no escape from my men. He didn't fall off that motorcycle. My men forced him off the road. And they say he died with your name on his lips."

The officials said Kaos was speeding and hit a slippery patch of road or a small object, skidded twenty feet or so, and hit the wall of an overpass. I cried for days just thinking about how much pain he went through before he died. People tried to comfort me by telling me that the head injury probably killed him instantly, but he was wearing a helmet, and I believed he may have had a shot if he hadn't hit a wall of steel and concrete.

"You're lying," I say.

"No," Mikhail says. "No lies. I gave you time to grieve. I watched you. I admired your ambition. You had fire. I wanted you. You were a sexy piece of ass, and I knew that one day under the right circumstances, I'd have you."

"You planned all this?" I ask him.

"Oh yes, for years. It was very well planned. I just never thought I would have to kill you. I thought I could tame you. Why, I've known just about every move you've made since your boyfriend's little accident. It's amazing how things fell into place. I like to think of it as providence."

"Fuck you," I spit.

"One thing I can't stand about you, Bobbi, is that you have such a limited vocabulary," Mikhail tells me. "A limited vocabulary is proof of a limited mind."

"Fuck you," I say again. "Why?" I ask him. "Why me?"

"Why not?" he asks me. "You were beautiful, and you were easy. You were hungry. I fed you. You came back for more. It was simple."

"I have to admit that I was so jealous at first," Rebeca pipes in. "When Mikhail told me that he wanted to fuck some little black bitch, I was livid. I still don't see what's so special about you. I never knew why Mikhail was willing to go through so much to have you. Do you know that he had the original owner of Babylon killed so that he could buy it?"

"I thought he died of an overdose," I say. "But now I see that's just your preferred method of killing people."

"It is so easy to pull off in Miami. Everyone is on drugs," Mikhail says.

"I knew you were trash from the first time I saw you. I knew it would be a matter of time before Mikhail realized it too," Rebeca says.

"Arrgh!" I scream in frustration as I struggle to free myself from the duct tape that is wrapped around my wrists. I can't sit there any longer and just await my fate. I am boiling with anger and refuse to die like a sitting duck. Mikhail had my friend and my fiancé killed and those deeds were not going to go unpunished. I will fight until my last breath to avenge their murders and try to prevent mine; unfortunately, my last breath seems too near.

"Stop struggling. It will all be over soon," Mikhail says. "I promise you. And because I love you, I'm going to make sure that your death is as quick and as painless as possible."

"Fuck you," I shout.

"Oh, but I've grown so bored of fucking you," he says coldly. "That's why I've been fucking Rebeca here. She is loyal. She doesn't lie."

It has always amazed me how Mikhail can go from hot to cold. It used to turn me on, but now it just scares me. He's liable to snap at any time. "You're a bastard," I tell him. "The two of you deserve each other."

"Much like you and your cop boyfriend deserve each other," Mikhail replies.

"Cop boyfriend?" I ask. "You're making a mistake, Mikhail," I say.

"Dimitri," Mikhail shouts. "Bring in our little piggy."

"Bobbi?" I hear Q's voice call out to me. There are footsteps on the cinder floor, and I strain my neck to see him. When he comes into view I can't believe my eyes. His face is bloody and swollen so bad that he's barely recognizable.

"Oh my God! What happened to you?" I ask. "What did they do to you?"

"Bobbi, I'm sorry," he says through his puffy lips, a line of drool mixed with blood hanging from them.

"Are you okay?" I ask. "What have you done to him?" I ask Dimitri. Dimitri says nothing; he just looks at me as if I am the scum of the earth.

"Isn't this a touching reunion?" Mikhail asks. "Too bad it will be short-lived."

"I didn't tell you the whole truth on Christmas," Q says to me. "I'm sorry. You have to believe me."

"Shut up! No one told you to speak," Dimitri barks, and kicks Q to the floor next to me. We sit next to each other on the pile of rags, bound and bloodied.

"You thought you were so slick," Mikhail says. "But you couldn't fool me, Bobbi. I told you when we first met that I have ways of finding things out."

My first instinct is to deny everything.

"It isn't what you think," I say.

"Lying bitch!" Dimitri says, and kicks me in the ribcage. I cough and spit up blood.

"That's enough, Dimitri," Mikhail says. "I promised her it would be quick and painless." Mikhail kneels down beside me and strokes my hair. "You're such a beautiful girl. I don't know why you couldn't just play the game," he says. "Why couldn't you be satisfied with showing up at the club and looking pretty? I handed you a life women would kill for!"

"Mikhail, nothing happened between us," I say. "We're just friends. Mikhail, you're mistaken. Q, tell him he's mistaken. He thinks you're a cop."

"You mean you haven't told her?" Mikhail asks. "My, Bobbi, aren't you the naïve one? First you get used by Amara, we certainly used you to our advantage, and then you get used by this pig?"

"What are they talking about?" I ask Q.

"I'm sorry, baby," he says. "You've got to believe that I wasn't using you."

"You're a cop?" I ask him.

"Yes," he says with a nod.

My heart sinks to the pit of my stomach. "You told me you worked for Mikhail. You said you would protect me," I say before I realize I'm saying way too much.

"What did he tell you?" Mikhail asks me.

I look from Mikhail to Dimitri to Rebeca to Q. I realize that the only person I can trust in this room is me. Everyone here has lied to me. I say nothing.

"I would strongly advise you to tell me what you know," Mikhail warns. "Don't make this harder than it has to be."

I still don't say anything.

"Do you know what I believe?" Mikhail asks me. "I believe that you knew that he was a cop all along," he says.

"I didn't. I swear," I tell him.

Mikhail walks over to me and clasps his hands around my neck. His strong hands squeeze my neck like a python. I struggle and gasp for breath, choking and sputtering.

"Let her go, motherfucker," Q says to Mikhail.

"Fine, I will," Mikhail tells Q. He lets go of my neck and my body goes as limp as an overcooked noodle. Mikhail moves from me to Q, and starts to strangle him. Q doesn't make any choking sounds as he squirms beneath him. His eyes are cold as steel as he glowers at Mikhail. I know he has to be struggling for breath and I am so afraid for him. Q may have lied to me, but I don't want to see him die right before my eyes.

"Better talk, Bobbi," Mikhail tells me. "Or your boyfriend here is going to die. Do you want his blood on your hands?"

I know that Mikhail is probably going to kill Q no matter what I say. But I can't just sit there and not attempt to save him.

"He said you were laundering money. He told me he'd help me get out of our relationship and that he'd protect me. I didn't know he was a cop. I swear. I didn't tell him anything. He did all the talking. He told me he was a drug dealer who worked for you," I blurt out quickly.

"That is what he pretended to be," Mikhail says, letting go of Q's neck. "He infiltrated our organization via another rat that we have since disposed of. He's good too. He's been working with us for a few years now. He brought us a lot of money. We never knew that we had a snake in our midst."

I look at Q in disbelief. "How could you?" I ask him. "You used me."

"Bobbi, I wasn't using you," Q says softly.

"Everything you say is a lie. I bet you didn't even know my Kaos, did you?" Q hangs his head.

"Bobbi, I've been undercover for three years. I was against involving you like this. And I didn't want to play with your feelings, but I couldn't figure out another way to get close to you. I was against involving you in the first place. That's why I tried to keep the wall up between us, but I couldn't. But I promise you that what I feel for you is real."

"You two shut up," Dimitri says and delivers kicks to both of us. I yell out in pain.

"Oh, baby, are you okay?" Q asks me.

"Do I fucking look okay?" I screech. Dimitri looks as if he's going to attack us again, but Mikhail prevents this simply by holding his hand up.

"Dimitri, that's enough," Mikhail tells him. Dimitri looks

disappointed but backs off, choosing instead to punch a wall. Plaster flies everywhere and his hand is bloody, but he doesn't flinch. He just looks at us and licks his own blood. This motherfucker is crazy!

Mikhail's cell phone rings and he begins to speak into it, turning his back on us. But Rebeca keeps an eagle eye on us. After a few minutes on the phone, Mikhail disconnects the call and he and Dimitri go back and forth in Russian. Their tone is angry but I have no idea what they are saying. I wish I'd been able to pick up at least a little of the language, then I'd have an inkling as to what was going on around me. At least maybe then I wouldn't feel like the biggest fool in the world.

I've slept with the enemy. Both of them. Mikhail had my beloved Kaos murdered, and Q is a fed who was using me. Even Amara got over on me. And now it appears that I'm going to die. Well, I can't let it end like this. I size up my surroundings and look around the room for any possible escape route. A getaway seems impossible. My hands and feet are bound, as are Q's, and I'm outnumbered and outgunned. There are no windows. The door is made of iron or steel. And each of my captors is certifiably criminally insane.

The only advantage I have is that now I realize exactly where I am. Mikhail hasn't taken me to some out of the way, unknown location. He's taken me to a storage area of Babylon, where we keep all the empty boxes and crates from deliveries and where we keep lots of miscellaneous junk. It makes sense that he wouldn't move me far because when he pistol-whipped me, there was still plenty of staff around. The pile of rags I'm sitting on isn't a pile of rags, but old and dirty tablecloths and linens from the club.

Mikhail and Dimitri are still bickering back and forth and

Rebeca is glaring at us, practically licking her chops in anticipation of our deaths.

"Bobbi," Q whispers through gritted teeth. "Bobbi, I love you."

My head snaps around as fast as that chick from *The Exorcist*. I look in his eyes, which are nearly swollen shut, and I know that he's telling the truth. He has no reason to lie now anyway. The end is inevitable.

"I love you and I need you to trust me," Q says in a hushed tone. "We're gonna make it out of here."

"Trust you?" I ask. "How can I?"

"I had nothing to gain from using you. You didn't know anything."

Mikhail and Dimitri stop arguing and Mikhail hands Rebeca a gun.

"Rebeca, I need you to watch these two. If they try anything, pump them full of bullets. Don't hesitate," Mikhail says.

"Leaving them with her is a mistake, cousin," Dimitri says, clearly angry. "Let me take care of them now."

"If what our source says is true, we may need to use the cop as a bargaining chip," Mikhail says.

"Well, then let me stay here," Dimitri says.

"I may need you," Mikhail tells him sternly. They lock eyes for a moment, and although Dimitri is the larger and crazier one of the two, he backs down. Mikhail is clearly the man in charge.

"What's going on?" Rebeca asks.

"Nothing," Mikhail says quickly. "Just do as I have told you. I will chirp you with any information if I need to."

"Okay," Rebeca says. Mikhail gives her a passionate kiss before he and Dimitri exit the room. While they're kissing, Q whispers to me, "Distract her," and I nod. With Mikhail and

Dimitri gone, there's no way we aren't going to take advantage of this opportunity. Dimitri was right. Mikhail shouldn't have left us here alone with Rebeca.

"Mikhail is such a good kisser," she says to me after the door closes. She's got a smug look on her overly made up face. We'll see who ends up smug.

"So is Q," I tell her. "He's better. Q has a bigger dick too."

"Too bad you won't get to fuck that big black dick anymore," Rebeca says snidely.

"I want you to know that you're going to rot in hell, Rebeca," I tell her.

"Maybe, but you'll be there before I will," she says.

"You're not going to get away with this, Rebeca. For all you know, Mikhail will do the same thing to you that he's doing to me. You always had it twisted. You shouldn't have been hating on me. I didn't know jack. But Mikhail knew everything. That's who you should have been hating on."

"That will never happen," she says. "Mikhail loves me."

"Right. He loved me too," I tell her.

"Shut up," she says. "Mikhail was using you."

"You want to think that he was just using me. But you know he loved me. Look at all he did for me. He gave me the world. He used you to make the money and he spends it on me. You're a worker," I tell her.

"You know, I could put a bullet in you right now," she says.

"But you won't."

"Oh, won't I?" she asks.

"Nope. Because you're too sprung to think for yourself. You need Mikhail to tell you what to do."

"Shut up," Rebeca orders.

"Why don't you come over here and shut me up?" I say.

She walks over to me and slaps me in the mouth, hard. I

fall back on the pile of rags and Rebeca climbs on top of me, straddling me. Whatever Q plans on doing, he'd better hurry up!

"I don't like you like that, Rebeca," I say, turning my head in disgust. Out the corner of my eye I can see Q jerking his shoulder like he's having a seizure and arching his back like a fish out of water. I try not to stare because I don't want Rebeca to turn around, but I really want to know what the hell he's doing. Rebeca grabs me by the face and points her gun at my forehead.

"I could blow your brains out," she says. "You should be begging me for your worthless life instead of talking shit."

"Okay, Rebeca," I say meekly. "Can you just take that thing away from my head? I promise I won't say anything else," I tell her.

"That's a little better," Rebeca says, backing off a bit, a satisfied smile on her face.

What occurs next happens so fast that it's a blur. Q is as swift and nimble as Jackie Chan. Like some kind of contortionist, Q brings his arms from behind his back and under his feet as if he were jumping rope. With one swift motion he balls his fists and brings them down sharply on top of Rebeca's head, knocking her unconscious.

"What the fuck?" I shout. "Oh my God, what the hell just happened?"

"I'm getting us the fuck out of here, that's what happened. I don't know how much time we've got."

"So what, are you some kind of supercop?" I ask him. "You're on some old MacGyver, James Bond shit," I say.

"Something like that," he says. Q rips the duct tape from his wrists with his teeth. He takes off my stiletto and uses the spike heel to rip apart the duct tape around his ankles. Then he helps free me from my bonds. There's still a little tape on my wrists and ankles because some of it didn't come off easily and Q is trying not to rip my skin. I kick away my other shoe and dust myself off.

Q takes Rebeca's gun and checks the bullets.

"We've got a full clip," he says.

"Good," I say. "Now bust a cap in her ass."

"Come on," he says, ignoring me.

"I'm serious. I know that you're a cop and all, but that isn't going to protect us in the long run. We've got to kill these motherfuckers."

"I can't just kill people, Bobbi," he says.

"I can," I tell him. "Give me the gun."

Q grabs me by the arm and opens the door.

"Stay against the wall, and stay alert," he says. "That phone call Mikhail got was a warning. There's about to be a takedown."

"How do you know?" I ask him.

"I'll explain later. We've got to move. If Mikhail is still here, he's monitoring the surveillance cameras."

Q opens the door and we move quickly through the rear end of the club with our backs against the wall. We're almost to the service entrance when I hear gunshots coming from behind me. I'm paralyzed with fear. I don't know whether to drop to the ground or run. Q steps around me and starts to shoot at Mikhail and Dimitri, who are headed toward us, guns blazing. I feel searing hot pain burn through my thigh, and I know that I've been hit.

"They hit me," I say to Q. I look down at my leg to see a stream of blood pouring from a gash about a half-inch wide. I don't believe that the bullet is lodged in my skin; it's just a graze. But it hurts like bloody hell and just the sight of the blood is making me want to pass out.

There's a loud clap that sounds like thunder and the service door is blown off the hinges. A team of men in black uniforms wearing helmets and carrying shields infiltrate the club. Bullets are flying as I slide to the floor and cover my head. I feel like I'm caught in the middle of a battlefield as the SWAT team swarms in and exchanges fire with Mikhail and Dimitri. I'm light-headed; there's so much blood coming from my wound. I'm on the verge of consciousness and unconsciousness as I see Q go down. I reach my hand out to him, but before I can touch him, I'm placed on a gurney and wheeled out of Babylon.

# OUTRO

W HEN THIS SAGA ALL BEGAN I HAD ONE GOAL: TO BECOME
a star. I wanted to make a name for myself, but getting caught in a web of international intrigue wasn't a part
of the plan. So many details were uncovered as the media
got ahold of the story. The fall of Babylon and the Petrov
crime syndicate has been the talk of the newspapers and
television for weeks.

Mikhail and Dimitri suffered some serious injuries, but
both of them survived their wounds and were taken into
custody, along with Rebeca. Her dumb ass didn't even realize that Mikhail was using her until the end. He and Dimitri were going to make their escape and leave Rebeca holding
a loaded gun as the feds infiltrated the place. As soon as
detectives questioned him, he promptly placed everything
on her.

I wish that I could say that Q made it out okay, but I
can't. He lost his life trying to save mine. I'm pretty con-
flicted about it all. He lied to me, played me like a guitar.
And there's still a part of me that feels so used. But he
claimed his love for me until he took his last breath. I don't
know how I'm going to deal with the fact that two men in

my life died because of Mikhail. I'm pretty screwed up and I don't see that changing. Physically, it turns out that the bullet that grazed me actually hit a major artery in my leg. If I had gone any longer without medical attention, I may have bled to death. I had to have a couple of surgeries, but I should come through everything okay. My only lasting scars will be internal . . .

Surprisingly, my family rallied behind me once they found out what was going on. Thanks to my father, and Q's reports to the DEA before he died, I'm not going to be charged with conspiracy. I realize that I'm getting off a whole lot easier than most people in my situation would. But it isn't without a price. I will have to testify in court, some shit that I am not looking forward to.

And the RICO laws are a motherfucker. I lost the club, but I'm sure that it's better that way. No one is going to try to attend any event associated with me for fear of getting caught up in some kind of mafia vendetta, so for the time being, my career is on hiatus. Babylon is going up on the auction block eventually, and some other shady character will buy it and the whole thing will start all over again. But that's South Beach for you.

The famous Ms. Bobbi is dead. No more long nights partying with celebrities, no more jet-setting to the most exotic locales around the globe. I'm over the club scene; I've got bigger mountains to conquer, like the music industry. Maybe when all the dust clears I can do some production, or maybe start my own record label. I still have plenty of money, though I've had to go to unbelievable lengths to hide my assets while this case is still open. But who am I kidding? Chances are, I'm going to have to enter some kind of witness protection program. What good will money do me, if I don't have a real life?

Most of the Apostles had charges brought upon them, but the authorities only cracked the tip of the iceberg in regards to dismantling Mikhail's organization. A couple of the Apostles fled their countries and are on the run. And then there are all the lower-level members of his organization. Mikhail had crews everywhere. For all I know, there's a hit against me, so making plans for the future is something I will have to do one day at a time.

My father assures me that they will take every necessary precaution, and that everything will be all right. I've been staying in a leased home in a gated community, with personal around-the-clock security, compliments of the U.S. government. There are motion detectors and surveillance cameras and all kinds of high-tech security systems, thanks to good old Uncle Sam. But it doesn't stop the nightmares. It doesn't prevent me from thinking that mercenaries have arrived to finish me off in a Scarface-styled bloodbath every time someone comes to the door.

Every morning I look at the sunrise and the memories bombard my brain like floodwaters raging through a breeched levee. I marvel at the Miami skyline and the famed coastline in all its majesty, so deceivingly beautiful. Every now and then I see a rainbow, and I'm reminded of how I vowed that I was going to claim some pot of gold at its end the day that I won the DJ Spin-Off at the Winter Music Conference. I went for the gold all right and I got plenty, but I've lost more than money can replace. I debate if it was worth it, if the good times outweigh the bad. But the story is still being written, so I can't give a concrete answer. It was what it was.

It's going to be a long time before I can even pretend to be "normal" again. I've had and lost all the money in the world. Everyone knows my name, and while it was good, it was very good, but that's no consolation. Because of Mikhail I've lost my fiancé, my friend, my lover, and my career. But for one brief shining moment, I was the queen of Miami, and I reigned over Babylon, the best club South Beach has ever seen. And although Babylon has fallen, at least I'm alive.

*Babylon is fallen, is fallen;*
*and all the graven images of her gods*
*he hath broken to the ground.*
                                    *—Isaiah 21:9*

# ABOUT THE AUTHOR

Méta Smith was born in Philadelphia and raised on the south side of Chicago. She attended Clark Atlanta University, where she majored in mass communications, and later transferred to Spelman College in Atlanta, where she received a bachelor's degree in English.

Her adventurous spirit took her to Miami on a vacation that turned into a six-year residency. In Miami she fell in love with the South Beach club scene and worked a myriad of jobs to support her nightlife addiction, including waitress, promotions coordinator for the local UPN affiliate, middle-school English teacher, nightclub promoter, exotic dancer, and music video model. The latter two positions inspired her to pen her debut novel, *The Rolexxx Club*.

Méta has also worked extensively in the field of fundraising for philanthropic causes, using her social skills and her gift for writing to raise millions of dollars for a variety of non-profit organizations, including the United Way and the Benedictine Sisters of Chicago, an order of monastic nuns. She lives in Conneaut, Ohio, with her fiancé and son.